BLOOD AND MAGIC

HISTORICAL PARANORMAL ROMANCE — WITH A STEAMPUNK EDGE

ANN GIMPEL

Edited by
ANGELA KELLY

CONTENTS

BLOOD AND MAGIC

COVEN ENFORCERS, BOOK ONE

Historical Paranormal Romance—With a Steampunk Edge
By
Ann Gimpel

Tumble into a supernatural version of the Old West with
heart-pounding romance

Magic didn't just find Luke Caulfield. It chased him down, bludgeoned him, and has been dogging him ever since. Some lessons are harder than others, but Luke embraces danger, upping the ante to give it one better. An enforcer for the Coven, a large, established group of witches, his latest assignment is playing bodyguard to the daughter of Coven leaders.

Abigail Ruskin is chaperoning a spoiled twelve-year-old from New York to her parents' home in Utah Territory when Luke gets on their stagecoach in Colorado. A powerful witch herself, Abigail senses Luke's magic, but has no idea what he's doing on her stagecoach. Stuck between the petulant child and Luke's raw sexual energy, Abigail can't wait for the trip to end.

Unpleasant truths surface about the child. While Abigail's struggling with those, wraiths, wolves, and dark mages launch an attack. Luke's so attracted to Abigail, she's almost all he can think about, but he's leery too. The child is just plain evil. Is Abigail in league with her? It might explain the odd attack that took out their driver and one of their horses. In over his head, he summons enforcer backup.

Will they help him save the woman he's falling in love with, or demand her immediate execution?

PROLOGUE

If we can know how to die, we'll learn how to live.
James Hillman

A *village west of* Boston
1830

LUKE RAN as if the devil dogged his heels. Breath caught in his throat. His lungs burned. Running and crying weren't a good mix, but Ma was dead and he couldn't help himself. The thing Ma had turned into danced behind his eyes and filled his mind with terror. His foot twisted sideways into a pothole and he nearly fell. Panting, he came to an abrupt halt and sucked air hard into lungs that had forgotten how to cooperate. When the world quit spinning, he straightened and rubbed his eyes until Ma disappeared and all he saw was the rocky, pitted road, slimed with mud from the rain.

"Good thing I stopped," he muttered. The turnoff to Aethelred's was behind him—not by much, but any time wasted wasn't good. Luke always avoided the town wizard with his long, white hair and penetrating dark eyes that looked right through you, but today was different.

Pa's words rang in his mind. "Run like the wind, son. Bring Aethelred. He's our only hope…"

Luke shoved strands of wet black hair out of his face and started up the steep hill to the school where some of the village youth studied mage craft with the wizard. Branches grabbed at his damp wool clothing almost as if the trees were alive. Shudders wracked his body. Magic made him uncomfortable. He didn't trust what he couldn't see.

Darkness closed as he huffed up the hill, and Luke's heart stuttered in his chest. Was it night already? If it was, then he was too late. He twisted his head wildly about. Trees were blocking what little light the gray day provided.

Thank Christ! I still have time.

He winced and tried to take back the *Christ* word since he wasn't supposed to swear. Once his Ma would've scolded him, but not anymore.

The hill ended abruptly. At the far side of a clearing stood an imposing stone house with smoke curling from one of its chimneys. Shutters covered the windows. The air around the house shimmered, but Luke ignored what felt like a warning to stay away. He pelted across the scrub grass and up the front steps. Before he could knock, the door creaked inward.

Aethelred eyed him shrewdly. "Well don't just stand there with your mouth hanging open, lad. Did you finally come to your senses about your magic?" The mage quirked a brow, his black robes fluttering about him.

"Pa sent me, he…" Luke choked out, but his tongue had taken root and refused to form words. He tried again. Wizard or no, Aethelred couldn't read his mind. Or maybe he could. Luke cringed away from the uncomfortable thought and forced his next words. "Pa said you've got to come. There's trouble—"

Aethelred drew his brows together into a thick, white line. "Wraiths. I see them in your head. Tell me quick, lad. Who'd they get?" He blew out an annoyed-sounding breath. "Your Pa's a right fool to send you off so close to dark. Is he wanting to lose his only son too?"

"Ma. They took Ma." The words burst out of him. Luke squeezed his eyes tight and bit down hard on his lip.

"Get inside." Aethelred yanked on Luke's arm and slammed the heavy oak door behind him. "What'd your Pa do?"

"Nothing yet. He said we had to burn her. That you'd have something to add to the fire so she'd, uh, stay dead." In a burst of brazenness he didn't know he possessed, Luke tugged at the wizard's sleeve. "Come on. We've got to hurry."

"You should've arrived earlier. They walk at night." Aethelred shrugged Luke's hand off. "Too late now, lad. We'd never make it back to your farm in time."

Luke ran for the door, intent on flight. If the wizard wouldn't help, he needed to get home, be there for his Pa and sissies. He pulled the latch, but it wouldn't open. Aethelred's arms closed around him from behind.

"Damn you," Luke cried, struggling to get free. "I've got to warn Pa and the girls. We never had wraiths before. Pa, he didn't know. He thought he was supposed to let Ma rest through two nights."

To his shame and horror, great gasping sobs tore out of him, leaching the air from his lungs. Luke didn't want to be fifteen anymore. He wanted his mother back, wanted the world to be right again, where your parents knew what to do. Where whether your family lived or died didn't rest on a half-grown kid's shoulders.

"It's not fair." Aethelred apparently read his thoughts easily, which amplified Luke's discomfort a hundredfold. "But if you go back to your farm, your Ma will get you. You'll end up one of *them.*"

"Come with me."

"I think not." Aethelred released him and turned away.

"But you know magic…" Luke's voice trailed off.

A very large raven perched on a rafter squawked, "Know magic, know magic."

Luke startled. He hadn't noticed the bird until it spoke.

The wizard snorted. "Of course I know magic. It's a precarious magic, though—and not within my ken—that'll save someone from wraiths once they've risen."

"I can't abandon my family."

Aethelred looked hard at him. Luke tried to meet his gaze, but couldn't. It was as if the old man was sifting through his soul, hunting for something. "You have talent for magic," the wizard said. "I've told you that before. I could train you, but you must welcome the call to waken your power." He hesitated for a long moment and then asked, "Are you willing?"

Luke shook his head. "No. The answer is still no. I've got to go home. Try to help." His shoulders slumped. "I still wish you'd come."

Aethelred sighed. "It doesn't work that way, lad. If we go, you'll be the first one your Ma singles out."

"Not you?"

"Not me," Aethelred agreed, then added, "I'm not her blood."

"If you can protect yourself, do the same for me," Luke demanded, anger edging out fear.

"It doesn't work that way," Aethelred said sadly. "You're her blood kin. Blood calls to blood from the other side."

Luke moved a few steps farther into the wizard's home and paced in a restless circle, his hands clasped behind him. Mercifully, Aethelred let him be.

It didn't take long to solidify his decision, and Luke stomped forward until he stood dead center in front of the wizard. He forced himself to meet the man's dark gaze. Despite being taller, it was painful to hold his ground. Power fairly oozed from Aethelred until the air thickened with the feel of it.

"I'm going home," Luke said. Terror ground at the edges of his sanity, eroding it one filament at a time. Looking at the wizard hurt his eyes, so he gave up and dropped his gaze to his boot tops. "Is there something—anything—I can do to protect myself?" Luke's heart hammered against his ribcage. His breath came fast and hard.

The wizard blew out an annoyed-sounding grunt and muttered, "I suppose I can at least do that much for you." He unfastened a heavy gold chain from about his neck. "Take this. When you run into trouble—and you will—grasp the stone and call for the goddess. She may help you. Other than that, light a torch. Wraiths avoid fire, unless they've summoned their own to hurt you." He pursed his lips into a hard, flat line. "They have to be wraiths for a while before they learn to call upon fire of their own, so you're likely safe on that front."

Luke gazed at the smooth, dark stone hanging from the chain. Something warm and inviting glimmered in its center. His fingers shook so hard he had trouble with the clasp, but he finally managed to tuck both stone and chain beneath his wet top. They felt soothing against his skin. "Thank you," he managed through suddenly chattering teeth. "I've got to leave now."

Before I lose my nerve and can't go at all.

The door behind him opened, scraping against its hinges, even though no one had touched it. Spinning sharply, Luke ran for all he was worth out the door and down the steps.

The raven's cries of, "Fool, fool, foolish lad," followed him until he was well into the trees.

Panting and with a stitch in his side, Luke didn't slow until he was almost home. So much time had slipped away, it was long past full dark. He'd puked up what little was in his stomach hours before, but the taste of sickness lingered in his mouth. Leaving the road, he crept along a familiar path that led to a cave he went to when he wanted to get away from everyone. Some of the straw there might make a torch—if it wasn't soaked through.

It had been tough to manage his fear while he'd been running. Once he slowed to wend his way under low-hanging evergreen boughs, terror threatened to paralyze him. What if his cave was some sort of channel the wraiths used to emerge from their underground lairs? What if…?

Stop that, he chided himself. *I could've stayed with Aethelred. I didn't.*

Luke bit the inside of his mouth until he tasted blood. The coppery tang broke through his inertia and he surged forward, pulling rushes and tree limbs away from the cave's hidden entrance. A faint, wavery light shone from within. Horror gripped him, tightening his gut, and he spun on his heel to flee.

"Pa? That you?" His sister's thin voice surprised him. Tamra sounded terrified, as if she was barely hanging on.

Yanking more of the cover back from the cave's entrance, Luke called, "No. It's me."

"Luke!" she exclaimed, followed by, "Where's Pa?" Her seven-year-old voice shrilled with fear.

"Don't know."

Gotta be careful, they might've gotten her...

Luke paced the length of the cave. Warily, he watched his sister and the smoky fire sputtering next to her. Aethelred said wraiths avoided fire, so maybe, just maybe, Tamra really was his sister, not some undead horror in sister form.

"Luke—" She gazed up at him out of eyes the same bright blue as their mother's. "Hold me," she whimpered. "I'm s-scared."

Unable to deny his littlest sister—not when she sounded like *that,* so anxious and so alone—he swallowed his dread and knelt next to where she huddled under a tattered blanket. The minute he was on the ground, Tamra threw herself against him, mewling with fright.

"Hush, hush," he murmured, smoothing her hair and reassured by the all-too-human warmth of her small body. Ma had been cold as death after the wraiths took her. "Tell me what happened."

Tamra pushed herself slightly away from him. Her wispy, blonde hair stuck out at odd angles, and her eyes shone with tears. "We—well, Pa—was waitin' for you to get back..."

"Waiting," he interrupted, and then he kicked himself. What earthly difference did her grammar make now?

"You been to school, I ain't."

He hugged her. "Go on, Tam. Sorry."

"It was gettin' dark." Tamra cleared her throat. "Pa, I think he figured it'd been wrong to send you off so close to dark and all. And he was just pacin' up and down the cabin somethin' fierce. Then...then..." Her voice trailed off. "I can't," she mumbled and squirmed back against him.

"You have to. I need to know."

Her small head nodded against his chest. The rest of her body trembled. Voice muffled against him, she went on, her words halting. "Ma, she walked into the big room just like always, even though she'd been laid out dead in the bedroom all day. She was smilin' and she sort of sidled up to Pa and put her arms 'round him. He had this…look on his face. It was awful. He screamed at me, told me to run.

"I…" Her voice broke. She tried again. "I wanted to go to Ma. So bad. But I did what Pa said."

He tightened his arms around her. "Where're Lilly and Marta?"

"Pa, he sent 'em to the Waverlys' farm so they'd be safe. I was supposed to go too, but I didn't want to leave Ma. So I snuck back."

My sisters. They're all still alive. Thank the goddess I came back.

"Did you ever tell anyone about this cave?"

She shook her head. Tamra had followed him one day, tracked him without him knowing. Lilly and Marta weren't nearly as adventurous, preferring to spend their time spinning, cooking, and sewing when they weren't in school. Because Tamra was youngest, their mother kept her home, saying she'd be lonely if all three girls were gone. Tamra had chafed at Ma's edict, and Luke planned to tutor her once the winter crops were in. Suddenly that felt like another world.

Was it safe to spend the night here? Maybe, if he stoked the fire… When dawn came, they could head for the Waverlys' house, half a league away. Tamra wriggled in his arms.

"We need to build up the fire, sissy. Where'd you get something dry?"

"Didn't. That's why it's smokin'."

"What'd you light it with?"

"My flint."

"I've got to get some tinder in here. Do what you can to keep it burning till I'm back."

Tamra let go of him. "I understand," she said, her quavering voice solemn.

Luke's heart went out to her, and he swore he'd do whatever he had to, if it meant keeping her safe from harm.

He stayed within a few paces of the cave. Every rustle in the thick undergrowth made him jump. He longed for a torch, but darkness was his friend. As soon as he was back inside, he whittled strips of wood, paying them into the fire. Tamra wrapped herself in the ragged blanket and fell into an uneasy sleep, twitching and moaning.

He tried to stay awake, but the fire warmed the cave, and he caught himself dozing a time or two. When he woke again, his mother and father stood on the far side of the flames with bodies like tall, thin puffs of smoke, their eyes gleaming unnaturally bright.

"Luke," Ma cooed, holding out her arms. "We found you. Come here so I can hold you, son of mine. I'm lonely."

Mouth agape, Luke glanced from one to the other. Pa's eyes were strange, tracking in opposite directions, and they weren't blue anymore, but a muddy charcoal. Luke looked closer. Ma's eyes were the same red-rimmed smoke shade and both his parents had long, blood-red claws where their fingers used to be. Luke's stomach clenched. If it hadn't been empty, he'd have vomited.

"Your Ma, she told you something," Pa said, his voice gravelly and odd-sounding.

Out of the corner of one eye, Luke saw Tamra edge toward their parents. "No," he cried sharply and snaked out his arm to grab hold of his sister. "You have to stay on this side of the fire."

When he pulled her close to him, she was shaking, her eyes round as small moons.

"I-I think I was knowin' that," she whimpered. "It's just…"

"Hush," he said. "I understand."

Luke's hand crept under his woolen tunic. He grasped the amulet and called for Danu, mother goddess of the Earth. Aethelred just said to call for the goddess. Since he hadn't said which one, Luke hoped against hope Danu could help them.

A hissing intake of breath from the far side of the fire shocked him. "I'm your ma. You pay attention to me." The wraith didn't sound nearly as friendly this time. Nor anything like his mother.

Closing his eyes, Luke sought Danu again, begged for her protection—and her wisdom. He thought he felt…something from the amulet, but he could've imagined it.

The things that had been his parents roared their fury from the far side of the fire pit and reached out with spectral arms. Tamra made another run for Ma, and he dragged her back. Nerves on edge, frayed like old rope, he finally turned away since he couldn't bear to look at what had become of his parents any more. Tamra tried to talk to him, but he shushed her. He didn't want to disrupt what had become an internal litany as he pleaded with Danu for help.

Hours passed. Luke paid out the wood, a bit at a time. He maintained a thin line of flames between them and the wraiths, but the feeble fire flickered ominously. Could it last through until dawn? That was looking less and less likely. Fear for his other sisters nagged him, but he reasoned if Ma and Pa were here, they weren't at the Waverlys' farm, so Marta and Lilly should be safe. He added them to his prayers as a hedge against a phalanx of unknowns.

Luke cast a desperate eye about for something else to burn,

but didn't see anything. Tamra had used up the straw to get the fire going. Only a couple chunks of wood remained, and it was still black as pitch beyond where Ma and Pa had planted themselves.

"We're runnin' out," Tamra whispered, clutching his arm and pointing to the few remaining shards of wood.

The husks of his parents leaned closer, their mouths curved in feral grins.

They're practically salivating. They've figured out there's not enough wood. Soon as the fire wanes, they'll be on us.

Luke cursed himself for a fool, his anger flaring. All his prayers had done was keep him from coming up with a real solution.

Tamra twisted and stabbed a grimy finger in front of her. "What's that?"

An odd light, all colors, and yet no color he could name, oozed through the rocks at the rear of the cave. "I don't know," he muttered. As he stared, mesmerized, the otherworldly glow grew to such a brilliance it hurt his eyes. The amulet, still clutched in his hand, warmed and began to throb.

The fire made a wet, gurgling noise and guttered. Like a hunting dog on red alert, his father jumped the pit, grabbed Tamra, and hauled her toward the mouth of the cave. His sister wailed piteously, writhing and kicking in Pa's grasp.

"No!" Luke screamed. "Nooooo…" He let go of the amulet and lunged after the pair, grabbing Tamra's feet and yanking as hard as he could. Tam screamed louder. Luke kept on tugging. As Ma lowered her face for the kiss that would steal Tamra's soul, the amulet turned red hot against his chest.

The brightness coming from the rear of the cave pulsed with energy.

His father cursed, words he'd never used before spewing

from him, but at least he loosened his grip on Tamra. Luke sprinted toward the rear of the cave holding his sister close. His mother shielded her own body with her hands, but the light curled around her, creating noxious-smelling smoke.

The brilliance was so intense, Luke had to shut his eyes. When he pried them open, Ma and Pa were gone—and so was the mysterious light. The cave sat empty, except for him and Tamra, who was dangling from his hands and still screaming.

Repositioning his sister, he cradled her against him. "Ssssh, hush," he murmured over and over.

"I wet myself," she sobbed, face buried against him.

"Never mind. I would've too, if it'd been me."

"Put me down so I can get my drawers off."

A burnt smell, different from the fire pit, rose and he realized it was his own flesh, scored where the amulet rested against it. He rubbed at his breastbone, but that made it hurt more.

"They're gone," Tamra mumbled from somewhere behind him. "You saved us, Luke." She was still snuffling, but seemed in control of her fear.

Luke readied himself to sit out what remained of the night. He'd just settled against a damp, curving wall when an unpleasant thought struck. "The wraiths. We ran them off here, so they've likely gone after Marta and Lilly." He recognized the ring of truth as soon as the words were out.

A dim version of the curious light in the cave returned, almost as if it agreed.

"If Ma and Pa are truly gone," Tamra sounded much less scared than she had earlier, "we might could take the horse to the Waverlys.'"

Of course. Why didn't I think of that?

"Great idea." Luke realized he should've taken the horse when he went after Aethelred—not that it would have altered the outcome. But Abel was a plow horse and rarely ridden, so it never occurred to him.

He pushed heavily to his feet. "Let's go get Abel. We'll toss a blanket over him. In fact, bring that one." He pointed to hers, wadded in a heap near the wall.

Nodding, she scrambled up. "Think it's safe?" she muttered and peered at the odd light, still suffusing the cave with its comforting warmth.

"Truth?"

"Yes, I'm wantin' the truth." Tamra drew herself tall, a solemn light in her eyes.

"I don't know how safe it is." He swallowed hard. "Probably not safe at all, but we have to warn the Waverlys." He hesitated. "There's something in this cave taking care of us. Let's hope it follows us out of here." He took Tamra's hand. "Come on."

It was black as pitch outside. And cold, but at least it had stopped raining. A slender thread of the multi-hued light floated out of the cave and wrapped itself around the two of them, rather like a length of shimmery rope. Its soft glow was welcome, and Luke managed not to stumble as he led the way to the moss-coated shed where Abel was tethered.

Clucking softly to the horse, Luke tossed the blanket onto his broad back. He untied Abel's halter, and then boosted Tamra up. She ducked to avoid the shed's low-hanging roofline. Luke led the horse out, vaulted onto its back, and turned its head toward the Waverlys' farm. They bounced unpleasantly once he whipped Abel into a ragged trot. When he looked down, Luke was surprised to find his free hand still clutching Aethelred's amulet.

A lighter gray painted the far horizon, and pink streaks formed, pale as seashells. "Hurry," Luke urged, gripping Abel with his knees. "Hurry." Tamra's small body, rigid with determination, pushed against him. He stared down the deserted road, willing the Waverlys' farm to appear.

The glowing rope unwound itself and stretched outward into a straight line.

"I think it means for us to walk from here," Luke muttered, not understanding how he could possibly know that, but knowing it all the same. He wrapped his arm around Tamra and jumped down.

"Abel's leaving," Tamra whispered urgently.

"It's all right. He knows the way home." Luke looked around nervously and followed the ghostly light's trail, with his sister clinging to his side. The amulet warmed again in his hand. He clutched it so hard it cut into his flesh, and blood trickled down his palm.

The road turned a sharp bend. Light shone from the windows of the Waverlys' rambling, two-story farmhouse. Folks used lanterns sparingly because it took a lot of work to render the fat to fuel them. Did all that light mean Ma and Pa were somewhere close? The fine hairs on the back of Luke's neck stood on end, and he combed the dark for any sign of the wraiths.

Tamra gasped, "Luke! Look there," and clung even tighter to his hand.

Outlined in the light of the coming day, Ma and Pa grinned at them from the far side of the Waverlys' front yard. They weren't as…solid as they'd been in the dark of the cave, but they leered and beckoned, calling for their four children.

"Blood knows its own," Ma crooned, her voice simple and terrible. "I birthed you all. Come to me now." The farmhouse door opened, and then thudded shut. Luke heard raised voices inside and understood one of his sisters tried to go to Ma, but had been pulled back. His parents shambled toward the farmhouse, their eyes glistening brightly.

"Go," he hissed at Tamra. "Run onto the porch and get inside." He placed his body between his sister and his parents. Acid curdled his empty stomach and tears stung his eyes. He wanted Pa to be, well, his Pa again. And Ma… She'd fed him, cared for him… How could she have turned into the atrocity advancing across the yard?

Tamra's footsteps pounded as she raced for the porch and safety. Another slam of the door told him she was in the Waverlys' capable hands. With the glowing rope of light in place around him, and apprehension chewing a hole in his guts, Luke shut out the rest of the world and faced the wraiths.

"You shall leave here," he called out sternly, except it wasn't his voice. Someone else spoke through him. It terrified him, but that didn't matter. What did was sudden understanding he'd been picked to kill the wraiths that had been his parents—or be killed trying.

His head whirled, but power humming through him kept him on his feet. Things grew disjointed after that. Pa leapt toward the porch. Before Luke could react, Ma jumped him and he had to push her chill weight off himself again and again. Then it was Pa he grappled with, and then Ma again. In a distant corner of his mind, Luke wondered which was worse: killing his parents or letting them kill him.

He struggled to his feet for the hundredth time, or maybe it was the thousandth. He'd lost count. His head pounded, and his heart ached as if he'd been stabbed.

The amulet grew hot, blazing hot, and the shimmering cord tightened about him. Fire erupted from his outstretched hands, but his parents—and something else he couldn't quite make out

—were finally fading, scattering in the light pouring off him. In moments, they'd be gone.

"Ma, Pa," he moaned, surprised to hear his own voice. "I love you. I'm sorry, so very sorry…"

Something constricted his throat, choking off his air, and the other voice took over his vocal chords again. "You are banished from the light," it shouted. "You shall not return. Not ever."

After that, saying anything became a struggle because the magical cord cut off his wind. The stench of his own burning flesh filled his nostrils, gagging him. Gasping for air, he collapsed in the wet mud of the yard.

WHEN LUKE CAME BACK to himself, he lay on a sofa in the Waverlys' familiar front room. Aethelred bent over him, wrapping soft bandages around his hands. "You came after all," Luke said weakly.

"That I did," the wizard replied. "You called for the goddess, and she sent me to help things along. Hold still now so I can finish with your hands. One was burnt nigh on down to bone."

"Are they gone?" Luke was almost afraid to ask, but he had to know.

"Yes," Aethelred replied, and a savage note chimed beneath that one word. "You did it, lad. They'll not be bothering any of us, not ever again." The wizard hunkered down and looked right into Luke's eyes. The amulet was back around his neck and this time his piercing gaze didn't hurt. "I'm sorry they're lost to you, but we saved your kin from the half-life of the damned. There couldn't be a better outcome."

"Others," Luke croaked. "There must be other wraiths." He

looked blearily at the wizard. It was hard to think because his brain felt swaddled in wool.

"Yes, there are other undead, but they're not your kin. It makes a difference. Once you're better, we'll—"

"Can we see him?" Tear-stained voices interrupted the wizard.

Aethelred frowned against his white beard. "Those sisters of yours have been nattering on ever since I carried you in here and laid you down."

Footsteps clattered on wooden risers. In a flurry of long hair, wet cheeks, stroking hands, and soft words, his sisters surrounded him.

"All right," Luke said gruffly. "I really am all right. No need to fuss so." He disentangled himself from the bevy of embraces, afraid he'd cry.

Recognition of something wrong sank slowly into his befuddled brain, and his eyes widened. "Tamra, where's Tamra?" He staggered to his feet and stared stupidly at the corners of the room as if she might crawl out from under a piece of furniture.

Joad Waverly moved in front of Luke and placed gnarled, work-stained hands on his shoulders. "It was my fault," he said. "I wouldn't let her in."

"But I heard the door—" Luke began.

"Yes, and I slammed it. I'm sorry, son." Joad's nostrils flared. "Tamra'd been out of doors in the dark with…with what was left of your folks. Couldn't risk it." He shook his head sharply. "I had Clare and your other sisters to think of." The big man let go of Luke and turned away.

Luke sat down hard because his legs shook so violently they refused to hold him upright. The tears he'd fought against earlier rose hot and bitter. Anguish roiled through him and he sobbed helplessly, beyond caring if it made him look weak. Marta and

Lilly hovered, trying to stand in for the father and mother all of them had lost.

"Once you're a bit better, you'll be coming with me." Aethelred spoke as if it were fact.

Throat thick, Luke swiped ineffectually at his streaming eyes with a bandaged hand. "I can't," he croaked. His littlest sister, the one he'd sworn to protect, was lost to him. "I've got to take care of them." He gestured toward Marta and Lilly wedged on either side of him.

"Where would you be taking him?" Joad asked, and pushed a hand through his thick, dark hair streaked with gray. His brown eyes caught the wizard's gaze and held it.

"To my school."

Joad nodded. Exchanging glances with his wife, he blew out a sharp breath. "Me and Clare, we thought as much when we saw all them lights out in the yard. We'll look after the girls and both farms till Luke can get back here. Least we can do."

Shaking long, gray hair out of her lined face, Clare echoed, "Yes, it's the least we can do."

"I couldn't let you," Luke protested. "My family's my responsibility."

"Go, son," Joad said. "Soon as you're strong enough. Things will be all right here."

A strange desire mingled with Luke's grief. It was so foreign it took him a few moments to sort it out, to realize he wanted to learn about magic, *needed* to learn. Just like he needed to eat and breathe. Whatever he'd awakened in the cave called to him, sang to him, dared him to pluck the strings holding his inner knowledge captive.

"I feel it too, lad." Weariness creased Aethelred's forehead, yet his eyes shone with hope. "It won't go away. You have no choice after tonight. The call, it comes to each of us in its own fashion.

The way your magic found you, well, it was harsher than most." He exhaled softly, his dark eyes full of warmth as they rested on Luke. "Rest now. There's time yet before we must leave."

Luke's eyelids felt suddenly heavy and he let them close. The warmth stealing about him was probably Aethelred's doing, but he didn't fight it. Burned, weary, and heart sore, he called up images of his parents and sister. Once he'd bid them farewell, he let the wizard's spell carry him away.

*entral Overland Stage Route, East of Salt Lake City
1860*

THE UNMISTAKABLE STENCH of spoiled meat, mixed with fresh excrement, wafted into the stagecoach. Abigail Ruskin knew that smell. She covered her nose with her handkerchief, but it was just as saturated with dust and grime as everything else and she sneezed.

The coach swayed alarmingly, rocking on the leather straps that dampened its lateral motion.

She thrust the heavy leather window curtain out of the way, so she could see how bad things were outside. Usually wraiths left you alone in the daytime—but not always. There'd been a time when they did, but dark magic fueled them these days, making them more dangerous than when they'd just been shades of the dead.

"Damn!" The word escaped despite her effort to stifle it.

"What is it, Miss Abby?"

"Nothing dear." Abigail patted Carolyn Giraud's hand. She was only twelve, and there was no need to alarm her about the wraiths. Without magic, Carolyn wouldn't be able to see them anyway—at least not as anything but gray shadows. Unfortunately, that wouldn't stop them from killing her.

"I want to look." Carolyn craned her neck, but Abigail slammed the curtain back into place. "I really did want to see." Petulance rode beneath the girl's words, reminding Abigail just how privileged and spoiled she was. "My parents employ you. You have no right to tell me *no*." Pain blossomed in Abigail's arm, and she realized the girl had pinched her…hard.

"Now, now. We'll have none of that, young lady." It took all her forbearance not to haul off and slap her young charge.

Abigail settled Carolyn firmly back into her seat and pushed the girl's blonde hair out of her blue-gray eyes, arranging it behind her shoulders. Curves were just starting to show beneath layers of finely woven woolen clothing. Maybe incipient womanhood was responsible for the girl's foul temper—and near inability to follow directions.

"Naught to look at," Abigail said, rubbing her arm. "I must've been half-asleep when I pulled that curtain aside. I'm sure we'll be on the other side of this mountain range in no time and in Salt Lake tomorrow or the day after that."

Unless the wraiths decide to attack. That could push our schedule back quite a bit.

She arranged her mouth in an approximation of a smile to settle her apprehension. The boning from her stays poked uncomfortably into her sides. Abigail did what she could to alleviate the pressure, which wasn't much with the man sitting across from her staring.

"I don't like you." Carolyn crossed her arms over her chest and glared at the floor.

Abigail blew out an exasperated breath. It had been clear from the first day of their long journey from New York City that Carolyn's parents denied her nothing. Gifted witches in Abigail's Coven, they'd hired her through the Coven network to chaperone their only child cross-country to their new family home in Utah Territory. The journey had been quite an odyssey, and it wasn't over yet. They'd traveled by train—three different rail lines—to St. Joseph, Missouri, and then gotten on the Central Overland Stage.

If the goddess kept a kind eye out, the elder Girauds would have their little darling back in short order.

Good thing too, or else I'd kill her.

Abigail's instructions had also included providing tutelage in the magical arts, which was probably why the elder Girauds hired her and not some non-Coven-linked governess. She'd tried, but Carolyn had absolutely zero aptitude, not even enough ability to light a candle. Strange, given how powerful her parents were, but not unheard of since witchcraft didn't follow genetic patterns of inheritance.

Abigail shook her head. She wasn't looking forward to being the one to tell the Girauds their daughter didn't even have a future as a hedge witch, let alone a stronger practitioner. In truth, she was surprised they hadn't already figured it out on their own.

"Like me or no, you'll be rid of me soon enough." Abigail aimed for a cheerful tone. "I'm certain your folks will be delighted to be reunited with you."

"Unless those danged Indians cause more problems," the other occupant of the stagecoach spoke up.

Luke Caulfield was a fortyish gunslinger, who hadn't said much since introducing himself when he boarded back in Sterling, Colorado. Twin colts graced his hips, and rows of bullets crisscrossed his broad chest in leather bandoliers. Black hair fell straight as a stick past his shoulders. Unsettling green eyes stared right through her, almost in invitation to reveal her ability. At times, she'd caught him fairly vibrating with power. Others, no matter how hard she looked, he was as unremarkable as a rain-washed windowpane—at least in terms of magic.

No living, breathing woman would ever consider Luke unremarkable in any other way. Muscles bulged under his form-fitting leather clothing. He was so masculine he made her squirm, and Abigail pressed her thighs together, suppressing thoughts of what she'd like to do with that leather-clad body.

She laced her fingers tightly in her lap, thinking she'd be damned glad to get off this stage and away from both Carolyn and Luke. The child was a pain in the rump and the man too sensual to even consider. He probably had women in a dozen cities across the country drawing straws to see who got to warm his bed. Not that she wouldn't like to be one of them, but he was a complication she didn't need right now.

"Oooh, Indians would be exciting," Carolyn trilled. "Do you really think they might attack us or something?"

"Of course not." Abigail jumped into the breach and shot what she hoped was a meaningful look across the small, enclosed space.

"Do you have to ruin everything?" Carolyn snarled, and reached out with pincer-like fingers.

Abigail anticipated her, though, and caught the girl's hand before she could strike.

"If you try that again," she snapped, "I'll tie your hands behind your back."

Or feed you to what's outside this carriage.

"You wouldn't dare—"

"Oh yes, I would. It's what we do to young ladies who refuse to behave as such."

"I'd tell."

Abigail grabbed the girl's chin, forcing her to look up and meet her gaze. "Yes, and so would I. I scarcely think your parents would be pleased by your behavior." That earned her a sulky silence. When Abigail glanced at Luke, the corners of his mouth were twitching. "Ever raised one of these?" She waggled a finger toward Carolyn.

"No ma'am. Can't say as I have." He chuckled. "Not looking like a very attractive proposition, watching you."

The stage ground to an abrupt halt, throwing her forward and then back against the seat cushions. The hum of brass gears, which worked as an assist to the horses through rough terrain—and that she'd been powering with a steady stream of magic—fell ominously silent. Luke tensed his jaw into a worried line. One of his guns found its way to his hand so quickly, Abigail didn't see him draw it.

She quirked a brow, but he shook his head and said, "I don't know why we stopped. We're not due at the next station for an hour."

"I'm going outside to look," Carolyn announced and lunged for the door latch.

"The hell you are, youngster." Luke's other hand closed around Carolyn's wrist, and the girl yelped. She tried to draw her hand back, but Luke held fast.

Carolyn wailed. Abigail, edgy because she had a bad feeling about what was happening, grabbed the girl's shoulder. Not hard, but enough to get her attention. "You will be quiet," she hissed. "Do you want to advertise your presence to whatever's out there?"

"What'd you see outside?"

Luke's question was so quiet, she wasn't certain she'd even heard it. The shriek of a horse whinnying filled her ears. It sounded like it was dying. The stagecoach canted crazily from side to side as the horses pulled against their harnesses. Luke tapped her leg with his pistol.

"Quick. Tell me."

"Wraiths."

He drew his lips back from his teeth in a snarl. "Figured as much from the smell. You need to help me or none of us'll get out of this."

"What are wraiths?" Carolyn sounded more like a frightened child than a surly almost-teen.

"Never you mind," Luke shot back. "Didn't anyone ever teach you to stay out of grownup conversations?"

"What do you have in mind?" Abigail asked, ignoring his question to Carolyn. She felt power pour off him, and wondered why he bothered with his six-guns. The horses started shrieking again.

"You and I are going out there to take on whatever's stopped us. This isn't a time to hide what you are."

"Carolyn." Abigail kept her voice low. "You will stay inside the coach. No matter what. Do you understand me?"

The girl hesitated before stammering, "Y-yes."

"I don't want to have to explain to your parents that you were killed because you didn't do what I told you."

"All right. I'll stay here," the girl muttered sullenly. "Just go outside and get rid of whatever it is."

Child always has to have the last word.

"Ready when you are." Abigail reached deep, down to the reservoir that held her power. Thank the goddess she'd eaten and rested. Magic was persnickety. It knew when she was worn down.

"I'll take this door." Luke gestured. "You go out the other one. Blast the holy crap out of 'em. Watch out for the horses. Sounds like we only have three left."

"Were the horses how you knew about my, um, abilities?"

He rolled his eyes. "As if I couldn't hear the gears whirling. Driver didn't have a lick of power. 'Sides, most coaches need six horses to pull these grades. We only had four. Now get the hell out there, woman, before we lose another horse."

His door slammed open, clunking against its stops. The last thing Abigail saw before she leapt out her door was Carolyn cowering as far back as she could get against a seat cushion.

Good! Hope the little bitch stays there.

Cursing her long skirts and cumbersome petticoats, Abigail used magic to skip the coach steps. Power blazed from her hands before she could see what she was aiming at. She was afraid if she took even a few seconds to hunt for a target, something would get her. Being dead wasn't desirable, but it was better than the other things wraiths could do to her. Those turned her blood to ice chips.

With her booted feet planted firmly on the ground, Abigail finally got a good look at the wraiths. She drew magic from deep in the earth and sent it chasing after them when they jumped sideways to evade her magic. Insubstantial as tall, thin puffs of smoke, they had glowing charcoal eyes. Long, blood red claws graced what passed for hands. Binding their victims with fiery strands was a favorite trick—just before they sucked your soul right out of you, leaving a handy vessel for one of their masters to occupy. Wraiths used to feed only on the living, making them into new wraiths. They'd been bad enough then, but now they functioned as hired thugs for practitioners of the Black Arts. It lent them the ability to operate in broad daylight. Abigail wondered which group of sorcerers this crew worked for. The Alchemical Council? Black Magick?

Good God but there were a lot of them. *Why?* Surely they weren't interested in the contents of the coach, which only carried mail and Carolyn's substantial luggage. Ducking and spinning to escape being entwined in a blazing net, she thought about the girl's steamer trunks. Abigail only helped pack two of them. The third had been locked and ready to go. Could that possibly be what the wraiths were after?

She shut off her thoughts so she could focus. The ragged sound of her own panting thrummed loud in her ears as she chucked one killing blow after another. Bolts of blue-white light flared from both hands. No point in running anything less than wide open. For each wraith she obliterated, three more showed up to take its place. Her chest ached from breathing sooty air and wraith stench.

Heat seared her back. Damnation! Her skirts were on fire. Abigail funneled magic behind her to quell the flames, but it didn't work. Smoke stung her nostrils. Fire had already eaten a long gouge in one of her hands. If she dropped to the ground to deal with her burning clothes, the wraiths would pounce. Terror licked at her along with the flames.

In spite of her brave thoughts earlier, she didn't want to die. Not here. And not like this. She cursed her corset. It was hard to get a decent breath. If she'd known she was going to have to fight—

"Keep after 'em," Luke growled from behind her. "I have your dress under control." She felt him drape something heavy around her shoulders—a lap robe he must've snatched from inside the coach—and press it close against her with his body. Gratitude wrapped warm tentacles around her. Having him right next to her made her already pounding heart do flip-flops, but she forced herself to focus on something other than all those rock-hard muscles jammed against her back.

"Are they all on this side of the coach?" she wheezed, still struggling to breathe. Between the smoke, her stays, and Luke's body so near, it was a losing battle.

"Pretty much. Guess they want you more than me. Actually, they've been trying to get to the trunks up top."

A discordant warning note sounded in the back of her mind. What the hell was in the girl's luggage that would draw wraiths? Her back wasn't hot anymore, so she assumed the fire was out.

That fire, maybe. The one inside me is just getting going...

She squirmed from more than the smoke and struggled not to turn around and press the front of herself against Luke. They had bigger problems than his undeniable charisma. Luke didn't seem to be in a hurry to move away, though. He remained front to back with her, and she absorbed power flowing from him. Damn, but he was strong. What she wouldn't give for that kind of magic.

It would help if I could breathe...

With difficulty, Abigail forced her mind away from Luke's charms. "The driver?" She hadn't been round to the front of the wagon to check.

"Dead."

"Ever driven one of these things?"

"Concentrate on killing, woman. If we can't get shut of the wraiths, 'twon't matter a diddly damn."

Anger flashed through her at Luke's highhandedness. She stepped away from him, and the lap robe slithered to the ground. Raising her hands, she pulled magic and killed three more wraiths. It was convenient they didn't hang around. They just sort of winked out once hit. For all she knew they weren't dead at all, just returned to some sort of central depot for reanimation. A flash at the edge of her vision set off alarms, but her reflexes were sluggish, and she was a hair too late. A wraith closed, slashing deadly nails down her already-burned hand. Abigail howled with pain. Luke's gun roared, making her ears ring, and a hole opened in the wraith's chest that got bigger and bigger until the thing folded in on itself.

"Thought you couldn't kill them with bullets," she gasped, staring at the place the wraith had been.

"Silver does the trick. I mix it with iron in my gunpowder, just to be on the safe side." Taking aim, he fired again.

Her breath came in little pants. She had a stitch in her side. Her face burned, and her injured hand was gashed so deep bone showed. Wraith fire was deadly like that; once it gained a toehold, it could burn a body to cinders. Thank the goddess, the flames attacking her were all extinguished. She twisted her head from side to side and looked for more wraiths, but couldn't find any.

"They're gone. Must not have liked the odds." Luke holstered his guns.

"Bravo. Nicely done." Clapping came from one of the open stagecoach doors.

Abigail looked toward the coach through eyes that were hot, gritty, and stinging from smoke. Carolyn sat on the floor of the stagecoach with her legs dangling. Something inside Abigail snapped. She raced to her charge and grabbed a fistful of her blonde hair with one hand, wanting to slap her. Hanging onto Carolyn made her wounded hand ache something fierce, but she didn't let go.

"You ungrateful little girl," she snarled. "What do you think this is? A sporting event?"

Blue eyes huge as pinwheels, Carolyn twisted in her grasp, trying to get away, but Abigail held tight. "You've needed your behavior reined in for years. While we're at it, what's in your luggage?"

"Good point," Luke muttered from somewhere close behind her. "We should take a look in there."

Carolyn screamed epithets no well-bred child should even know, and shock slammed Abigail in the guts. "If you don't stop that right now," she gritted, "I'll use magic to bind you." The threat seemed to work because the girl shut up.

Abigail stepped back from her and eyed a stream running by the road. She stumbled over to it, knelt, and threw water on her face and hands. It felt good, cooling the places her skin was charred and split. She pulled the pins out of her hair, bent forward, and soaked the singed, sooty strands. They floated in the current like exotic, dark red seaweed. What she really wanted to do was loosen her corset, but she'd need to strip down for that. Not something she could do in front of Luke.

"I won't look," he said.

Giving her hair a final dunk, she pulled it out of the creek, and wrung as much of the water out as she could manage. She straightened and met his gaze. "You have the mind reading gift?"

"That and other things." He turned away from her. "Go ahead. We've got some hard work ahead of us. It'll help if you can get a straight breath into you."

Unbuttoning her dress, she pulled at the laces holding her stays. She'd planned to just loosen them, but once they were undone, she let the whalebone-reinforced undergarment slip under her skirts where she could just step out of it. She inhaled all the way to the bottom of her lungs and smiled grimly.

Yes. More like it.

"You took your underthings off in front of a man." Carolyn sounded scandalized—and fascinated.

Abigail stomped back to the coach and tossed her stays

inside. "And you just cursed a blue streak. We need to have a talk, but not right now."

Her wet hair soaked through the bodice of her dress, but at least the day was warm enough it didn't matter. She twisted and looked over both shoulders assessing just how damaged her dress was. The thick linen fabric was singed, but not so badly she couldn't still wear it. Good thing, since she'd only packed three others. She focused a few strands of magic to dry everything and moved to the front of the coach.

One of the horses was, indeed, dead. Drawing a knife from her belt, Abigail cut it free from the others with a great deal of difficulty. The remaining three pranced, eyes rolling as they attempted to distance themselves from their fallen companion. She tried to soothe them enough so they wouldn't kick her. When that didn't work, she reached into their minds with a strong suggestion they settle down. *Now.* While she waited for the horses to stop snorting and pawing the ground, she diverted a trickle of magic to patch up the worst of her injuries. There wasn't time to truly heal herself, but she did take a bite out of her pain. She also retrieved the lap robe and stuffed it back inside the coach.

"How should I hook them up?" she asked Luke, finally satisfied she could approach the horses safely.

He'd already pulled the driver off the box and was piling rocks over his body. "One in front, two behind. I'll help you once I'm done here."

As Abigail worked, she speculated just how much more magic it would take to run the gears that powered the wheels and helped the horses over the steep parts. That had been one of the attractive parts about this journey: getting paid twice. Once for shepherding Carolyn, and again for helping with the stagecoach. Still panicked, one of the horses nipped her with its broad, flat teeth. She thwacked the side of its head and wondered what was keeping Luke.

As if in response to her thinking about him, Luke materialized by her side and started tightening the leather straps. "Looks like you've about got it."

"Thanks. Same thing I thought. Should we open her luggage?" Abigail feared what they'd find.

He laid a comforting hand briefly over one of hers. "Nah, let's wait until we're well clear of this spot." Luke jumped onto the box and gathered the reins. "Get inside with the hellion—ah, I mean the girl." He laughed, but without much warmth. "She's not what she appears, but there's not time to talk about that right now."

CHAPTER 2

*A*bigail dragged her tired body to the coach. She slammed one door, and then went around and got inside through the other. She'd barely gotten the door latched when the stagecoach lurched forward. She paid out magic to the gears, seeking a balance point. Once they were humming along nicely, she turned her attention to Carolyn.

The girl stared defiantly at her. "You have witch eyes. Are you going to hit me, witch?"

"Not if you do what I tell you." Abigail trained her hazel eyes on the girl. "Why make a fuss about magic? Your parents are part of my order."

"I'm not their daughter," she said sullenly.

That might be why she doesn't have any magic.

Abigail waited, but Carolyn held onto an edgy silence. Finally, she asked, "Who are you?"

"Goody Osborne." The girl smirked, as if daring Abigail to challenge her.

Skin stretched along the sides of Abigail's face as her eyes

35

widened. *She can't be Sarah Osborne, the witch from the Salem trials* — "What'd you do with Carolyn?"

"Can't tell you."

"Why not?"

The girl shook her head. Abigail considered using magic to force truth out of her, but saw in the girl's eyes that she'd die before giving up her secrets.

I need Luke. Maybe he can read what's in her head.

"Don't try it." Something shadowy and feral flared from Carolyn, darkening her blue eyes to almost black.

Abigail did a double take. The girl didn't have Coven magic. The power she'd taken care to cloak—until now—came from the other side. From the devil worshippers and their ilk. Understanding dawned. "You called the wraiths. You or whoever you work for."

"Did I now?" The girl mimicked her inflection.

Abigail's skin crawled. The thing sharing the carriage seat suddenly felt like consummate evil. Was there any way Sarah Osborne could have taken possession of Carolyn? Spirits did that, body hopping for centuries to give themselves corporeal form.

"What if I'm lying to you?" the girl-thing piped up. "Maybe I really am Carolyn Giraud. After all, I look a lot like the girl in all those pictures you helped me pack. The ones where my parents had their loving arms around me."

The girl smiled. Something about her expression froze Abigail's blood. Her grip on sanity slipping, she focused on the gears, wondered how close the next stage station was, and prayed like hell it would come soon.

The girl eyed her appraisingly, almost as if she was considering some sort of direct attack. Abigail's magic was depleted from fighting the wraiths. Likely Carolyn knew it.

"When did the other side start using children to fight their battles?" Abigail asked. Beneath her discomfort with the girl, she felt sickened, outraged.

"It's logical. People trust us."

"What were you going to do after the wraiths killed us?" Abigail wove a small spell into her question, hoping for at least a halfway truthful answer.

"Well—" the girl leaned forward as if to impart a secret "—I hadn't counted on that man joining us. If it weren't for him…" Her words trailed off.

"Where were you going to slip away to?" Abigail persisted when it became apparent the girl wasn't going to say anything else. "It's pretty unforgiving country out there."

The same supercilious smile crossed the girl's face. Abigail gave up. It was possible part of the child's assignment was to take out the Girauds. At the top of the Coven's hierarchy, they'd be a worthy goal. Did Carolyn look enough like their true daughter to pull off something that bold? Abigail thought it unlikely. Maybe she really was their daughter, conned by inducements from the other side. Or else possessed.

"What do you want me to call you?" Abigail asked.

"Why, Carolyn. It *is* my name." Innocence practically bled from her pores as if their earlier conversation had been a hallucination.

Abigail fought a sick sensation that raised goose bumps, and she stifled a shudder. She needed to do something, but what?

The stagecoach slowed, and then stopped. Abigail withdrew her magic from the gearing mechanism. When she pulled the curtain back, she saw the stone wall of a stage station. Thank God. They'd pick up another driver, though it might be a bit of a wait for the stage company to send one.

"I'm getting out," Carolyn announced. She pushed one of the doors open and trotted nimbly down the metal steps.

"I don't think so. You come back here right now," Abigail countered, but Carolyn kept right on going.

Abigail considered shouting after her to not stray too far from the station, but bit her tongue. Frankly, she hoped to never see the child again. Then she thought about the inadvisability of letting something that wicked run about loose and hurried outside. The earth, packed hard by stagecoaches and horses, felt welcome after the swaying carriage. For once, it wasn't windy, but the November day was growing much colder as evening neared. She caught up to Luke as he emerged from the small office.

"Gave the driver's packet to the station manager," he said. "Fortunate for us someone's here."

"Are they going to send another driver?"

He nodded tersely. Taking her arm, he pulled her off to one side. *"Can you hear me this way?"* he said into her mind.

"Yes."

"I listened to the conversation you had with the kid. Deucedly unsettling. Our safest course is to kill her."

Abigail started to protest that Carolyn was just a child, but the words curdled in her throat. Maybe a child in years, but scarcely in any other way that counted. Still… *"I'm not sure."* She sorted through her thoughts, cataloguing pros and cons.

Luke started talking again before she'd come to any sort of conclusion. *"I sensed something was amiss with her the minute I got on in Colorado. It's like there's two of her, 'specially when she's asleep and her glamour slips."*

Possessed.

Damn! I knew it.

"You got that right." Luke's dry voice intruded. *"She is possessed. Good you recognize it."*

Abigail kicked herself for being gullible and a fool. She'd never thought to question the child of someone so high up in her Coven. *"How long will we be stuck here?"*

"A day. Maybe two."

She met Luke's clear, green gaze. *"What are we going to do with her? I don't trust her not to harm us while we sleep."*

"Humph. Maybe something in her trunks will tell us more." Even his mind voice sounded dour. It was obvious, if he had things his way, he'd murder the girl, douse her in mage fire so she stayed dead, and be done with it.

"Good idea. With everything that's happened, I nearly forgot about the trunks."

No matter how appalled Abigail was by dark sorcery luring children to serve them, she didn't want to have to kill Carolyn unless there weren't any other options. The girl had gotten sucked into something far too sophisticated for her to understand. Maybe Sarah Osborne really had possessed her.

Or maybe Carolyn was just the Girauds' child out for revenge —and power. Some kids were rotten through and through without any assist from magic.

"Come on." Luke put a hand on each of her shoulders and shook her lightly. "You'll never get it sorted out. There're too many *what ifs*. I'll get the steamer trunks down and move them into the coach, one at a time."

Closeted in the stagecoach, Abigail used magic to defeat the locking mechanism on the last trunk. The first two had proven to be the ones she'd packed back in New York. Luke checked for hidden panels, but found nothing.

"What are you doing?" Carolyn screeched, catapulting into

the coach. "Those are mine. Mine. Why are my other trunks outside in the dirt?"

"You will leave now." Luke's voice held compulsion. The girl's slight frame rocked backward before she turned to climb down. "Won't hold her for long," he told Abigail. "Best hurry."

She pushed the lid up, and it creaked on unhappy hinges. Her mouth fell open and she drew back, feeling the bite of foul magic immediately. The trunk was full of ancient books. If they were all like the ones on top, they dealt with arcane magick and the Black Arts.

"No wonder it was so heavy." Luke reached out a hand and turned a leather-bound volume on its side. *Alchemy for Dark Wizards, Volume I*, sprang into view in gilt lettering, edged with red. His mouth set in a hard line, he picked it up and flipped it open.

"Go ahead, look through it." Carolyn's face was framed in the open doorway. Her lips were parted and spots of color rode high on both cheeks. "That's one of my favorites. You can read to me." She paused. "I like it when men read to me, probably 'cause my daddy read to me a lot."

Abigail blanched at the fascination in the child's voice. When she turned to stare at her, she was horrified to see Carolyn bouncing up and down, vibrating with eagerness to hear a tale fraught with evil. "Luke—" she began, but he'd noticed too and dropped the book. It made a slithery, slapping sound before the thud of the trunk lid slamming shut drowned it out.

"Oh." Carolyn's voice bled disappointment. "You've gone and closed it." An uncomfortable look flitted across her features. "What I said about Daddy… He'd read me school books and such."

Feeling ill, Abigail opened her mouth to try to talk with the girl, but Carolyn turned and fled. Abigail gathered her skirts close and started out the door. "I hate the idea of her next to me," she said to Luke, "but we can't just let her run off."

Luke latched a hand around her arm. "We can catch her later," he muttered. "Devil's spawn. There'll be no saving that one." He eyed Abigail, a resigned expression on his face.

She tried to shake off his hand, but he held tight. "I really think I ought to go after her."

"Stay put. Please." He softened his tone. "We need to talk. This won't take long."

She stared at the place Carolyn had disappeared over a draw and sucked in a tense breath before meeting Luke's gaze. "I suppose you're right. How hard could it be to track a child—even one who's possessed? Frankly, I'm more worried about the parents. Whose side are they on?"

"She already told you she's not theirs."

"And then she told me she lied." Abigail hesitated a beat. "I'm fairly certain she's a Giraud because I used magic just now to check." She frowned and bit back a string of curses at what a mess this had turned into. "I didn't get all that far inside her, but far enough to sense the parents' blood. And something else too." She blew out a harsh breath. "The more I think about it, the more I believe Sarah Osborne possessed her. It's the only explanation that makes sense."

Luke shook his head and a resolute expression hardened his features. "It doesn't matter. We need to find her and...alter things. Did you see that unnatural hunger in her eyes? I've known kids like that before. Can't salvage 'em. Waste of good magic to try."

"Yes. You already said that." Abigail closed her eyes. Something about having all those books right next to her did odd things to her mind. The trunk must have been spelled to contain their wickedness, but enough had leaked out to make her light-headed. She gripped the handles and helped herself down from the stagecoach.

"Come on." He followed her out and took her arm, but she shook him off.

"Let go of me," she bristled. "I need to think. I'm tired and hungry. Besides, I don't know a thing about you other than you have magic."

He pulled a battered, leather wallet out of a pocket. From within its folds, he extracted a thin, wooden card. It had two five-pointed stars encased in circles with a triangle scribed about everything. The unmistakable signature of their founder scrawled across the triangle from lower left to upper right in faded red, which was likely blood. Luke flipped the card over. His name was engraved across the back. She recognized the insignia, felt power ooze from the slender piece of sacred balsam wood. Coven enforcers carried those. She narrowed her eyes. "I thought I knew all the enforcers."

He shrugged. "Guess you missed me."

"Is that why you picked this stage? To protect the Girauds' child?"

He looked at her for a long while. "You know I can't answer questions about Coven business. I wouldn't have identified myself, but I need you to trust me. I can take care of the girl by myself, but it would be easier if you helped." Balancing on the upper stagecoach step, he heaved the book trunk back onto the roof and barked a command to seal it from prying eyes.

By the time he stood before her again, she'd made up her mind. Swallowing her reservations, she set off on foot with Luke in search of Carolyn. They hunted for hours, magical senses on full alert, with no sign of her.

"Goddammit! She's playing us for suckers." Luke pulled the black cloak he'd tossed over his leathers closer about himself. "It pains me to admit it, but you were right about going after her earlier. She's close, but she moves whenever we do, and we're wasting our time."

Abigail glanced at the moonlit terrain, all shadows and scrub oak and sagebrush. "I need to eat something and sleep. I don't have enough magic left to call a mage light." She shivered. Once she'd stopped moving, the chilly night air sank into her bones. Lots of places hurt too. She hadn't been able to spare any magic to fix herself up since right after the wraith attack.

He nodded, draped an arm around her shoulders, and steered her back toward the stage station. The stationmaster had told them they could sleep on the floor of the office with him, but the coach at least had cushions. Luke helped her inside, and Abigail dug some nuts and dried fruit out of her valise. She chewed automatically, washing everything down with half a water skin.

"Here." He handed her a silver flask. Whiskey burned as it tracked down her throat to her stomach, but it warmed her, too. "Sleep. I'll take first watch."

"She's not anywhere near here," Abigail protested. "We hunted for hours. You could probably get some rest."

Luke shook his head. "Nope. She's around. I feel it. Soon as we bed down, she'll show herself, hopefully not with reinforcements, but I wouldn't put it past her."

"Wake me if that happens." Blackness closed about her almost before the words were out.

CHAPTER 3

*L*uke listened to the rise and fall of Abigail's breathing. Even asleep, tension fairly bled from her, and he sent threads of magic to soften her agitation. The current turn of events was damned upsetting. The child, Carolyn, reminded him of an older version of Tamra, in appearance not actions, but still… For her to look so much like his sister and be chockfull of wickedness was unnerving. His current assignment from the Coven was to guard Carolyn against harm on her journey, a duty he'd been ambivalent about since getting on the stagecoach and sensing the girl's disturbing dual nature.

HE'D TRAVELED a long road since that hideous morning in the Waverlys' living room when he'd discovered his favorite sister was dead. At first, he'd thought it a kindness for Aethelred to take him in, but the mage quickly disabused him of that notion. The older man's primary interest in him was honing his magic to the sharpest possible edge.

"There's a war coming," he'd told Luke. "There won't be near enough of us, so each of us'll have to do the work of ten."

Luke shook his head and stifled a sigh, lest he wake the woman across from him. One of Aethelred's talents was prophecy. Luke had spent ten years with him. In that time, wraiths had turned from an occasional annoyance to an outright scourge. Their alliance with Black Magick lent them an even more unnatural power. When he and Tamra had cowered in the cave near his home, scared half to death, fire provided a hedge. Not anymore. Not only were wraiths unafraid of fire, they used it as a weapon regularly. And not just those who'd been dead for a while. Newly turned wraiths were just as likely to burn their enemies as those who'd been dead for a hundred years.

His thoughts returned to Aethelred. Once he discovered if it weren't for his magic, the wizard would've left him with the Waverlys, he'd resented him, but then he'd grown up. What had wakened in him that awful night when he was fifteen was shockingly powerful. If it hadn't been for Aethelred, he might have gone mad. As it was, he'd cried himself to sleep many a night, a thin pillow stuffed into his mouth to muffle the sound. Magic raced through him like lightning, setting his teeth on edge and his nerves on fire. He'd railed against it, tried to jam it back into whatever box it came from, but nothing worked.

One long, winter night after he'd been with the wizard for more than a year, Aethelred had come into his room. It was one of the bad times, and Luke's pillow was wet from his tears. Usually, he did a better job controlling them, but that night things had gotten away from him, maybe because he'd visited the Waverlys and his sisters, and seen the house all decked out for the upcoming Christmas holiday. It had driven home the fact he'd never have a family again, or anyone to care about him. It wasn't that Lilly and Marta had forgotten him, but they'd settled into the Waverlys' household. Despite Joad's words about keeping up both farms until Luke returned, he knew he'd never be back—and so did Joad.

His narrow cot had creaked when Aethelred balanced on its edge. "I'm sorry," the wizard said. "I wish things were different, but they aren't, and they never will be. You are…altered and it sets you apart from everyone you ever loved."

Luke sat up then and called a mage light, one of the first magics he'd learned and by far the easiest. He didn't try to hide his tear-blotched face. "I don't begrudge them moving on…" His voice faded, because it wasn't true. Not really.

Aethelred narrowed his eyes. "In a corner of your soul, you do, though. Change is hard. You didn't just lose your folks that night, and the one sister. You lost your family, and the reality of that is just now sinking in."

Luke's throat thickened, but he pushed past it. "They looked at me funny when I was visiting today. Like they didn't quite trust who—or what—I am."

"They don't," Aethelred spoke flatly. "Those without magic don't trust us. What we can do makes them uncomfortable." He heaved a sigh and quirked a shrewd brow. "Remember how you felt about me? And not so very long ago."

Luke winced. He did remember, and it wasn't pretty, but reality often wasn't. It was one of the things he'd learned that he wished he hadn't. He opened his mouth, but the wizard waved him to silence.

"I had a family once. A wife and children, since my power came to me much later than yours." He blew out a haunted-sounding breath. "I still remember the day Hagan, my wife, told me she was going back to her folks—and taking the children with her. They were from her first marriage, but I loved them all the same. Magic terrified her."

Luke stared at Aethelred then, really seeing his mentor for the first time, and he felt ashamed. He swallowed around the lump in his throat and forced his next words. "I've been so sunk in feeling sorry for myself, and wishing my life hadn't gone to hell, I haven't appreciated much of anything you've given me." Remorse swamped him. "I'm sorry. Truly I am."

Aethelred held up a hand. "Stop. You owe me nothing, least of all apologies. We were part of something bigger than both of us when you lost your sister and your folks. Never forget that. The goddess brought you to my door that night, and then she chivied me out after you. So long as evil lurks, there will be those like us to fight it." The wizard had leaned close then. "If we die out, there'll be no hope for humankind."

THE CRY of a night hawk out hunting brought Luke back to himself, and he looked around the dark stagecoach. He'd turned a corner that night in his little room under the eaves in Aethelred's rambling house and learned to focus on what was important. The boy in him died, making room for the man he would become. He'd developed his magic, embraced it for the gift it was, and helped tutor Aethelred's students. None of them had much ability, but he'd found grace and patience for those less skilled than he.

On his twenty-fifth birthday, the wizard had given him a horse and told him it was high time he made his way in the world. He'd known the day would come, welcomed it because it meant he'd be leaving the relative safety of Aethelred's compound and testing his mettle against whatever fortune threw at him.

He'd freelanced for a while, and then the Coven had hired him as an undercover enforcer, which was why Abigail hadn't recognized him. It was useful for the organization to have those like him—and there were an even dozen—to do jobs the Coven needed to distance itself from. He hadn't been slated to keep an eye on the Girauds' child, but the man who'd drawn that duty had been killed in an unexpected skirmish.

The Girauds' child.

Luke pressed his lips together. When she'd leaned in the stagecoach door blazing with fervor over what was in the books, it had taken all his will power not to throw a bolt of magic that would stop her heart. What she'd said about her father had been chilling too. Little twit. Dark magick had its claws into her so deep, there wasn't a way out. Whether the girl had been turned, or whether she was truly possessed by one of the Salem witches mattered little. What did was finding her and annihilating her, preferably with mage fire so she'd stay dead. Once that was done, he could worry about her parents and which side they were on.

Abigail sighed in her sleep and repositioned herself. Her leg fell against his, warm and enticing, and his breath hitched. She was a damned attractive woman. He'd kept pretty much to himself, except for the odd dalliance, mostly with fancy women who wouldn't want anything from him but coin. Abigail might change all that. He wondered about her. She didn't wear a ring, but she could still be married, or have a special man tucked away somewhere. There hadn't been much chance to talk about anything personal, but he'd felt drawn to her from the moment he got into the stagecoach.

Having her dress turn practically transparent after she soaked her long, red hair in that creek hadn't helped. Her full, firm breasts, with puckered nipples, had been visible through the linen fabric of her shirtwaist. He'd kept his word and not watched while she slithered out of her corset, but knowing what she was doing had given him a hell of a hard on.

His current line of thought wasn't helping. He reached down and rearranged his straining cock so it wasn't bent double against his too-tight breeches. Luke tried to think about other things, but his body wasn't interested in cooperating. He inhaled Abigail's earthy scent: jasmine, vanilla, and musk, and wished he could take care of himself unobtrusively, but there was no way. Any motion would make the coach rock on its straps and waken Abigail.

He settled for smoothing a few stray hairs off her cheeks. She had an arresting face with sharp cheekbones and a strong jaw. Even though her eyes were closed just now, they were an intriguing multi-hued hazel, shading from brown to violet to green depending on how the light hit them. Her brows were a deep auburn color and they winged across her forehead, giving her a haughty look. Full lips covered very straight, white teeth. He pegged her for around thirty, but witches didn't age if they didn't want to, so she could be much older than that. Not that it made any difference. Magic wielders lived a long time. If she found him as attractive as he found her…

Luke shook his head, disgusted with himself. They had to get out of the mess they were in. First and foremost, that had to be his primary focus, or they likely wouldn't survive. He told his engorged cock to stand down. There might be an opportunity for its needs later. This time, it wasn't quite so difficult to wrench his thoughts away from his body and address the problem at hand.

Where was the damned girl?

Why hadn't they been able to find her?

When he fanned magic about, he felt her particular, putrid emanations, but couldn't pinpoint quite where they were coming from. Luke took a deep breath. He'd played this game many times before, where you were either hunter or hunted. He was confident if he lay low, the girl would show herself. He shut his eyes for the barest moment to rest them. They felt hot and gravelly, but sleep was out of the question. When Carolyn showed herself again, he'd be ready for her.

Toward that end, he deepened Abigail's slumber so the coach's canting wouldn't waken her, and let himself outside. Once there, he wrapped a protection spell around the sleeping woman and faded into shadows, magic at the ready. It would be easier to deploy a defensive strategy from where he crouched, hidden by sagebrush, than from inside the enclosed coach.

CHAPTER 4

It wasn't Luke but a long, drawn-out shriek that brought Abigail thumping back to consciousness, her heart hammering triple time in her chest. Eyes wide and staring against the darkness, she warded herself just in time. Strong magic battered her. She tried to sense Luke, but that was the problem with wards. They protected by forming an impenetrable barrier that corralled her magic inside.

Whatever was pummeling her first lessened and then faded entirely. Abigail waited, but it seemed to have given up. She risked chinking a very small hole in her warding to send a tendril of magic outward because she needed information. When it came, it terrified her so profoundly, her heart stuttered.

Dark things surrounded them. Humans who'd sold their immortal souls for forbidden knowledge drove wraiths and mad wolves—creatures turned to serve the other side—into a fury. Had the girl rallied them? How could she possibly be that powerful?

She's not, but Sarah Osborne is.

Luke didn't seem to be anywhere. Abigail hoped he'd

concealed himself out of harm's way, because the two of them couldn't make the slightest dent in the dark horde outside. The stagecoach rocked, and she realized someone was climbing onto the roof. Throat so dry she could barely breathe, she mended her warding.

The books. That's what they want... Let them haul the miserable things out of here.

She should risk heaven and hell to keep such knowledge out of dark hands, but Abigail didn't see how throwing her life away would alter the outcome. She heard voices speaking the demons' tongue, and then dragging sounds as someone transferred the trunk to the ground.

Luke shouldn't have bothered to put it back up top, she thought grimly.

What had the Girauds been doing with such arcane tomes in the first place? She supposed there was the slightest chance they'd been protecting them from falling into the wrong hands.

Yes, by all means, let's give Coven members the benefit of the doubt.

Except it was a stretch of anyone's credibility, and she didn't know who the hell to trust anymore. She waited until it was absolutely still outside. A tentative scan told her the dark host she'd sensed earlier had moved on, and she loosed her wards. The minute she did, she felt Luke's energy.

He pulled open one of the coach doors. "I scared up a couple of horses from a nearby farm. We need to go after those books—and the girl."

She fought down the protest that rose to her lips, but it slid out anyway. "There aren't enough of us."

"Fixed that problem too." He smiled grimly. "I can ward you if you want to stay here, but if you're coming we need to get moving. Don't want to let the trail grow too cold." From the smirk in his voice, she knew he was being sarcastic.

She sent her magic spiraling outward and felt the books pulsing with evil. No way *that* path would ever get cold. "Why couldn't I feel them this strongly before? I know the trunk had to have been spelled, but still…"

"The trunk was spelled, and by someone with magic to burn. It's over in those trees. I guess Carolyn's minions were in a hurry and didn't have a wagon."

Abigail felt like a rube. The book trunk had already been packed and sealed when she'd picked Carolyn up in New York. She'd never even thought to examine it. "Did you see Carolyn?"

"Yup." He curled his upper lip into a sneer. "Caught a glimpse of her riding a mad wolf and laughing her fool head off."

"Do you suppose there's some way we could separate her from Sarah Osborne?" Abigail bit her lip nervously.

Luke shook his head. "Even if we could—and I don't think it's possible—there are too many unknowns. Her parents might've been turned. If that happened, the kid could've embraced evil before it entered her body. By the time we sorted all that out, the dark would have one too many chances to kill us."

Abigail winced at the unvarnished truth in his words. Any residual doubts she held about the necessity of destroying the girl frittered away. "Yes," she said through clenched teeth. "I'm coming with you."

Luke boosted her onto one of the horses. She pulled her skirts out of the way. It was a normal saddle and this was scarcely a time for modesty. Luke vaulted onto his horse, kneeing it, and they took off up the Central Overland Stage Road at close to a full gallop.

"We're making too much noise," she sent.

"Doesn't matter. They'll expect us to come after them."

She clung to the horse with her legs, enjoying the feel of not having to ride sidesaddle. Luke's horse was larger, faster, and soon pulled so far ahead she could barely see him. She kneed her horse, urging it to greater speed, but the animal shied, and then reared. Abigail struggled for balance and called magic to calm the spooked animal. Something sprang at her and knocked her to the ground. She sent killing magic to stop its heart before realizing what it was. Panting, she crawled out from under a black and gray mad wolf with blood dribbling from its nostrils.

Abigail glanced warily about. There had to be more of them, so where were they?

Carolyn stepped from the shadows. It looked as if she was alone, but Abigail suspected otherwise. "What do you want?"

"Simple enough. I plan to use you to get rid of Breana Giraud —and others." A sneer twisted the girl's features into something unpleasant. "You think people don't know you're part of Coven government?"

Abigail set her mouth in a hard line. "Fine. So the other side knows about me. Question is, who are you really?"

"Don't you recognize me?" Carolyn stepped closer and turned her face from side to side as if posing for a photographer. "I gave you my name, but I am far more than that."

She's arrogant. Perhaps I can use that in some way.

Abigail spread her hands in a placating gesture. "Because I'm used to seeing you as Carolyn Giraud, I'm not certain who you are, but I'm very interested." She paused for emphasis. "I'd like you to tell me."

"Certainly." A feral grin made the child look like something out of a nightmare. "It's always better to know who your adversary is." Her voice turned soft and silky. "I have access to magic you would kill for. You may not know it, but you'd like to work for us." She laughed, but it sounded more like broken glass shattering against itself than a twelve-year-old girl's mirth. "We have real power, not that paltry tripe the Coven settles for."

Abigail waited. When Carolyn didn't say anything else, she urged, "I'm listening…and considering your offer. Life is always better than the alternative."

"Ha! They said you couldn't be turned, but I told them they were wrong. I am The Promised, resurrected out of legend. Sarah Osborne was but a start, and this little girl is merely a convenience." Something like an outraged squawk followed the words, but Sarah silenced Carolyn almost immediately. "What I really want is you, Abigail Ruskin."

Shit! She can't be The Promised…

"You mean the Dark Messiah? The one who's supposed to show up to lead Black Magick mages to some kind of glory at the end of days?" Abigail scrunched up her face and held her breath, hoping against hope she'd gotten it wrong.

"The same." A supercilious expression etched into the girl's features. "At least the other side has heard of me. Warms my black, black heart."

"The books—?" Abigail hunted for a connection while she rode herd on terror that threatened to immobilize her as it clouded her judgment. If ever she needed a clear head, it was now, but her mind raced feverishly.

"They weren't doing the girl's parents any good moldering away in that underground chamber. I'd actually been searching for them for years." She flashed a sly smile. "They used to be mine."

Understanding flooded Abigail like a sour tide. "You led Carolyn to the books, corrupted her, figured out how to defeat the Girauds' warding, and—"

"Not exactly, but then you don't need to know everything."

"No, I don't suppose I do." Abigail ground her teeth together so hard she was surprised they didn't splinter.

She was trying to come up with another question to stave off what was feeling inevitable when the thing in Carolyn's body cut her off coldly. "Will you switch allegiance?" A knife materialized in her hand. "I would bind you with your blood."

"Why me?"

"Once I absorb more Coven knowledge, I shall be the most powerful sorcerer the world has ever known, strong enough to kick the gates of Hell open. Using your body, I can get close enough to Coven members to kill them. Once they're dead, I'll soak up their magic too."

Abigail clenched her jaws to keep from screaming. "If I say no?" Once she gave her blood and her word, she'd be stuck. She sent magic spinning outward to discover what lay hidden by darkness and found mad wolves and wraiths.

"They'll kill you—after I've emptied your magic." The girl laughed shrilly. "I can make use of you, no matter what you decide. I could simply force my way inside you, but you'd fight me tooth and claw and I'd have to keep my guard up every single moment." She shrugged. "It's scarcely worth the trouble."

Desperate for time to think, Abigail tried for a deferential tone. "May I have a moment or two to consider?" Once Sarah abandoned Carolyn's body, the child—who was really nothing more than a victim—would be helpless.

"Not more than that."

"What happens to the girl?"

A nasty smile crossed the thing's face. "I'm surprised you even have to ask."

Another outraged squawk, presumably from Carolyn, was cut off midstream.

Abigail turned in a slow circle, assessing just how many she faced. She thought about Luke, but couldn't risk calling him because Sarah would pick up her mind voice.

"Choose now, witch. Power or death."

Abigail sucked in an uneven breath and blew it out, her eyes on Carolyn. She felt the sizzle of magic build in the air and recognized her own death, hovering, just waiting for an order to release it. She threw wards up, but didn't think they'd hold against the enormity of the power thrumming about her. In spite of herself, awe filled her. What would it be like to command that much magic? Maybe she should sign on with the dark—just until she learned their secrets. Surely there'd be a way to break free after that.

No!

She shook her head hard to clear it. Sarah must be using compulsion on her, but it was so subtle and sneaky it almost slipped past her guard. Abigail had just opened her mouth to ask for a little more time when a blast nearly deafened her and a shriek tore out of Carolyn, terrible to hear in her still-childish voice. Hands raised to call power fell to her sides, and blood sprayed from the hole ripping its way through her midsection.

What the hell?

Abigail scanned the darkness for Luke, but didn't see him. Loosing her wards, she pulled earth magic. It rampaged through her as she sent death spiraling in all directions. An odd sensation filled her, boosting her power tenfold, and her myriad injuries healed immediately. When she realized what had happened, a corner of her mouth twitched downward in horror.

Against all reason, the Salem witch hadn't died with Carolyn. She'd fled in time to blast her way right through every single one of Abigail's wards. Her moment of indecision—the one where she'd wondered about signing on with the dark for long enough to learn their secrets—had been her undoing.

"Get out," Abigail shrieked, feeling violated—and helpless. She started to claw at her midsection, but stopped, knowing it wouldn't change a thing.

"Make me," Sarah smirked from a place deep inside Abigail.

Luke and six men who looked a lot like him—tall and powerfully built, with cold eyes—closed behind her and jumped from their horses. Coven enforcers. She recognized most of them. The night came alive with light as power blazed from their hands—and guns. After putting up slightly more than token resistance the dark creatures scattered, apparently not willing to sacrifice themselves without someone driving them.

"Stupid little girl." One of the enforcers walked to Carolyn's corpse, muttered a spell, and the body caught fire. His leathers creaked when he moved and he'd braided his dark hair, probably to keep it out of the way.

Another man, who could've been twin to the first, snorted. "Yeah, from what Luke said, we need to make certain that one stays dead."

"Plan to. I'll remain until I'm certain. Then I'll catch up."

Abigail watched the flames, feeling she'd failed in some elemental way. If she'd been sharper on the uptake, maybe she'd have come up with a way to salvage the child, never mind circumventing the pickle she was in. She pressed her lips together into a thin, worried line. The Girauds would be devastated, but once they'd heard the story, Abigail was nearly certain they'd understand.

Maybe not. Depends whose side they're actually on.

Sarah had said she wanted Breana's blood, but not Don's. Abigail tried to puzzle out what that meant, but her brain wouldn't cooperate.

The other enforcers mounted up and left in a clatter of hooves and dust. The noise cut into Abigail's bleak thoughts. So did Luke when he placed an arm around her. He smelled of sweat and magic, a welcome change from the stench of burning flesh. "We still have to round up those books."

Abigail turned and looked right into his eyes. Sarah's power swelled inside her in dark, alluring waves. The Salem witch clearly liked men. Abigail waded through revulsion and sick knowledge that Sarah had cut through her defenses as if they were nothing but air, and managed to toss a weak smile Luke's way.

"I'm coming," she muttered.

"Of course you are," Sarah nattered from her ringside seat. *"You're going to save those books."* Abigail cringed and struggled to maintain a neutral expression.

Luke must not have noticed because he nodded. "Thought you'd see it that way. Besides, once we've got that little problem cleaned up, I'd like to find a decent hotel and buy you a meal."

She swallowed a desire to shriek as Sarah urged her to accept and cocked her head to one side. "I'd like that. Can't remember when I last had a gentleman caller."

"He's no gentleman." The enforcer who'd torched Carolyn chortled.

Abigail made a huge effort to forget about Sarah, which wasn't easy because the Salem witch had opinions about everything, and forced her weak smile into a grin. She continued to focus on Luke's amazing green eyes and let him fill her thoughts. Gentlemen were a dull breed. It was a little too soon to tell, but despite her earlier concerns, she thought she wanted someone just like Luke, or she would want someone like him if she could jettison the Salem witch. Danger and power lurked beneath his sanguine surface, and the combination heated her blood. Unfortunately, Sarah wanted him too, which posed huge problems. Abigail drew her horse back with a thread of magic. It whinnied as it trotted over.

She snapped up the trailing reins and did her damnedest to appear normal. When she'd turned her attention away from the abomination inside her, she'd actually been able to think clearly. Maybe, just maybe, she could control a two-hundred-year old spirit and bend it to her will. She glanced at Luke, infusing a hint of promise into her gaze. "Ready?"

"Whenever you are." Luke boosted her up. His hand rested on her rump a shade too long, and she leaned into it. Throwing him an even wider grin, she urged her mount after the other enforcers.

Coven and dark power too... If I get really lucky, I can harness the best of both worlds.

Maybe.

From somewhere deep inside, raucous laughter clawed at her innards. Her earlier misgivings rose to mock her and clouded her mind, but Abigail pushed them aside and rode hard. If she gave in to her fears about what the Salem witch could do, she'd sink into madness. The only way to deal with Sarah was with stealth, since the witch could read her thoughts. She'd sort out exactly how to wend her way through the minefield her body had become as things played out. For now, it might be best not to think about anything. The better Sarah got to know her, the harder it would be to fool the Salem witch.

And if I can't trick her somehow, I'll never get out of this alive.

CHAPTER 5

*L*uke vaulted onto his horse and galloped down the road. His hand still tingled from the jolt of sexual energy he'd sensed helping Abigail mount up. She certainly hadn't seemed like a loose woman before. Had getting out from under babysitting her charge freed up a different side of her? He peered through darkness and sent magic ahead to make certain he was following the others. Not as much as a hoof beat broke the silence surrounding him. He didn't see how Abigail could've gotten so far ahead, particularly since his horse was faster than hers, but he was sure he'd catch up soon.

His body was on fire. Heat licked at his loins, and his cock ached where it pressed against his tight, leather breeches. What was the matter with him? He hadn't had such a visceral response to a woman—ever. What he felt was ten times as intense as his sexual arousal when she'd drowsed across from him in the stagecoach.

Partially because of the need to maintain a low profile, and partly because he detested group gatherings, he'd avoided Coven get-togethers. He'd heard reports about raucous group sex from

63

some of the other enforcers, though. They were forever nagging him to come along and try out some of the randier witches. Before he knew what he was doing, his fingers had tugged the lacings of his pants open. Chill air blowing against his suddenly exposed cock brought him to his senses.

"What the hell?" he muttered, and stuffed his erection back under cover. "Was I just going to do myself out here in the open?" Because he couldn't put his pants back together one-handed, he looped the reins around the saddle horn and quickly set himself to rights. His imagination needed a bucket of cold water, and he could use a shot of whiskey. Maybe if they got those books burning, he'd forget about his cock. Fey magic was afoot; he felt it all around him, and it iced the marrow in his bones.

Luke forced his mind away from sex. Discipline, the product of long years of imposed structure resurrected itself, but it didn't happen as smoothly as he might've liked. Perhaps dinner with Abigail wasn't such a good idea after all. Maybe the woman had…done something. Cast some sort of spell to snare him. She didn't seem the type, but he had to admit he barely knew her, and things had been tense almost from the time he'd gotten onto the stagecoach because of the girl. Or maybe it wasn't Abigail at all, but those damned books. He hoped so.

He kneed his stallion to greater speed, thinking he should have caught up to Abigail by now, let alone the rest of the group. The servants of the dark had left on foot, for chrissakes, unless someone had met them and spirited them—and the books—to another location. He pounded a fist into his thigh and willed the horse to run faster. Those books needed to be wiped off the face of the Earth. There was more than enough wickedness in the world, and the knowledge in those books would swell the ranks of evil he'd sworn to destroy.

Finally, he caught the sound of hooves ahead. He opened his mouth to call Abigail's name, but stopped himself. His head had cleared and the almost sick sexual tension drained away. If touching her had that kind of impact, he'd do well to steer clear…

"There you are," Abigail cried as he rode alongside. "I waited and waited, but you never did—"

"Seen any sign of the others?" he broke in and reined his horse so it trotted next to hers. His voice sounded gruff, but he wasn't in the mood to modulate it.

"I haven't passed them, but you'd know that since you came the same way."

Luke winced. He'd asked a stupid question, and she'd just rubbed his nose in it. "Humph. You given any thought to the girl's things?"

She turned her head to glance his way. "My, you're not sounding very friendly." Her tone was mild, but a chiding note grated against him.

"Sorry. It's been a rough night. Carolyn's trunks?" he prodded.

"I haven't thought much about them. Why?"

Surprise speared him. It seemed odd she'd have to ask. "Her kinfolk will want them back, since it's all that's left of their child."

After a hesitation that felt a shade too long, she said, "You're right, of course. Uh, guess I'll have to go back to the stage station and give the stationmaster instructions—and figure out when the next stage leaves, assuming it has room for me and those steamer trunks."

Luke had been listening carefully. Her last words sounded different, more like the woman he'd spent hours searching for Carolyn with. He shook his head. Maybe he was imagining things. He sent out a telepathic call to the other enforcers. One thing at a time. If they didn't run those books down now, they wouldn't get a second opportunity. He could figure out what was going on with Abigail later.

"Say—" Abigail's voice tone changed again "—since you brought it up, I could return the books to the Girauds. After all, they apparently kept them safe for years."

"Bad idea. Besides, we have no idea how long they had those books. One thing's certain, if they'd done that good a job, we wouldn't be out here in the middle of the night tracking them. Nope. We get hold of the damned things, they're headed for mage fire. It's the only way. Moreover—" he darted a glance in her direction "—neither of us are exactly sure which side the Girauds are on. We could be delivering coal to Newcastle, or even worse, weaponry."

A hissing intake of breath startled him. Luke twisted in the saddle to look at her, but she sat the horse straight as an arrow. If the noise hadn't come from her, then where?

"Where the fuck are you, brother?" rang through his telepathic connection to the other enforcers. The bond was blood driven and stronger than most magics.

"Pull up," Luke snapped.

Abigail tugged on the reins. "Why?"

"Something's not right."

"Where are you?" Luke shot back.

"You oughta know. You galloped past us about five minutes ago."

"I'm turning around. Next time you see me, if I keep going, come after me."

"What—?"

"Don't know if I can explain it, since I don't fully understand myself. Just do it." Luke closed off the mental channel linking him

to the other enforcers. His horse had already slowed to a walk, and he drew on the reins to turn his mount around.

"What's going on?" Abigail walked her horse next to him. "We just came from that way." She reached across the space between the horses and wrapped her hand around his arm. "I heard you talking to someone just now. Couldn't quite make the words out, but—"

Liquid heat rolled from his arm to his belly. His erection from earlier returned with a vengeance. He turned to face Abigail. Her mouth was half open, her eyes heavy-lidded. Sexual energy emanated from her in dusky, provocative waves. He had just enough presence of mind left to jerk his arm free and back his horse a few paces away. "We rode right past the group. I'm going back. If you still want to help, come along. Otherwise, I'm guessing you can find your way back to the Overland Station."

"I thought you liked me, Luke." The way she said his name was entreaty and censure rolled into one.

"I thought I did too, but you've got to stop trying to force things with magic." He clenched his hands around the reins. There. He'd said it. Maybe it wasn't the most romantic thing. Other men wouldn't give a crap, as long as the woman was willing, whether she spelled them to fuck her or not. But he did.

She encouraged her horse to walk close again. He didn't want to hear whatever she had to say. The texture of her magic hung heavy in the air. It felt different somehow. Wrong. Kneeing his horse, he took off down the road. Usually, he enjoyed working alone. Tonight, having the group of enforcers for backup suddenly felt critical. If he didn't watch it, he might slip into something he couldn't extricate himself from.

～

"*Nice work,*" Abigail snarled at Sarah.

"*What do you mean?*" the Salem witch inquired archly. "*We almost had him.*"

"*I don't know whose body you shared before you picked on that twelve-year-old child, but we never even got close to having him.*" Abigail blew out a breath and kicked her horse into a gallop after Luke. "*Men like to do the courting. You scared the living shit out of him.*"

"*He was hot. I smelled it,*" Sarah insisted. "*More important. You can't let them burn those books.*"

"*What the hell am I supposed to do to stop them?*"

"*We could kill all of them.*"

Abigail battled an impotent rage. After her initial disgust when she'd sensed the Salem witch's power, she'd racked her brain trying to figure out how she could've barred the wicked presence from her body—and hadn't come up with a thing. The way events were shaping up, death would've been a better choice. She took a steadying breath.

"*Enforcers are all mind-linked. I don't fully understand the way of the spell, but they can communicate over distance. There's no way we could kill this set of enforcers before one of them sent out a distress call. They know me.*" Sour smelling sweat ran down her sides. "*Before the night is out, every Coven member and enforcer would be out for our blood. Whatever you hoped to gain by using my body to get close to Breana Giraud, or anyone else, will have vanished.*"

Sarah laughed long and loud. Just when Abigail was afraid her slender hold on sanity would shatter, the witch said, "*How quaint. You believed me.*"

"*Believed you about what?*" Abigail asked, but Sarah didn't answer. Abigail shifted the reins to her left hand and rubbed her temples with her right. Her head throbbed, and she felt as if she'd gotten sucked into an insane asylum where nothing anyone said made sense.

The horse's pounding hooves were a welcome distraction. She waited for whatever argument Sarah might launch, after her reminder about evil and truth not being good bedfellows, but it never materialized. The logical next step would be for Sarah to simply dump her body and move on to someone more malleable, but the Salem witch didn't propose any such thing.

Damn!

So long as Sarah didn't kill her leaving her body, it would be such an easy solution—for everyone. Abigail considered suggesting it, but bit her tongue. For one thing, she didn't like the idea of foisting Sarah off onto anyone else. Look how she'd corrupted Carolyn, an innocent child. Abigail ground her teeth together. Maybe there'd be a way to capture the vile creature within her and figure out some trick to declaw her forever.

Sarah maintained an edgy silence. Abigail sensed her restless energy, but no more words came. Feeling like she might have gained a slender toehold, she added. *"If you want Luke in our bed, you have to lay low. He suspects something, and he's too old and too canny not to guard himself. It was pretty stupid of you to spell him so he passed his cronies without noticing them. Besides,"* she added slyly, *"that's where your precious books are."*

"For all the good they'll do me." Sarah sounded bitter. *"You'll smell the smoke in a minute. They're already burning."*

A low, keening moan rose in her mind. Abigail almost pointed out if Sarah hadn't played that stunt on Luke, she'd have arrived before the books went up in flames, but it probably wasn't wise to bait her. Abigail sniffed the air. Smoke mingled with a putrid, spoiled miasma, as if the books were more than leather and parchment.

So that's what evil smells like when it dies...

"You win for now," Sarah growled. *"Get the man in our bed. Do it soon or I'll dump you for worthless, just like I dumped the Giraud brat."*

A grim smile split her face. *"I'll do the best I can. If things aren't happening fast enough for you, think twice before you empty buckets of magic around him. No matter how hot he is, he'll bolt the second he senses he's being forced."*

The twisted magic that had pulsed around her fell away. The night felt cleaner somehow, and the stars shone brighter. Abigail gazed through darkness, following the smoke smell, and saw an enormous pyre. Against her better judgment, she was intimidated by the amount of raw power Sarah commanded. To be able to manipulate something so vast defied reason.

Luke veered hard right onto a track leading a short way into the forest and pulled up at the outer edge of the circle of enforcers. She followed him, but not too close because she didn't want to spook him again. Luke didn't trust her for the best of reasons. It would take a great deal of finesse to move past Sarah's damage, and it probably wouldn't happen in the space of an evening. Best she could hope for might be a dinner—or breakfast at this point—where they might begin to patch things up.

She slid to the ground and gave her horse freedom to go where it wanted. Like all horses, it didn't care much for smoke and trotted off into the darkness, presumably to join the other mounts. One of the enforcers stood next to a stack of books. He and another man took turns feeding the flames.

"This all of them?" Luke asked

Another man shook his head and spat into the dirt. "Nah. Maybe a quarter. Rest of them got away."

Deep inside Abigail, Sarah hooted, hollered, and yipped with delight. *"Let's see if I can save the rest of them,"* she screeched.

Rotten meat smell, mixed with shit, hit Abigail full on. "Wraiths," she shrieked and spun, hands raised to call magic. The

Coven enforcers cursed roundly. One of the men chucked the remaining half dozen books into the fire and pulled a six-shooter. Luke jumped down from his mount and joined the other enforcers. Wraiths poured out of the woods, their red-rimmed eyes brilliant with hunger for warm, living flesh.

Power flared from the enforcers, cutting a swath through the disgusting undead creatures. Abigail tried to summon power, but Sarah blocked her.

"You have to let me fight." She panted. *"The men will know something is wrong if I don't help."*

"They're my creatures," Sarah said sulkily. *"They obey me."*

"Well then, figure out a way to separate your magic from mine. And do it damned quick."

Abigail swallowed down bile. Sarah had summoned the wraiths to salvage her precious books, but how the hell had they gotten here so fast? Abigail swallowed again, wincing against the burning sensation at the back of her throat. The longer she shared her body with the Salem witch, the sorrier she was, and the more frantic to do something—anything—to get away from her.

She pulled power again. This time, feeble light formed around her fingertips. *"You're on the right track,"* she gritted out, *"but I need more. Lots more. And it has to feel like me, not you."*

Heat tracked down her back. She twirled and came face to face with an enormous wraith. Biggest one she'd ever seen, it had to be over seven feet tall. The thing drew its lips into a hideous snarl, exposing black teeth. She reached deep, gave it everything she had, and was gratified when jolts of power flew from her fingers.

The wraith stumbled and reached for her. She sidestepped it, knowing it might kill her yet, but at least she wouldn't die tonight at the hands of the enforcers. They maintained order and weren't averse to killing witches who went rogue. They'd chuck her into mage fire in a heartbeat if they suspected what was really going on.

Abigail hurled more power at the wraith. It howled with pain. A gunshot nearly deafened her, and a hole opened in the wraith's chest. It folded in on itself and faded away. She didn't have to look to know Luke had shot it. She felt his energy pulse behind her. He had to be able to feel hers too. It was how he'd known she wasn't what she seemed, that something had changed.

As quickly as they'd arrived, the wraiths retreated. Abigail waited for the next rush of mad wolves, or humans who served the dark, but it never came. The fire, while still burning, had shrunk as it consumed its fuel. She sent magic spiraling outward to sense if anything lurked beyond the borders of her vision. Nothing. The only bad thing left was inside her.

Luke strode to the other enforcers. They formed a circle, obviously talking, but she couldn't hear what they said. Didn't want to. Abigail stood quietly in the dark, waiting and watching the malevolent books erode to cinders. She was ecstatic they'd destroyed even a fraction of the miserable things, but she took care to keep her mind neutral. Taunting Sarah, who raved disconsolately inside her, was a terrible idea. Abigail had the upper hand—for now. She had to make certain it stayed that way.

The enforcers broke from their tight formation. One clucked for the horses, and another stirred the still smoking bed of coals. Luke strode to her side, a harsh, unpleasant expression on his face. "We talked about things," he said without preamble and without making excuses for not including her. "What we came up with is this. We think you should ride the stage, with the Giraud child's things, to Salt Lake as planned, meet the Girauds, and explain what happened to their little girl." He pressed his mouth together into a thin, flat line. "If you're not wanting, or able—" he skewered her with his green gaze "—to do that, I will."

"Of course I'll do it." Abigail squared her shoulders. "I owe allegiance to them. It's the least I can do."

Luke drew his thick, black brows together. "Not quite the tune you were dancing to earlier."

Abigail shook her head. Now was the time to do whatever she could to convince him she'd come to her senses. On the one hand, she wanted to shriek at him to run as far and fast from her as he could, but if she did that, she'd be all alone—with Sarah. And the enforcers would kill her. She dredged up a chagrined look. "I, um, I'm sorry about what happened back there. I have no idea what got into me. I wasn't very respectful—to either of us, but especially not to you." She didn't have to try very hard before a tear slid down one cheek. They were near the surface from stress and fear.

He shrugged and didn't address her apology. "One of us will be on that stagecoach with you, to make certain the Girauds get their girl's things back. I volunteered, but if you'd rather one of the others, just say the word."

She blinked away more tears. Damn, but Luke was a decent man. If Sarah hadn't forced her way inside her body, Abigail would have liked to get to know him better. She fired a mage light so he could see her clearly and raised her gaze to his. "I'd be most grateful if you joined me. It's going to be hard telling the Girauds what happened. Carolyn was their only child."

Abigail considered engaging Luke in further discussion about the Girauds and their possible alliance with evil, but bit her tongue. She didn't want to tip her hand any more than she had to. Sarah might have some way to reach out telepathically and warn them.

Maybe she'll do that anyway to try to worm out from under any responsibility for their daughter's death.

Luke's voice cut into her thoughts. "Telling them will be a bitch." He hesitated. "I had a sister once. Looked a lot like Carolyn. Wraiths got her. Made what happened back there all that much harder."

"Thank you for telling me."

"I'd like to hear more about you." His voice softened a little. "We'll have a couple of days on the stagecoach."

"My life hasn't been all that interesting, I'm afraid."

Luke turned and took her horse's reins from one of the other enforcers. Instead of addressing her last comment, he asked, "Do you need help?"

She shook her head, angled a stirrup, and mounted. If he was ever going to trust her, she'd have to proceed really, really slowly. She hoped to hell Sarah wouldn't get impatient and blow the lid off things. Abigail waited for Luke to say his goodbyes to the other enforcers.

They galloped off down the road in the opposite direction from the stage station, all except one who stayed to tend the last of the fire. Luke walked his mount to her side. "No need to rush," he said. "If we arrive at the station around dawn, the stationmaster might have breakfast, or at least something we could cook."

Abigail just nodded and let her horse amble next to his. An idea was forming in her mind. Sarah obviously read English and demonspeak, the devil worshippers' tongue. Maybe she didn't know any other languages. Schooling had been a hit-or-miss affair in the seventeenth century, particularly for girls.

If Abigail could write something in French or Spanish or Latin, and give it to Luke, maybe he could bend his magic to helping her find a way out of her dilemma, assuming he knew any of those languages himself. Maybe there'd be an indirect way to sound him out on that. Of course, there was also the chance he'd kill her on the spot if he knew her secret, but she'd just have to risk it. She'd die soon enough anyway if she couldn't get out from under Sarah's presence inside her.

One thing at a time.

For now, it was enough that some of the books were destroyed, and Luke hadn't totally blocked her out.

CHAPTER 6

$\mathcal{L}$uke glanced at the angle of the sun through the stage station windows. It was getting on toward midafternoon. Abigail drowsed in a chair, her head cradled in her arms. She looked exhausted, with dark smudges beneath her eyes. The stationmaster hadn't been there when they returned, but the station was open. They'd let themselves in to wait after dragging Carolyn's trunks to a spot where they wouldn't be pilfered, in case any riders happened past on the road.

He'd hunted down a couple of rabbits and gutted them, and she'd made a stew out of greens that grew next to a nearby creek, mixed with the fresh meat. Once they'd eaten, she fell into a restless sleep. It was getting late enough, a new driver and fresh horses probably wouldn't show up until the following day. He wasn't sure quite why, but the specter of spending another night with Abigail bothered him. Since she seemed pretty out of it, he cautiously draped a net fashioned from magic around her. Maybe he'd be able to sense something, and if he was subtle about it she'd never find out.

The first step was deepening her slumber so he could take a good, hard look into her mind. She'd behaved impeccably since her last seduction charade in the middle of the darkened road last night, but he didn't trust her as far as he could see her, which didn't bode well. He had to sleep sometime. He could swathe himself in wards, but it almost defeated the purpose of rest, since any protections worth their salt required huge infusions of energy.

He probed ever so gently at the edges of her consciousness. Abigail's energy thrummed beneath his touch, fragrant and sweet. Honey and summer wildflowers. It didn't feel anything like the murky power she'd sent spiraling into him. Christ! That energy had practically torn his cock from its moorings with wanting her.

Luke checked to make certain she was still deeply asleep. He anchored that segment of his casting to keep her that way and dug down another layer, but very delicately. If she housed the evil he suspected, his *sleep now* spell could shatter in a flash. Something skirted just at the edges of his questing magic. More than skirted. It leapt forward, toyed with him, and retreated. Dark and hot, it tightened his muscles and made him ache with wanting a woman's heat around him.

As quietly as he'd entered her mind, he withdrew, keeping his movements small, silent. Abigail writhed in her sleep. Color bloomed on her pale cheeks. Her breath hitched, and she jammed a hand between her legs.

Knowledge slammed into him with all the subtlety of an out-of-control steam engine. He and the other enforcers may have killed the Giraud child, but the Salem witch had jumped ship before losing her essence to mage fire when they torched Carolyn. Remorse smote him. He'd shot Carolyn through the chest, so she'd been dead before they consigned her body to the flames, but still... He'd have to tell the Girauds the truth, and they'd have every right to be furious with him for not trying harder to save their child, particularly since Sarah Osborne, or whoever the fuck she really was, was still at large.

At the very least, they'd have expected him to figure out their daughter no longer hosted evil, didn't require burning, and could have been returned to them to mourn and bury—if they hadn't been turned by evil themselves. He pressed his tongue against his teeth. If the Girauds had joined the dark side, who knew how they'd feel about their daughter's death? That she'd met her end in the purification of mage fire would probably incense them beyond measure.

He tried not to look at Abigail writhing against the fingers playing beneath her skirts. Had she invited Sarah Osborne into her body? He resurrected the sequence of events and considered his question. He'd been ahead of Abigail, realized she was missing, and retraced his steps to investigate. Once he located her and the child facing off against one another, he'd hung back in the shadows for long enough to determine what was going on. Somewhere along the way, Sarah had inveigled her way inside Abigail.

He pulled magic from his *sleep now* spell. Maybe if Abigail rose nearer consciousness, she'd realize what she was doing... He cast a practiced gaze her way. If she hadn't already come, she was damned close. Her nipples were visible through her top. She was panting, and though he couldn't see through her skirts, it seemed she was moving her hand faster and faster. If she woke now, she'd be unutterably embarrassed. Luke got to his feet, making as little noise as possible, and slipped outside the stage station. At least that way, she'd be spared the humiliation of having frigged herself in front of him. He kicked a rock, feeling frustrated. It flew a few feet and *thunked* against a corral stave.

Fragments of what must have happened clunked into place, but the result was so disconcerting it stole his breath. Regardless of how Sarah managed it, she'd possessed Abigail. Luke kicked another rock, grunting when pain shot through his booted foot. He couldn't let her know he was onto her, because it would spell her death. Sarah had jettisoned the child when she wasn't of any further use.

Abigail's only hedge was that she was highly placed in Coven government. The Salem witch could use that to get close to people like the Girauds. Even so, once Coven members started dying under mysterious circumstances, Abigail wouldn't be useful for very long because the other witches would figure out she was responsible. If he couldn't come up with some way of luring the Salem witch out of Abigail's body, her days would definitely be numbered.

Too restless to stand still, he paced to the end of the corral and hunkered next to a creek that ran fast and clear. He threaded the icy water through his hands and tried to think. For whatever reason, Sarah had backed off. Abigail must've come up with a rational argument to squelch her, but he'd seen enough of the Salem witch in Carolyn to understand that any détente had to be fragile. Sarah was half-crazed with wanting power. Standing by while some of her books burned must've damn near killed her.

Another even more disturbing thought formed. The last wraith attack couldn't have been accidental. As long as Abigail played host to Sarah Osborne, they were likely to have run-ins with all manner of dark creatures. The water was cold enough to make his hands ache, but he kept them submerged to clear his mind. When he'd chatted with the enforcers over the burning books, they'd discussed having two of them accompany Abigail, but it had seemed like overkill.

Not anymore.

He flirted with calling one of his associates through their mind link, but discarded the idea because it would look suspicious. Bad enough he'd tipped his hand by delving into Abigail's mind. He wasn't certain if Sarah had actually caught him.

If not, it had been perilously close, and he couldn't risk having her intercept a telepathic transmission to other enforcers. If Sarah suspected he was onto her, she wouldn't hesitate to kill Abigail and look for another host.

Luke straightened, shook water off his hands, and flexed his fingers to get some feeling back into them. He hoped Sarah had been asleep, right along with Abigail. And the energy he'd felt trifling with his own was an automatic response to anything male in Sarah's immediate vicinity. He snorted derisively. The Salem witch must've been hell on wheels before the witch trials. He wondered how many men she'd mowed her way through as a young woman.

"Do you think the new driver will show up today? And what on earth happened to the stationmaster? He wasn't here when we got back, and he still hasn't returned."

Luke started at the sound of Abigail's voice. "Not sure—about either of those things, but I'd wondered about the stationmaster myself." He turned slowly and glanced at Abigail, framed in the stationhouse doorway. The dark rings beneath her eyes had morphed into purplish smudges, and her hair tangled in ropes around her. Though she clasped her hands together, they shook a little. Counter to his better judgment, his heart softened. It was all he could do not to rush to her side, gather her into his arms, and tell her everything would be all right. She looked so vulnerable, and yet so resolute, he vowed to help her any way he could.

The chill voice of reason intruded.

I'm going to have to destroy her if I can't figure anything else out.

His gaze scuttled sideways. Although he'd just now allowed the thought to surface, he'd understood his duty the minute he discovered Abigail's dual nature. If another enforcer were here, he'd probably insist they strike immediately and remind him the battle against evil always left a string of collateral damage. It was too bad about Abigail, but fighting wickedness was a thankless business, not for the squeamish or weak-minded...

"What? Did I do something wrong?" Abigail's voice dragged him out of the morass his thoughts had become. She plucked at her skirt with restless fingers.

He sent a weak smile her way. "Not you. This time it's me." He inhaled deeply. "Tell me about yourself. Looks like we've got the time."

She looked longingly at the creek. "Do you mind if I take a bath first? There's a pool I can see from here, where it would be easy to warm the water. If I don't bathe before the sun goes down—and it gets too cold—I might not have a chance tomorrow if the driver shows up early."

His heart hammered and his throat grew thick. She hadn't invited him to share the water with her, but... Luke brought himself up short. He was starting to recognize the feel of Sarah's castings and waved a dismissive hand. "Go ahead. I'll get some more wood inside. If we're here for the night, and it's certainly starting to look that way, we can fire the stove. I used up all the tinder inside the station when you made our breakfast."

He didn't wait for her to say anything else, just strode away from the water and left her to her bath. It was difficult, but he didn't peek back over his shoulder when he stopped for a small axe leaned up against the station. While he chopped and ferried wood inside, images of Abigail's body bombarded him. Even though he couldn't see her, his imagination was ripe with possibilities. Lush breasts, a round bottom, and the dark, private place between her legs tormented him. The wood box was nearly full, but he made one last trip into the nearby woods. Mouth dry, cock desperate for relief, he lost himself in a dense grove of trees and wound magic thickly around both the trees and himself before he unlaced his breeches.

His cock practically jumped into his hand. What he was doing felt wrong, yet if he didn't, he wasn't at all certain he'd be able to resist Sarah if she used Abigail to try to seduce him again. He closed his hand over his shaft, shut his eyes, and drove all thoughts of Abigail from his mind. She was beautiful, but until she was herself again—if that ever happened—he'd be better off with cascading images of bouncing breasts and damp pussies that belonged to anonymous women, a collage of ones he'd known over the years. It only took a few strokes before his penis jerked in his hand, spewing semen onto the ground. Once his breathing steadied, he sent tendrils of mage fire to obliterate his seed. If the other side got hold of his essence, they could use it to bind him.

ABIGAIL HAD WAKENED to a powerful orgasm pounding through her. When the last vestiges of sleep fell away and she'd found her hand beneath her skirts, she'd been mortified, until she discovered she was alone. Thank the goddess. Maybe her wantonness had gone unobserved.

"What the hell are you doing?" she asked Sarah.

"We needed that. Want to do it again?" The witch sounded as if she was smirking.

"No. I'm just damned glad we didn't get caught."

"Oh, but we did."

"We didn't," Abigail insisted. *"He's not here."*

"He was, but he left."

Thinking she could capitalize on that, Abigail muttered, *"See. He's a gentleman. Watching me touch myself made him uncomfortable..."*

"He's a damned coward. Most men know what to do when their cocks get hard."

"I told you—" Abigail spaced her words out *"—he suspects something's not right. If you push him, he may just kill me."*

"Pfft. He wouldn't. You're on the same side."

"Why do you think the Coven employs enforcers?"

"I have no idea. Witches didn't need them in my day. We handled our own dirty work." Sarah sounded insufferably smug.

"They do quite a few things, but one of their functions is to keep rogue witches in line."

"Fascinating."

"Isn't it?" Abigail mimicked Sarah's tone. *"It's why I asked for access to my magic last time you called the wraiths. If I hadn't fought back in some sort of credible fashion, the enforcers would've put one of their silver bullets through my heart—which would have killed you too —and made sure our remains joined your books in mage fire."*

"Oh."

"That's all? Oh?" Abigail waited. When Sarah didn't answer, she forced a courage she was far from feeling and said, *"I'm going to go outside and find Luke. You're going to behave. I want to get through tonight without incident."*

Satisfied she'd done all she could, Abigail moved outside. While a bath had been her idea, Sarah added her own touches to things. When Luke stalked off to get wood, Abigail breathed a huge sigh of relief. For whatever reason, he was one man who didn't let his cock rule him, and she respected him for that.

A little scouting turned up bear onion, otherwise known as soap root. She found a pool, warmed the water with magic, and soaped her body and her hair. Most of the way through drying herself, also with magic, Sarah burst into satisfied laughter.

"What?" Abigail asked.

"The man. He's not so pure as all that. He's out there frigging himself. Damn if he didn't shroud himself in magic. I'd love to get a good look at his cock."

"Stand the hell down." Abigail shinnied into her pantalets, chemise, and petticoats, tugged her dress over her head, and fastened its buttons. *"He's a decent man. You leave him alone."*

"Decent, eh?" Sarah cackled. *"You just said he wouldn't hesitate to kill us."*

"Yes, I did say that. Last time I checked, you were our enemy. He likes me, but he wouldn't let that stop him from doing his duty to keep wickedness at bay."

Sudden pain flashed through her. Her heart stuttered. Breathing became a struggle, and her vision faded at the edges. She shouldn't have said what she did, but there was no taking it back now. Would Sarah kill her where she stood?

"Where will you go if my body dies?" Even her mind speech sounded choked and breathy.

The pressure inside her chest let up. Abigail sucked air, filling her lungs. After a time, the tingling in her extremities lessened. Desolation racked her, followed by anger. She'd gotten herself into this mess by being sloppy way back in New York when she hadn't checked the third trunk. By God, she'd get herself out of it too. Waiting for either Luke or Sarah to kill her wasn't her style.

"Everything all right?" Luke's voice drifted from the other side of the stationhouse.

"Fine. I'll be there soon. Want me to gather some more greens?"

"Sure. We'll be needing something for supper."

Abigail finger combed her long hair. She could finish drying it inside. Fury at the Salem witch curdled her stomach, but she pushed it aside. She'd told her the truth, and look where it had gotten her.

Yeah, almost killed. If I hadn't reminded her she had nowhere to go, I'd be face down in the creek.

"*Don't tempt me,*" Sarah snarled. "*You're starting to feel like more trouble than you're worth. It doesn't have to be that way.*" The witch's interior voice took on a wheedling quality, and Abigail recognized compulsion.

She swallowed back a sharp retort that she didn't bargain with evil. Instead, she kept her mind voice even. "*How would you like it to be?*"

"*Why, both of us being witches and all, we should be on the same side.*"

"*If I agree, will you lay low for the rest of the night?*"

Silence. Abigail ground her teeth together. Further conversation was probably pointless, but she'd never felt quite so helpless, or so exposed. Light leached from the day. Night was a prime time for wraith and mad wolf attacks. Though the other witch was inside her, Abigail couldn't divine her thoughts.

Probably just as well. If I knew what she had up her sleeve, it might drive me insane.

She plucked a few bunches of wild onions and watercress and trudged toward the stationhouse. Luke must've lit the woodstove because fragrant smoke wafted from the chimney. Abigail pressed her tongue against her teeth and pasted what she hoped was a neutral expression on her face. It was going to be a long night. She sent up a prayer to the goddess that she and Luke would live to see the dawn. Pushing open the door, she let herself inside and dropped the greens on a table.

"Hi. Thanks for firing the stove." She glanced his way.

"Hi, yourself." He'd braided his hair. Whiskers shadowed his strong jawline. Clear green eyes gazed at her, but the edginess that had made him seem like a prickly pear earlier was gone. "Do you want to cook, or are you okay with me making us something?" Without waiting for her to answer, he added, "I found some cornmeal in a sealed canister. There's still some rabbit left, and some grease from it. Thought I'd fry up some cornmeal mush with greens and the rest of the meat."

"Sounds wonderful. I'll cut up the onions and meat."

Emotion narrowed her throat. Abigail couldn't remember the last time anyone had prepared a meal for her, but beyond that, Luke was being kind. After the way Sarah had tried to manipulate him, he could look past it and treat her humanely. She resisted an almost overpowering desire to throw her arms around him and thank him, but that would put him squarely in Sarah's clutches. She fumbled in her valise for a pocketknife and positioned herself beside him to help make their evening meal.

"Thanks for bringing my things inside." She gestured toward her valise.

"You're welcome. While I was scouting to see what was here, I also found this." Luke cocked his head to one side and waggled a bottle of some sort of spirits. "Might be the stationmaster's private stash, but I can always have another of the enforcers repay him next time someone rides through here."

Abigail wasn't sure why, but a ray of hope lightened her bleak mood and she risked a grin. "Bet that poor fellow never leaves his station unmanned again."

Luke scraped rabbit fat from beneath the skin and placed it in a cast iron pot sitting on the woodstove. "You were going to tell me about yourself."

He nodded encouragingly, and her self-consciousness dropped away. She fetched a wooden board from near the pump and organized her thoughts as she worked.

CHAPTER 7

*A*bigail pared the tough parts from the wild onions, shredded the watercress, and debated where to begin. If she didn't watch it, she could bore him to tears with her less-than-interesting life.

"I was born when there were still colonies, just before the Revolution. You'd think I'd have had a whole bunch of adventures in the last ninety-odd years, but it hasn't exactly worked that way."

He scooped up the greens she'd chopped and added them to the bowl where he was mixing cornmeal with water. Grease sizzled in the pot and filled the small building with a pleasant odor. "Which of the colonies?" he asked, followed by, "Were your parents witches?"

"Virginia. Not my parents, but my grandmother." Abigail smiled in spite of herself, remembering. "Poor Ma. She never liked being raised by a witch, and when she gave birth to one, it must have been damned unsettling. Of course, she didn't find out right away, but still, neither of my parents were ever comfortable being around magic, and I'm sure it was a big relief to them when we left."

"Who's *we* and where'd you go?"

"My grandparents decided to head west well ahead of the wagon trains. They took me with them."

Luke must've noticed she was done chopping because he picked up the board and tipped everything into his mixing bowl. "How old were you?"

"Let's see." She looked skyward, thinking. "Eighteen, maybe nineteen. It was 1788 and most of the country was still overrun with Indians. Gran and Pop were headed for California, mostly on account of it might be a friendlier place to practice witchcraft undisturbed. It was a tough journey, much harder than any of us anticipated." She shook her head, eyes narrowed, remembering. "We never could have done it without magic. When we could find them, we followed Indian tracks. Finally, we gave up on the wagon. Pop finagled a few more horses from a local tribe and we transferred most of our goods, but we left a lot in exchange."

"After all that work, was California all you'd hoped?" Luke dropped dollops of his concoction into the hot grease. It spattered and hissed, smelling heavenly. Her stomach clenched, and she realized how hungry she was.

Abigail nodded. "For the most part, yes. People were grateful for what we could do. No one questioned us, or was frightened at all. The monks who ran the Mission de San Francisco de Asis mostly kept to themselves. When it seemed like we'd be able to make a life for ourselves, we built a log house in the woods. There were a few other settlers, but it was something like fifty-five years before the town of Yerba Buena came to be. Gran started midwifing and she did real well, between delivering babies and selling herbs for whatever ailed folk. She and the local Indian shamans got on famously. Pop got into lumbering.

"I mostly helped Gran and worked to develop my magic. Somewhere along the way Mother and Dad died. Remember, neither of them were witches. Gran and I wanted to go back east for Mother's memorial service, but by the time we found out, it had already happened. We didn't find out Dad was gone until over a year after the fact."

"Yerba Buena's the same as San Francisco, isn't it?" Luke glanced at her and quirked a questioning brow.

"Yes. It got its new name a few months after the Navy claimed California as part of the United States."

Luke turned the cornmeal pancakes and rustled through cupboards, coming up with a couple of dusty plates. She made a grab for them and went to the sink so she could pump water to clean them before the food was ready. He took the wet plates from her and set them atop the woodstove to dry.

"Thanks." He flipped the pancakes again. "Witches live a long time. Are your kin still there?"

Abigail nodded. "I stayed there too, for years, but there were so few people I got restless. Besides, a bunch of religious groups showed up in the early 1840s, and they saw Gran and me as little better than devils—same thing we left the eastern states to get away from. It took a little doing, but I signed on as a cook with some men and wagons heading back to the east coast. It took close to eight months to get to New York City, but at least the men behaved themselves. I showed up at Coven headquarters one day, and that's about it. I've been working for them ever since, maybe fifteen years. Gran and I write back and forth. Guess the gold rush of 1848 really made the city explode. She says I wouldn't recognize it because of how big it's grown."

He handed her a plate and she felt suddenly shy. "Thank you. It smells delicious. I'd been planning to visit Gran and Pop after I dropped Carolyn off in Salt Lake. Pop's getting really old. Gran's been extending his life with her magic, but he's finally getting to the end of things. Anyway, seemed like a good opportunity. I didn't know when I'd be so close again…"

Her voice trailed off. Cheeks heating, Abigail knew she'd said too much. What if he asked her more about that, or worse, offered to go with her to San Francisco? No way could she go to her grandmother's in her current state. She loved the old woman and Sarah might kill her. She pushed the stationhouse door open and sat on the top step, with her plate balanced on her lap. There weren't any forks, but she still had her knife and it was good enough to cut, spear, and transfer food into her mouth.

Abigail glanced over her shoulder. "What about you?" Maybe if she could get him talking about himself, he'd forget what she'd said about a side journey to San Francisco.

Luke tucked a sliver of wood beneath the door to keep it from slamming shut and sat next to her. "Not all that much to tell on my side, either. I was born in a village about a hundred miles west of Boston. Family was pretty darned normal. Me, three sisters, Ma, and Pa. We had a little farm and grew pretty much everything we needed. I didn't realize I had power until I was fifteen." A muscle twitched in his jaw. "Anyway, after that I studied with the village mage for ten years, wandered for a bit, and signed on to be a Coven enforcer."

She chewed and swallowed. Abigail wasn't quite sure how he'd managed with such humble ingredients, but the cornmeal mush pancakes were wonderful and she said as much. It was easier than telling him she knew he'd left out a few key things about his past. Thank God, Sarah wasn't kicking up a fuss, what with Luke sitting right next to her and all.

"Why'd you pick the Coven?" she asked.

He turned his head and smiled. He had very white, very straight teeth, and the smile transformed his stern features into something striking. "Easy enough. They're the largest organized group fighting evil. Other than a few splinter groups, the Coven is it. I wanted to be where I could do the most good."

Abigail thought about it and worked her way through another pancake. "You said you wandered. Were you part of one of the vigilante groups taking on wraiths and mad wolves?"

He nodded. "Rogue humans too. We weren't very well organized and didn't have a dependable way to tell if new recruits were what they claimed." His forehead furrowed. "One of the newer men sold us out and we lost three strong fighters. Those of us who were left went to the Coven and begged them to take us on."

"I'll bet they accepted you without question." She laid her knife on her empty plate.

"You'd be right, but how'd you know?"

"Because the Coven is fair and they'd never turn down anyone with power who could help our side."

He eyed her plate. "Would you like more?"

"Sure. Maybe you could bring that bottle of spirits back along with another couple of pancakes?"

"I'd be happy to." He pushed to his feet.

Abigail watched stars flicker and a harvest moon just cresting the horizon. She liked Luke. The more they talked, the more she appreciated his decency. He didn't just pay lip service to an honorable code; he lived it. She wondered what he'd left out of his life story. He'd said something about losing a sister to wraiths earlier. Maybe whatever he'd skirted over was wrapped up in grief so profound, it still hurt to talk about it.

He'd just settled next to her, and handed her plate back, when she caught the sound of distant hoof beats. "You expecting any of the enforcers?"

Luke shook his head. "No. If it was them, I'd feel it. It's not."

She exchanged a glance with him and got to her feet. They edged inside the stationhouse, quietly shut the door, and killed their mage lights. Until they knew who was headed their way, it was best to lay low. It might just be a late traveler, but that seemed unlikely.

LUKE LOADED his revolvers by feel from the ammunition belts crisscrossing his shoulders. Silver- and iron-laced bullets *snicked* satisfyingly into cylinders. The approaching horses could be something as benign as the stationmaster returning, but until he knew for certain, it paid to be on his toes. Sloppy got you killed. As he worked, he glanced sidelong at Abigail. He'd thoroughly enjoyed just sitting and getting to know her while they traded histories. Quite aside from being such a beautiful woman, it was hard to keep his hands to himself, she was a decent soul. There had to be something the two of them could do to defeat Sarah.

Cooking had given him a chance to think. While he wasn't totally positive what he'd felt inside Abigail was the Salem witch, she was the likeliest prospect. The energy matched what he'd sensed inside Carolyn, and coincidences were rare birds. A very slim possibility existed that another stray dark spirit had captured Abigail at the same time Sarah lost her home inside Carolyn, but Luke had never believed in happenstance. He'd be ready for anything, but he was as close to certain as he could be who his adversary was.

Thoughts of the Salem witch sent a chill down his back. If something malevolent was headed their way, he bet Sarah was behind it. He tightened his jaw and squared his shoulders. If Abigail turned on him, driven by Sarah's energy, he'd have a big problem on his hands. Shooting her would solve it, but he didn't want to do that unless there wasn't any other choice.

She called to something inside him, a part he'd shuttered the night Tamra died. Before he could delve deeper into his irrational desire to gather Abigail close and protect her from harm, they had to separate her essence from Sarah's. He opened his mouth, and then clacked it shut. He couldn't discuss the problem with Abigail without exposing his intentions to Sarah, which made things that much harder. Worse, he couldn't even come up with a subtle way to clue Abigail that he knew about her dilemma.

Luke listened intently, pulling magic to sharpen his hearing. Not only were the hoof beats drawing nearer, they'd turned off the main road and were headed right for them. Two horses, which probably meant two men. *Damn!*

It could mean a whole lot more than that. Wraiths and mad wolves don't need horses.

He glanced at Abigail. She'd retreated to a corner with her arms wrapped around herself and her head tilted downward. Luke wanted to go to her, crush her against him, and reassure her he'd take care of her, but he didn't. That much proximity would surely spur Sarah into something. Whether it was sexual or aggressive didn't matter. He didn't want to deal with the Salem witch unless she made her presence obvious.

Once she did that, she'd force his hand, and Abigail would be as good as dead.

Luke jammed his revolvers back into their holsters. He wanted to smash his fist through something. Frustration jangled his nerves. He'd never been much for cloak-and-dagger operations. No, he liked to operate with his cards face up. To have to pretend grated against every instinct he'd ever had. Plus, he knew he was playing with fire—and breaking all the rules—by not killing Abigail outright, but he couldn't bring himself to do it. Not yet.

"They're coming here." Abigail's voice was thin, strained.

"Ssht." He looked at her and shook his head, meaning for her to remain silent.

Luke padded to a window. He used magic to keep himself invisible and peered out. A bay and a black trotted into the Central Overland Stage yard. Two horses. Two men. He'd been right about that part. He split his magic to feel beyond the horsemen, and sent it hurtling into the darkness to sense what might be with them. Something blocked him, which gave him all the answer he needed.

He strode to Abigail's side and bent so his mouth was right next to her ear. "No matter what happens, you stay in here and shroud yourself with magic."

"I helped you fight before."

Her words didn't sound right, and she wasn't looking at him. "That was then," he murmured low. "This is now. I'm pulling rank on you. As a Coven witch, you're obliged to obey an enforcer's direct order."

Abigail's features twisted into something he couldn't quite make out in the dark. That she kept her face averted didn't help. He read anger in her posture, along with resignation. Luke turned away. By the time he made the door, he held a gun in one hand. The only way he'd make it through the next few minutes was by taking a hard offensive position. A quick glance out the window beside the door showed both men still on their mounts as if they were waiting for something, or someone else, to arrive. Too bad there wasn't a side door, but he'd have to work with what he had.

Abigail hadn't moved. *Good.* Luke pulled shadows around himself so he wouldn't be quite so visible, opened the door, and shut it behind him. He drew his second gun, keeping both low, half hidden by his body—and his spell. Magic would shield him, but not from astute magic wielders.

"Hey there!" he called out with false cheer. "You woke me. What can I do for you?"

"Stationmaster sent us," one of the men replied.

"Yup. We're the relief drivers," the other said. "Seeing as how we're behind schedule, we thought we'd get a jump on things."

The men were hazy, but it might have been Luke's spell. He sent shielded magic outward, but it bounced back again. "I'll wake the lady," he murmured, buying time. "We'll be ready soon as you get the horses hitched."

"You're the stable boy tonight," the first man snapped. "You get 'em hitched for us."

If Luke had any doubts about the men, they evaporated. Horses were sensitive to dark magic. If these men couldn't hitch up a team, it meant whatever they were riding had to be illusion. In one smooth motion, Luke swung both pistols to firing height and pulled the triggers. Screams ricocheted off the trees, shrill and horrible, and the men plunged to the ground, clutching their stomachs. Before the riot of noise faded, he lowered the guns fractionally and shot whatever was masquerading as horses. Neighs turned to snarls and the horses shimmered, becoming huge gray wolves writhing in death throes, surrounded by spreading pools of blood.

Luke was breathing hard. Still clutching a gun in each hand, he scoured the darkness with magic and his eyes. Had he missed anything? The door creaked open behind him. Abigail—or Sarah. He twirled, but he was a second too late. The woman launched herself at him, biting, scratching, clawing. Magic poured off her.

"Sorry. I'm so sorry, but I can't keep her under control," Abigail screamed, her face contorted in agony.

"No need for apologies. I already figured it out." Luke quickly holstered his guns.

He dragged her from his body, chucked her back inside the stationhouse, and pulled the door closed, turning the key to engage the locking bolt. Glass shattered, but he was ready this time and moved away from the window Abigail tumbled out of. An unholy shriek rose from her and she threw herself on the ground thrashing and kicking. Her body lurched upright, only to sprawl on the ground again.

A grim smile split Luke's face. Sarah was trying to leave, but Abigail subverted her by dragging their shared body downward. From the sound of it, Sarah was shredding the hell out of Abigail's innards. Luke felt proud of her for not giving in and letting the Salem witch have ascendency, even though she was obviously in pain. He ached for her, wanted to help her, but didn't know how.

A rush of magic buffeted him from two sides. He raised his hands to call power, and sent magic catapulting outward to see what he faced. Mad wolves. Lots of them. No doubt they'd risen to Sarah's summons, and they'd be furious when they raced into the clearing and saw their two dead companions. Luke ratcheted up his magic and loosed a distress call. He needed help. There'd be forest wolves here. Maybe they'd fight if he asked. Luke had been outmanned and outgunned before, but never by so large a margin.

Until the wolves showed up, assuming they heeded his summons, he cut a wide swath with his power, feeling it snuff out one mad wolf after another. Once he had allies, he'd have to be more careful so he didn't kill one of the good wolves by mistake. Thank Christ he'd had a decent meal. Magic wasn't a bottomless well. If he didn't pace himself, he'd run dry. Luke dialed back the intensity of his attack. So far, nothing had ventured within the clearing hogged out of the forest where the stage station stood. Distant howls from forest wolves, not mad ones, plucked at him and gave him hope. Even though they didn't know him, they were on their way.

He spared a glance at Abigail and sucked in a horrified breath. Deep scratches marred her face where she'd dug her nails in. Blood ran from her face and hands and arms. Had Sarah forced Abigail to mutilate herself? Worse, was Abigail trying to kill the body that housed them both? The thought sickened him. He raced to her side and pulled her out of the dirt. She twisted in his arms, trying to bite him. Hating to do it, but not seeing any other choice, Luke directed enough magic to knock her out. It took way more than he'd expected. When she finally went limp against him, he was scared shitless he'd killed her.

He laid a hand on the side of her neck, relieved beyond words when he felt her pulse still beating. He carried her to the porch and considered simply leaving her there, but thought better of it. Twisting the key, he laid her gently on the floor inside the station. Luke kissed her forehead, told her everything would work out somehow, and let himself back onto the porch, taking care to lock the door and pocket the key. If Sarah clawed her way through his spell, there was always the broken window she could use to escape, but he'd fight that battle when he had to.

A pack of wolves, normal ones, burst into the clearing, eyes bright, fangs bared. They twisted their heads this way and that, hunting for something to kill. Luke sucked in a steadying breath and spiraled magic in a huge circle so he could help his new allies. He sensed evil, but it was moving away from them.

He shook his head. It didn't make sense. Why were the mad wolves leaving? Sudden understanding filled him with elation.

Sarah was truly out of commission. Without her calling the shots and flogging them forward, her minions were rudderless, and had chosen the path of least resistance. Luke didn't blame them. They might dance to the wrong piper's tune, but they were far from stupid. Why die if you didn't have to?

He bowed to a large black and gray timber wolf, maybe the pack's alpha. *"Thank you, brother, for responding to my need. The wicked ones are leaving."*

"We thought as much." The wolf's tail plumed. His breath frosted the chill, night air. *"We will patrol for a while, in case they change their minds and return."*

Luke bowed low. *"I am in your debt."*

The wolf's tongue lolled, and lupine laughter rang in Luke's mind. *"If you're truly indebted, you won't mind if we help ourselves."* The wolf trotted to one of the dead men and nosed him with his snout.

"Feel free. At least they can fill your bellies and finally do some good with their sorry lives."

Luke turned and unlocked the door to let himself back into the station. Morning was still hours away. Regardless whether the relief driver showed up, he had to prioritize freeing Abigail from the Salem witch. The gig was up. Sarah must know he'd figured out what she was up to, which meant Abigail had become expendable.

Luke put out a telepathic call to any enforcers close enough to hear him. The odds of saving Abigail were thin, but without help, they'd erode to nil, and he'd have to kill the abomination she'd become. He paid magic into the spell keeping her comatose, knowing full well the deeper she went, the greater the danger she'd die anyway.

CHAPTER 8

Luke fetched a soft, woolen shawl out of Abigail's valise and folded it beneath her head. He didn't have much of a plan, but he'd try to keep her unconscious until one or more enforcers arrived, and they could come up with something better. Her hands were trashed with several nails ripped from their beds. Damn, but that must have been excruciating. He focused a slender thread of magic to heal the worst of her wounds, including her lacerated face. It was little enough, but doing something eased the ache in his heart when he gazed at her ruined body.

He tried to piece together what Sarah had hatched up for a strategy. The men riding the mad wolves were obviously servants of the dark. Maybe she'd wanted them to drive the stagecoach because they'd do what she wanted.

Had they killed the real stationmaster somewhere along the way? Was that why he'd never returned to his station?

If Luke had gotten into the stagecoach with the false drivers, he had no doubt he'd have been the next casualty, killed and dumped in a remote corner of the Central Overland Stage Road.

A knife in the ribs, or maybe a gunshot wound when he went into the woods to relieve himself, would've been simple enough to finesse. He couldn't watch his back constantly.

Time passed. The windows grayed with the dawn, and then got even lighter. Abigail still slept. Luke pursed his lips into a hard line. Which of the enforcers would heed his call? When would they show up? Most important of all, would they insist on taking the high road and killing Abigail's body to quash Sarah permanently?

Almost as if he'd broadcast his thoughts, a voice eddied in his mind. *"Sam here. You still with us, brother?"*

"Yes."

"Damn! Sounding pretty chipper. We'll be there in half an hour, maybe a little less. Rode most of the night, ever since we got your call."

Because he didn't know what else to say, Luke murmured, *"Thanks."*

Gratitude flooded him. The enforcer brotherhood was unbreakable. No one had a past, not one that mattered, but they were the best kind of family. Loyal to the core. He'd have knocked himself out too, if one of the others sent out a distress call. What Sam had called him wasn't accidental. The other enforcer was the closest thing he had to a partner, to a brother.

Luke settled in to wait. Abigail's ashen face made his soul hurt.

"Soon," he whispered. "We'll figure this out and free you." He wanted to draw her against him, but was afraid he'd wake her. Luke gazed at her and tried to infuse hope into some deep place Sarah hadn't touched. He stood guard until he heard hooves pounding and felt the unmistakable twang of enforcer energy drawing near.

He moved to the door and made a chopping motion with one hand so the men would be quiet. Sam, Joshua, and Chris dismounted. Like all their ilk, they were tall, rangy, tough as nails, and dressed in leathers. Sam was another of the undercover enforcers, which was why Luke knew him so well. While he recognized the other men, he had no sense how they might react to Abigail's problem. Using shielded speech, he synopsized what had happened, starting with Carolyn's death and the Black Magick books.

"What's this mess?" Sam pointed at places where the ground was stained red and blood still pooled.

"Oh yeah. Forgot that part," Luke said. "Sarah summoned men who'd been turned and mad wolves. Their bodies aren't here because the wolves that came to my aid must've dragged them away."

"So one of our witches is in there?" Joshua jerked his thumb toward the stationhouse.

"I know her," Chris said. "She's a good woman. Magic runs strong in her. I'm sure you've met her too, Josh." He shook his head. "It's a rotten shame, but we don't have much choice here."

Luke's hands had been balled into such tight fists they ached. Chris' words chilled him, but he'd been expecting them. He held up a hand. "Wait. Please. Isn't there some way we can get Sarah out of Abigail—and trounce her? I've racked my brain, but I'll be damned if I can come up with anything that won't kill Abigail right along with it."

"No. There's not," Chris said flatly.

Joshua walked closer. "We have to do the right thing and destroy her. Now. Before she wakes."

Luke turned away to shield his emotions from the others and waged an internal battle. He'd never felt such antipathy for duty before. Coming to a hard decision, he spun and let his gaze settle briefly on each man. "If there's anything, anything at all that might save Abigail," he said, "I'd be forever in your debt. I understand we can't let evil like that loose in the world, but I care about her. More than I've cared about anyone in a long time. I know if we try and fail, we'll have no choice, but..." His voice cracked. He stopped talking because he didn't know what else to say.

Chris and Joshua exchanged worried glances. Sam narrowed his blue eyes and shoved strands of hair out of his face. "Luke wouldn't ask if it wasn't deadly important," he told the others before turning his attention toward the stage station and furrowing his brow in thought.

He didn't speak for so long, Luke felt hope ebb and prepared himself as much as he could for a world without Abigail in it.

"It's risky, but the only thing I can think of is this..." Sam said at last.

As he listened, Luke's heart sped up. "If we do that, it should be me."

Joshua shook his head, making his red braids slap from side to side. "No. Sarah knows you're onto her. You said as much. If this is going to work, you have to stay in the background. We'll tell Abigail you left and hide you with magic. If things go to hell —" he snorted and rolled his hazel eyes "—feel free to jump into the fray. It won't matter then."

Chris clapped Luke on the shoulder, his brown eyes brimming with deviltry, and said, "No time like the present. Withdraw whatever you knocked her out with and let the games begin."

"Games, my ass," Joshua muttered darkly. "I'd rather be almost anywhere than here right about now."

Sam slugged Luke lightly in the arm. "We'll give it our best shot, bro." He spun Luke to face him, his blue gaze auguring deep. "You do understand if this doesn't work, we won't have any choice."

"Got it."

Luke forced breath past his narrowed airway into his lungs. They'd have to move fast if their plan blew up, before Sarah got away. He wasn't certain if she could inveigle her way into any of their bodies, but he didn't want to find out. In truth, Sam's suggestion was incredibly dangerous and required split-second timing. If Sarah caught onto them, she was more than capable of killing them all.

"Okay," Sam said to Luke. "Open yourself so this spell takes." He raked his fingers through blond hair that had been hacked off to uneven lengths, and walked in a circle around Luke scattering an invisibility enchantment. The enforcer stood back and cocked his head to one side, assessing his work. "What do you think?" he asked the others.

"Looks good to me," Joshua said.

Chris gave a thumbs-up sign.

Luke sent up a fervent prayer that things wouldn't turn to shit and reeled in the magic he'd pumped into Abigail. The other three enforcers sashayed into the stationhouse. Luke slipped in right behind them and stood off to one side. He trusted Sam's casting to both render him invisible and damp down his energy. Hopefully, Sarah would be distracted enough by the other men she wouldn't notice him.

The woman on the floor stirred. Sam strode to her side, gathered her into his arms, and pulled her to her feet. She wrapped her arms around him. Jealousy knifed through Luke, but he ignored it. Sarah was running the show, not Abigail. The Salem witch would have woken first. He hoped Abigail would remain out of it until their strategy played itself out.

"Well, lookee here," Sam crooned. "Say, it's not every day I find a sleeping beauty like you out in the wilderness." He laid his cheek next to hers. "You feeling all right, sunshine? What happened?"

"I'm fine. Must've just fallen asleep." The woman craned her neck around as if she was trying to work the kinks out of it.

"Can you stand by yourself?" Sam asked.

"If she can't, I'd be glad to help her." Joshua stepped forward, flanked by Chris.

"How you doing, sweets?" Chris flashed a grin and winked. "Been a while, but we met back at Coven headquarters a time or two."

She cast a blank look his way, murmured, "Of course," and tightened her hold on Sam.

Luke exhaled tensely. At least the Abigail part was still asleep since she'd have recognized Chris.

"Say—" the woman cast a crafty look about "—wasn't there another of you boys?"

"Yup." Sam patted her bottom and pulled her against him. "He left. Got orders he was needed elsewhere."

"It's why we showed up." Joshua said brightly. "To make certain you and the Giraud girl's things made it to Salt Lake."

"We'll be going with the stagecoach," Chris added.

"But it's not leaving anytime soon." Sam smiled. "Lots of witches like to have a bit of fun." He quirked a brow her way in obvious invitation.

Color stained the woman's cheeks. "Would it just be you? Or will the rest of you play too?"

Luke bit his lip so hard he tasted blood. Damn if Sarah hadn't risen to the bait. He felt elated, but sickened that Abigail was a pawn in this endgame. Even if she was asleep, it didn't make it any better.

"Whatever you want, sweetheart." Sam smoothed her hair back from her face.

"Ooooh, three of you would be…exciting." She licked her lips, eyes shining with anticipation.

"Maybe we could get to know one another a little better first." Joshua moved closer. "Chris knows you, but I've only heard your name. Tell us a little bit about yourself. I'm sure Sam's interested too."

A frantic look washed across Sarah's face, but it was gone in an instant. "Why most of us witches are pretty much the same," she murmured. "I've been with the Coven for years."

"Have you always lived in New York?" Sam pressed.

"Not always."

"Which of the women mentored you?" Joshua asked. "I've been around for a while, maybe I know her."

"Oh, I'm sure you wouldn't. I'm quite old and she, um, went back to England years ago." Sarah cocked her head to one side, a come-hither grin on her face. "There are quicker ways to get to know me, boys."

"Which ones did you mentor?" Sam went on as if she hadn't said anything.

Sarah rolled her eyes and leaned her body even closer to Sam. "Well, let me see. There was Eliza and Mary Jo…"

As the men fed Sarah questions, piling them atop one another, Luke felt anxiety pour off her. She stammered and stuttered as she tried to come up with answers to increasingly complex queries about arcane magics and spells. Chris stood behind the Salem witch, hands on her waist, trapping her between his body and Sam's. His brown hair fell across his face as he nuzzled her neck—and anchored magic inside Abigail's body.

It was damn near killing Luke, but he kept his gaze trained on the tableau unfolding in front of him. Sarah tried hard to maintain the charade she was Abigail, but lack of access to her memories was clearly frustrating her. Irritation joined anxiety, and Luke knew they had to make their move soon before Sarah's temper got the better of her.

Chris ran his tongue down her neck. "You've been really patient," he crooned. "We're not animals. We like to know a woman before we…do other things."

Sarah laughed, but it held rough, impatient edges. "Have I told you enough yet? You're a mighty attractive bunch of men. Worth waiting for, but not forever."

"I'm not sure." A feral grin split Joshua's face and he glanced at Chris. "Has she told us enough?"

Luke tensed. When Chris gave the word, it meant he'd finished laying the magical spadework within Abigail. Once that happened, they'd all pounce. It was the perfect time, the only time, to drag Sarah from Abigail's body. Chris nodded, which meant he had the requisite magic anchored deep.

"Yes," Chris drawled in case anyone hadn't seen his nod. "I think she has."

"Let's go!" Sam commanded.

Obviously assuming Sam meant something entirely different, the woman leaned her head back and tried to drag his mouth down to hers, but her body started to shake. A high, thin wail rose from her, and she shuddered against the hold Chris and Sam had on her.

"You bastards," she screeched. "Fucking bastards. You tricked me."

Luke and Joshua surged forward and poured magic into Abigail, along with Sam and Chris, to force the Salem witch out. Her shrieks changed from horror to terror to fury as she understood she'd left herself vulnerable. A shadowy essence formed behind Abigail's suddenly inert form, still supported between Chris and Sam. Luke didn't hesitate. He summoned mage fire. Sarah's spirit sputtered, burst into flames, and formed a conical pyre.

"Take her." Chris thrust Abigail's body into Luke's arms. "I'll tend the fire and make sure it has enough of a toehold nothing can interrupt it. Sam'll help me."

"Keep that fire burning," Luke growled. "We want that abomination deader than dead."

"We've got it," Sam said. "No worries on that front."

Luke clasped Abigail against him and met Chris and Sam's somber gazes. "Did she make it?"

"Not sure," Chris said.

"If she did, it'll be close," Sam muttered. "The Salem witch had her claws deep into that one. I felt things rip when we forced her out."

Luke tightened his hold on Abigail and carried her outside, away from the sickly taint inside the stationhouse. Mage fire wouldn't destroy anything except the Salem witch, but the stench of her evil was thick and cloying. He closed his mind to the possibility that after all they'd done, Abigail would die anyway. Fate couldn't be that cruel.

Oh yes it could. Remember Tamra? an inner voice mocked.

Luke kept moving until he was in an open spot next to the creek bank. He sat on some dry grass and cradled Abigail against him. It took a few minutes before he could force himself to lay a finger alongside her neck to check for a pulse.

"How is she?" Sam asked.

Luke looked up to see the other three enforcers ringed near him. He'd been so locked into his own misery, he hadn't noticed them approach. "Still alive," he gritted. "Barely."

"The Osborne bitch is well and truly gone." Joshua hunkered next to them. "Have you figured out what's wrong with Abigail?"

"I've been so busy holding her on this side of the veil, I didn't get that far."

"Mind if I look?"

Luke clung to Abigail, loath to turn her over to anyone else.

"I have some healing ability," Joshua said, his voice soft. "If Sam is right and she's tore up inside…" His words trailed off.

"All right." Luke spread Abigail tenderly in the grass and moved off to one side.

Joshua started at her head and let his hands travel the length of her body, but a few inches above it. His expression turned so grim, Luke's heart splintered. "What'd you find?"

Chris shook his head, dark eyes serious, and said, "Let him work. If he has to talk to you, it will distract him."

Luke felt the air thicken, saw it shimmer as Joshua summoned magic. A canopy of multi-hued air formed around Abigail's body. For the first time since Tamra's death, Luke prayed. He had no idea who he called out to, but he begged any deity who might be listening to a poor sod like him to spare Abigail's life.

Sam sat next to him. Chris hovered off to one side. Magic flowed from him, augmenting Joshua's healing efforts. Luke lost track of time, but the sun had nearly reached mid-heaven when Sam dropped a hand on his shoulder.

"Look!" His voice held an excited note. "Her color's better." He exhaled noisily. "I swear, up until just now I thought she was a goner for sure."

Luke's gaze had never left Abigail, but he sharpened his focus. Sam was right. Pale pink washed both her cheeks, and the rise and fall of her chest was visible, truly visible, not a product of him wanting her to be stronger. His throat thickened, but he swallowed back strong emotion. Enforcers were hard men, men who'd moved beyond the need for tears. No reason to shame himself.

"You care about her," Sam said softly.

"More than that," Luke said. "I think I'm falling in love." Heat rose to his face, as if admitting any feeling were a weakness. He shook his head. "Sorry, not sure quite where that came from."

"No wonder you didn't want to just kill her and have done with things. The boys and me, we wondered about that."

"You talked about it telepathically without me?" Luke felt taken aback.

"Had to." Sam narrowed his eyes. "You'd have done the same. Not that I didn't believe your story, but we made a field decision early this morning. Needed to be as certain as we could you weren't part of a trap."

"Thanks for trusting me." Luke looked at his hands. He'd thought the other enforcers might reject his plea to save Abigail, but it never occurred to him they'd see him as part of a possible plot to lure them to disaster.

"No problem. You owe me."

Luke bit back a grim laugh. "Anytime."

"She's coming around," Chris said.

Luke scooted to where Abigail lay. As soon as Joshua's magic dissipated, he gathered her into his arms and rocked her against him. "It will be all right," he murmured. "You're safe now."

Her eyes fluttered open. She gazed at him, and then at the other enforcers ringed round her. "What happened?" She shut her eyes, took a deep breath, and smiled weakly. "My God! She's gone. What'd you do to get rid of her? Last thing I remember is when she commandeered my body to attack you."

"It's a long story. The important thing is you're still with us," Luke said. He was grinning like an idiot, but couldn't stop himself.

Abigail struggled against him and Luke loosened his hold. "Would you like to get up?"

"Not sure I can." She closed her teeth over her lower lip. "Answer me this. Did you kill her?" She winced. "That was a stupid question because she's long since dead. My mind is fuzzy."

"I knew what you meant," Luke said. "Yes, I engulfed what was left of her in mage fire. She won't bother anyone again. Ever."

Tears welled, but Abigail didn't brush them away. "You'll have to tell me how you did it, but maybe not just now."

"You planning to introduce me?" Sam jabbed him with an elbow.

"Next thing I know, you'll be dropping *A Handbook of Etiquette for Gentlemen* into my saddlebags." Luke snorted.

"Now that you mention it…" Joshua laughed long and loud.

The sound was so robust, it reminded Luke of everything he was grateful for. "Let's see. This blond-haired fellow is Sam, one of my closest friends."

"I know Chris and Joshua," she interrupted. "Pleased to make your acquaintance, Sam."

Joshua knelt next to her and took her hand. "I healed you. Sarah did a lot of damage on her way out."

Abigail grimaced. "I'm not surprised." She shook herself free of Luke and Joshua and stood unsteadily. "Good that all of you are here. I— Well, that is, I need to be honest and this is as good a place as any to start."

Luke's gut tensed. Had she invited the Salem witch into her body? If Abigail had done that, no matter how he felt about her, he'd have to cut his losses. He got to his feet and moved so he faced her. "Go ahead." He motioned with two fingers. "We're listening."

"Remember when we went after the books the first time?"

When he nodded, she went on, "You were way ahead of me. A mad wolf knocked me out of the saddle. I killed it, but when I called my horse back, Sarah—except she was still in Carolyn's body then—accosted me. She told me I was surrounded by mad wolves and wraiths and that she'd kill me if I didn't let her bind me with a blood oath. I was trying to buy myself time, but the ugly truth is I came within a hairsbreadth of succumbing to her compulsion spell to play host to her."

Abigail squared her shoulders and met his gaze. "You showed up then and shot her. Somewhere in between that and Carolyn dying, Sarah abandoned the girl and climbed aboard me. I still have no idea how she whooshed through my defenses. She was inside me so fast, it took me a while to figure out what happened.

"At first I thought I could control her." Abigail's mouth curled into a bitter expression. "Figured out damn fast I wasn't strong enough. After we attacked you, once you'd killed the men and mad wolves, I tried to kill myself." She swallowed hard. "It was the only way to rid myself of her, and I didn't want to live with her inside me. That's how I got all these cuts and scrapes that I guess you or Joshua worked on since they're healing."

Abigail swayed from side to side and planted her feet more widely to balance herself. "I understand you'll have to let the Girauds know, and the rest of Coven government too."

"None of them will hold anything that happened against you." Sam stepped forward.

"What you told us was unvarnished truth," Joshua added. "I was checking."

"You're not the first witch who was snared by the dark." Chris smiled warmly.

The rigid set of her shoulders softened, and Abigail made her way to the steps leading into the stationhouse. She settled on the bottom riser and raked her fingers through her hair.

Luke walked over to her. "You need food and rest." Protectiveness swelled within him, but he also censured himself. If he hadn't ridden ahead after the books that night, maybe he'd have been able to save her from the hell she'd just lived through.

"I'll get us a meal together," Sam offered.

"With what?" Joshua countered.

"With whatever you and I can catch," Chris said. "Come on. Let's see if we can't scare up a rabbit or two, or a raccoon."

"I vote for venison," Sam called after their retreating forms, but they didn't even turn around.

"Thank you," Abigail glanced from Sam to Luke. "The words seem inadequate somehow, but if it wasn't for you two, and Chris and Joshua, I'd be dead."

"Aw shucks, ma'am, t'weren't nothing." Sam winked broadly.

Luke elbowed him. "About that etiquette book. Does it include a grammar section?"

"Wouldn't know. Never laid eyes on one. I'm going to make certain that fire's out." Sam trudged up the steps and pulled the door open. A putrid stench wafted out.

"Whew!" Abigail wrinkled her nose. "Guess we won't be eating in there. I could smell it some before he opened the door, but that's pretty awful."

"We can air it out so it's habitable again." Luke followed Sam up the stairs and propped the front door open. He held his breath against the reek of evil and walked from window to window, tugging them open. Once he'd done all he could, he went back to check on Abigail. She was leaned back against the steps with her eyes closed, dozing. Exhaustion scored her face and made him heartsick he hadn't been able to rescue her sooner. Luke reminded himself that his feelings for her might be one-sided. They hadn't really had much time together without Sarah as an unwelcome third.

I'll just take things nice and slow, he promised himself, and then knew he was lying. He wanted to stake his claim to the woman asleep on the steps. It would practically kill him if she wasn't interested.

$\mathcal{A}$bigail leaned against the stagecoach seat and adjusted the magic she paid out to the gears. Dust drifted in through the open window. They'd be in Salt Lake soon, probably within the hour. Three days had elapsed since the men rescued her from Sarah's clutches, and she was starting to feel more like herself. Her magic, which had taken the most time to recover, was strong enough to use again so they were making good time with just four horses.

The first day they'd remained close to the stage station, once it had thoroughly aired out. She'd dozed off and on, waking to share food and the bottle of spirits with the men. The relief driver had shown up early the next morning and disclosed the sad news that he'd found the stationmaster with his throat torn out about ten miles up the road.

They'd driven through the second day and night, switching teams and drivers at intervals. By this morning, she'd been able to help power the coach. Abigail moved to the bank of seats on the opposite side to stretch out her stiff muscles. It was closing on dusk again, and she'd be relieved to have the meeting with the

Girauds behind her. Whenever she thought about them, the fine hairs on the back of her neck trilled a warning.

All four enforcers were traveling with the stagecoach because of the doubts all of them harbored about the Girauds. If she quested outward with her magic, she could feel each of them, comforting and solid. She blew out a small sigh. Luke was a special man, but maybe she only felt that way because he'd stuck by her, even after he knew she housed the Salem witch. She'd caught him watching her when he thought she wasn't paying attention, though, his gaze warm and tender.

"Probably doesn't mean a thing," she murmured. "Good looking fellow like that. Bet he's got women waiting for him in lots of cities." He hadn't suggested dinner again, or really much of anything. Maybe he was afraid she'd sustained residual damage from Sarah's presence. Hell, she was worried about the same thing. That some taint remained, which would show up at an inconvenient time to sabotage her.

When she'd insisted on knowing exactly how the enforcers had ousted Sarah, he'd described what they'd done with enough tact and delicacy she hadn't felt uncomfortable, at least not very. It wasn't as if any of the men had actually done anything disrespectful to her body, beyond Chris nuzzling her neck and Sam keeping his hands on her bottom. Chris had to have physical contact to secure his spell, and Sam needed to divert Sarah so she wouldn't pay too much attention to what Chris was doing.

Abigail blew out a breath. Sam and Chris had taken a huge risk. Because they were actually touching her, Sarah could have killed them instantly—if she'd figured out what they were up to. Fortunately, the Salem witch had been extremely narcissistic. And desperate for male attention. It hadn't occurred to her that the three enforcers were engaged in anything beyond a courtship ritual, one she didn't fully grasp since she was from an earlier time.

Funny she believed them when she went to such great lengths to remind me not to trust a word that came out of her.

Abigail took a steadying breath. Even when she dug deep, she still couldn't dredge up even one memory between when Sarah forced her to launch herself at Luke and waking up in the grass near the riverbank. Probably a good thing, but the blank area in her mind bothered her and left her feeling not quite whole.

Abigail wondered what she was going to do after today. It depended on how the Girauds took her news and if they blamed her for their daughter's death, as they well might. If they booted her from the Coven, she supposed she'd go back to Gran's and live with her. San Francisco had grown; surely she could find some application for her witchy talents in a city that size.

If I do that, I'll never see Luke again...

The thought both tugged at her heartstrings and confused her. She'd always been self-sufficient. Even when she'd had the occasional dalliance, usually during one of the festivals like Beltane, she'd never yearned for a man before, but Luke was different. It was a rare moment when he wasn't in her mind, or close enough he may as well be.

He'd taken up residence in her dreams too. Her cheeks warmed. Some of those dreams had been so steamy, and so real, she'd woken to climaxes thrumming through her. At least the stagecoach afforded some level of privacy. She hoped she hadn't screamed, or writhed, or done anything to embarrass herself while they'd all still been at the stage station and her exhausted body kept drifting off.

The driver yelled at the horses to slow down, so she reeled in her magic and peered out the window. They weren't in Salt Lake quite yet. Why were they stopping? The coach rolled to a halt off to the side of a well-rutted roadway. She unlatched a door and navigated the steps, glancing about uncertainly. Maybe there was some sort of trouble, but she didn't sense anything amiss.

Luke got off his horse, tethered it to the rear of the coach, and walked to her side. "Mind if I ride the rest of the way in with you? There're things we need to talk about, things the boys and I got straight back on the road."

"It would be nice to have company." She turned and ducked back inside the stagecoach, doing her best to hide how pleased she felt. No need to make him uncomfortable by gushing over him. Besides, he hadn't exactly sounded romantic. *Things we need to talk about* smacked of business, not anything personal.

He waited until the coach was moving again and she'd settled the gears into a rhythm to assist the horses. "How are you feeling?" he asked.

She shrugged and pressed her lips together. "Nervous. I've been trying to come up with options in case they kick me out of the Coven."

"They might insist you return to New York for a trial."

Breath whooshed out of her. "What? Why would they do that? It isn't as if I killed her."

"Grieving parents aren't always rational." A corner of his mouth turned downward. "You didn't kill her. I did, and that's what we're going to tell the Girauds. The truth, or most of it, anyway."

"It would have to be damn near everything. They won't be so grief-stricken they'll forget to set a truth spell in play, once they realize Carolyn's dead."

"We thought of that," Luke went on. "The only part you're going to alter is when you realized their daughter was possessed. We're going to leave out our earlier suspicions and we're not going to tell them about Carolyn running off into the desert half-cocked and us hunting for her for hours. Or her pinching you, or disclosing she was Sarah as soon as she did." He tapped an index finger toward her. "None of that."

Understanding threaded through her. In a spontaneous gesture that embarrassment caught up to later, she reached across the coach and laid a hand over Luke's. "You're going to spare them the unpleasantness of what their daughter turned into."

"That's about the size of it. Nothing to be gained by giving them every single, grisly detail. Better to focus on you being possessed. Carolyn was already dead then, so there wouldn't have been a thing you could have done for her."

Abigail snatched her hand back. "Sorry. That was forward of me."

He gazed at her, his green eyes sparking with tenderness. "Don't apologize. I was enjoying you touching me."

She felt flustered, pleased, but uncertain. To avoid admitting she'd enjoyed touching him too, she retreated to safer ground. "Back to Carolyn. When did we figure out something was wrong?"

"When they came after the third trunk in the middle of the night. Didn't know about the books until then, either, mind you. We woke up, realized Carolyn was gone right along with the ungodly thumping that had woken us, and took off after her. We found a couple of the books and the spelled chest just outside the stagecoach, and put two and two together. The rest of things are just the way they happened, except you didn't suspect a thing about Sarah until after you killed the mad wolf and Carolyn stalked out of the woods."

Abigail rolled it around in her mind. "I think it'll work. Carolyn serving as a vehicle for that abomination for a very short time will be a whole lot more palatable for her parents than thinking Sarah had her claws into their child for months, if not years."

"It could well have been years," Luke agreed. "Sam and I kicked that around. Depends just how long the Girauds had those books."

Abigail narrowed her eyes. "Sarah did say they'd belonged to her originally. It makes sense she'd have tracked them, found the weak link in the Giraud chain, and wormed her way in." She exhaled wearily and shook her head. "I haven't let myself think much about it, but my escape was way too close for comfort. I still can't believe I was stupid enough to delude myself I could control something that wicked."

In a single fluid motion, Luke moved across the small space and sat next to her. He placed a hand on the side of her head and turned her so she looked right at him. "You were not stupid. You were fighting for your life. She would've killed you outright, she said as much. And she forced her way into you. It's not as if you were offered a choice. In situations like that, of course you'd try to put the best possible spin on things."

"It's kind of you to make excuses for me, but—"

He moved his hand from her face to her mouth. "Hush. I'm not making excuses. I know what it is to blame yourself." He hesitated a beat before caressing the side of her face again. "And I know just how hard it is to forgive yourself afterward. It took me years—" his nostrils flared "—and some days I'm not any closer to it than I was when I was fifteen and couldn't save my seven-year-old sister."

She looked at him then, locked her gaze onto his. "I'm sorry. You must've felt helpless."

He shook his head. "It was worse than that. I thought Tamra was safe, but it turned out I'd sent her to her death by telling her to knock on our neighbor's door. There were wraiths about. Our parents had been taken."

The corners of his eyes pinched with pain. "I didn't blame the neighbors for not letting my sister inside. Hell, I didn't even know what they'd done until later. I heard their front door slam and believed she was safe. It was a huge relief because things were turning to shit all around me. I fought with magic I didn't even realize I had, until everything blew up and I passed out. But if I'd been thinking, I'd have kept Tamra with me. If I'd done that—"

"Stop." She placed her hands over his. "You did the very best you could. You loved your sister and did your damnedest to save her." Abigail ached for Luke, understood he'd carted guilt around for years. "None of us are perfect. It's like what you were trying to tell me about Sarah, that I put the best face I could on things, once I realized what happened."

She hurried on, aware she was babbling, but the need to comfort him trumped everything. "You made what you thought was the best decision for Tamra. I'd have done the same thing and sent a child as far out of harm's way as I could, especially if the wraiths were our parents. Blood calls to blood. Keeping her close might've been worse." She stopped long enough to suck in a breath. "You have no idea what would've happened if you'd done something different. You only think you do."

Abigail clasped her hands in her lap and looked at them. What she'd just said had been incredibly blunt and forward. "Sorry," she mumbled. "I can be pretty opinionated when I get rolling."

"I respect that in people. Better than someone blowing smoke up my ass." Luke covered her hands with his. "I still want to get to know you better. I've been staying out of your way to give you a chance to recover a little, get your bearings back. I figured what the boys did to you while we were ousting Sarah might've made you squirm a bit, even if you can't remember it."

Warmth started in her belly and radiated outward. She risked an upward glance. His brow was furrowed and he looked determined, as if it had cost him to show any human need, but he wasn't going to let that stop him. She took a deep breath and squeaked out, "Me, too."

"Me too, what?" His voice deepened, rough with emotion.

She swallowed. "I want to get to know you better."

Relief lightened his expression, and he squeezed her hands hard enough to hurt. "Thank Christ! I thought you were interested, but then I told myself it was just Sarah and her insatiable need for men and sex."

"Sarah's gone. Really and truly. But it wasn't just her who liked you. I did too. Not did. I still do." Abigail grimaced. "It was one of the reasons I thought maybe she and I could coexist together." She shook her head. "I don't want to talk about Sarah, or think about her any more than we have to. How about if we start with that dinner you invited me to? Or maybe it'll end up being breakfast once we've talked with the Girauds."

"So long as you brought them up, we need to discuss one more thing." Luke frowned. "While we were riding, the boys and I chewed the fat over how…absent the Girauds have been. It's been at least a couple of years since they took an active part in Coven activities."

Abigail considered it, and then realized she hadn't been around enough to assess something like that. "I don't go to the council meetings," she said, "and I'm not very social, so I didn't notice."

"May have been why they picked you to escort Carolyn." He cleared his throat. "Anyway, just beware. We'll be playing this whole thing by ear once we get to Salt Lake."

"Carolyn did say something curious." Abigail narrowed her eyes, remembering. "She wanted to use me to get close enough to Breana to kill her, but she didn't mention Don."

"Mmph. Interesting. Maybe it means only one of them joined the other side."

An iron bar of tension settled between Abigail's shoulder blades. She hadn't exactly forgotten her doubts about Don and Breana Giraud, but she'd shoved them to a far corner of her mind. Surely evil couldn't have infiltrated that high into the Coven. She set her jaw in a hard line and gazed at Luke with sad eyes.

"I know." He patted her hands. "None of this is pleasant to contemplate, but I didn't want you going in blind."

"Thanks." She tugged one of her hands from beneath his and laid it on his shoulder.

He bent his head and closed his mouth over hers. The kiss was so tender and so inexplicably sweet, it melted her heart. His scent, amber and something definitely male, eddied about them. She wound her arms around him, wove her fingers into his hair, and opened her mouth to his questing tongue.

Luke groaned. He threaded his arms around her and pulled her against him, while his tongue explored her mouth. Her nipples formed peaks where they pressed against his hard-muscled chest. Something warm, fluttery, and melty moved through her, filling her with affection and need. She sucked on his tongue and then drew back to nibble his lips.

Abigail was considering rucking up her skirts and straddling his lap when she came to her senses and pulled away reluctantly. "We, that is I… Aw hell, this isn't right, not until after we get past talking with the Girauds."

"I agree. I wouldn't have let things go much further, but damn, woman, you just feel so good in my arms. Like you belong there." He shook his head. "Watching Sam and Josh and Chris go at you was one of the hardest things I've ever done, even if it was just Chris kissing you and Sam holding you. Had to keep reminding myself the real you was still deeply asleep. If I'd dashed forward and snatched you away from them like I wanted, Sarah would probably have killed Chris and Sam and you—"

"—and then she would've escaped," Abigail finished for him. "I'm glad she's well and truly finished. Evil spirits like her don't deserve their extended lives. I have no idea how long they can survive outside a living body."

Luke snorted. "Neither do I, but it's likely longer than we think since there're so many of 'em out there."

She grinned. "Look at it as job security. For me too. If there wasn't so much wickedness and misery in this world, humans would've burned all of us at the stake a couple hundred years ago."

"There've always been those who believed in us," he pointed out, still keeping her firmly clasped against his body.

"Yeah. It's the only reason any of us are still here." She laid her head on his shoulder and absorbed his energy, enjoying the way it complemented her own. "Back before you kissed me, you said you were afraid I wasn't interested in you. Nothing could be further from the truth. I'm not sure I understand, but you're almost all I think about…" She broke off, self-conscious she'd let quite so much slip.

"Now that's music to my ears." He laid his head atop hers for a moment. "Unless the Girauds need us to stay—or there's some other reason, like them joining up with the other side—the boys and I were planning to hightail it out of Salt Lake as soon as we could. You said you'd been considering where to go. What'd you come up with?"

"Depends on how the Girauds take things. If they're too

broken up, and they're willing, I might stay with them and help out, until they're past the freshest part of their grief."

"Where were you going to go if they kick you out of the Coven?" he prodded. "Or if they turn out to be evil incarnate?

"San Francisco."

"Ah, your grandmother. I remember you said something about that at the stage station the night I made us dinner. And then you clammed up real fast."

Abigail nodded and realized she was smiling at the thought of the woman who'd practically raised her. "I *clammed up* because, once I said it, I realized I couldn't visit Gran with Sarah inside me. I would never have put Gran at risk like that. She would've taken me in because she doesn't judge and she'd have wanted to help me, but it wouldn't have been fair to her or Pop."

"I think I'd like her. Sounds a lot like Aethelred, the wizard who taught me how to control my magic."

"You'll have to tell me about him." Abigail moved far enough away from Luke so she could look at him. "I want to know everything about you."

He rolled his eyes. "You only think you do."

"Yes, well, I figured my life story would bore you to tears too, but it didn't seem to."

He stroked the side of her face and tucked a lock of hair behind her ear. "Not that I'm any great judge of such things, but this feels like a good beginning—for us. We'll play what comes next as it happens. If you stay with the Girauds, I'll ask if they can find me some work here too."

"I'm sure they wouldn't turn you down."

"Probably not. But if I'm too visible, I won't be any good for the undercover work anymore."

"Would that bother you?" She closed her teeth over her lower lip and waited for his answer, casting the slightest of truth spells.

"No. Only thing that would bother me is being separated from you."

His words pinged sweet and clear off her spell, and joy cascaded through her. "I'm not certain how we'll do this," she murmured, "but we'll make things work."

"You damn betcha." He grinned and her world lit up.

"You should do that more often. It makes you look a whole lot less intimidating."

"Do what?"

"Smile."

"Tell you what—" his grin broadened "—I'll work on it, but just for you. And only so long as you don't tell anyone. Wouldn't want to ruin my image."

The driver shouted, "Whoa, whoa," and Abigail slowed the gears. She straightened in her seat and squared her shoulders. It was almost time to face the Girauds. Though she'd never had children of her own, she'd lived long enough to know parents never truly got over losing one of their offspring. She sent up a prayer for gentleness and compassion to deliver such horrible news. Then another for the equanimity she'd need if it turned out they'd been coopted by the other side.

"You won't be alone," Luke said resolutely, apparently having sensed her thoughts. "I'll be with you every step of the way."

CHAPTER 10

*L*uke pushed the stagecoach door open and looked outside. Breana Giraud with her long, golden hair and timeless features stood off to one side, draped in a colorful shawl and a black skirt. Her husband, Don, lounged beside her. Though neither of them were particularly tall, they oozed power. Don's copper hair was braided tight to his skull in many small rows and he wore his trademark black pants, shirt, and jacket. Stacked beside the couple were brightly wrapped packages.

Luke swallowed hard. Loving parents would bring presents to a joyful reunion with their only child, but being faced with the reality smote him. Breana rushed forward. "Carolyn, honey," she called. "I've missed you, child."

"Mrs. Giraud." Luke leapt to the ground. "I'm afraid we have bad news."

The smile on her face crumpled. "Bad news? Whatever do you mean?"

Abigail moved in front of him and held out her hands. "Oh, Mrs. Giraud, I'm so sorry."

"Is my baby's body in there?" Breana's voice held a strangled note as she raised a shaking finger to point at the stagecoach.

Don strode forward. His sharp, black eyes moved from Abigail to Luke. "I'm guessing the answer to that is no." He clamped his jaws together and glanced at the other three enforcers who'd dismounted and come close. "Get your things," he barked at Luke and Abigail. "We're not going to stand out in the street discussing this."

"No. Of course not." Breana sounded shell-shocked. Her tanned face turned ashen. She swayed on her feet, and Don threaded an arm around her waist, but she yanked her body away from his, an unreadable expression on her face.

"Our house is a few miles out of town," Don said. "Get on your horses and follow us.

Abigail went back to the stagecoach and pulled her valise from it. "Do you mind if I put this in the back of your wagon?" she asked Don.

He looked at the four enforcers and their horses. "Fine. I'll take it." He levered it from her grasp. "You can catch a ride with one of the men." He bent close and lowered his voice. "I don't want to talk about this until we're home. If any of you ride with us, Breana will drive you half mad with questions."

Don turned away. He stopped in front of the pile of presents and Luke could almost see him gird himself as he tossed Abigail's suitcase into his wagon. Hands freed, Don bent, scooped up his daughter's gifts, and placed them gently in the back of the wagon.

Abigail exchanged glances with Luke, her hazel eyes rimmed with anguish for what the Girauds must be feeling. To spare her the trouble of asking, he said, "You'll ride with me. Horse is plenty strong enough, plus he got a break this past hour."

Luke helped her arrange herself in the saddle and squeezed in behind her. Under any other circumstances, he'd have enjoyed the press of her body against his, but all he could see was the haunted look on Don's face when he'd put Carolyn's gifts into his wagon. The man had placed them as reverently as if they'd been his daughter's missing body.

Abigail twisted her head so she could talk with him once they started slowly after the wagon. The other enforcers rode in a rough row on both sides. "My God, but they're stoic," she said.

"Don pulled magic right after Breana jerked away from him. It's probably the only thing holding her together. Didn't you feel it?"

Abigail shook her head. "I wasn't looking, though. Those poor people. I've been racking my brain, trying to figure what I could have done, but the die was cast even before I showed up in New York."

"Hush." He shook his head slightly. "Don might be using magic to listen to us."

"I doubt it. For all his aplomb, he's shattered and probably blaming himself for not bringing the child when they first moved."

"You're likely right."

A sad, slow ache thrummed through Luke, as if their failure to protect Carolyn mirrored his loss of Tamra. They didn't talk anymore after that. Luke gazed at Don and Breana from time to time. Rather than sitting next to one another, as grieving parents might, they were just as far apart as they could get with one at each end of the wagon's seat. The ride felt as if it took forever, but probably not more than an hour passed before Don turned the wagon down a bumpy side road. In another half mile, a two-story log house sitting atop a rise came into view. The Girauds had picked a lovely piece of property on thickly-wooded land, with a rushing creek not far from the house.

Luke drew his horse up, jumped off, and made space for Abigail to dismount. The other enforcers joined them. "I'll hobble 'em near the creek," Sam said. "That way they can graze a bit and drink what they need."

"Don't be long." Luke recoiled at the pleading in his voice, but Sam's quiet strength rounded out his own. There weren't very many people Luke was comfortable asking for help, and something about the Girauds' ignoring one another on the drive didn't sit right. Not a single word had passed between them, either out loud or telepathically.

"No longer than I have to." Sam gathered four sets of reins and set off at a brisk pace with the horses trailing behind him.

Abigail pushed toward the Giraud's wagon and offered a hand to help Breana down. When the other woman was on the ground, Abigail opened her arms and Breana stepped into them. A sob escaped her, followed by another before she straightened.

"I am not going to do this," she said through clenched teeth. "I'll have years to mourn, the rest of my natural life. Right now, what I'm needing is information. What happened to my baby?"

"Maybe we ought to go inside," Don said, but he looked uncertain, as if getting them home had exhausted his strength.

Luke stepped forward. "Some stories go best in the clean, clear light of day."

"All right." Don sat heavily on one of the lower porch steps.

Breana stumbled to an upturned log end and sat on it, still maintaining an obvious distance between her and her husband.

Because he wanted to be at eye level with the Girauds, Luke hunkered in the dirt in front of them and motioned to Abigail to do the same. He took a steadying breath, met Don's direct, dark gaze, and started talking. "I got on the coach in Sterling, Colorado, just like my orders said. First thing that went wrong is we got attacked by wraiths. Abby and I, we did okay. Driver was killed, and one of the horses, but I hitched up the three that were left and got us to the next stage station. We were pretty done in, had a bite to eat, and went to sleep. The stationmaster offered to let us sleep inside, but I figured I could protect the women better if we stayed in the coach."

He stopped to clear his throat. "In the dark of the night, the coach began rattling and shaking something fierce. Woke us up and we saw right away Carolyn was missing. We sensed fell things, and I kicked myself for not setting a watch."

Abigail picked up the telling. "Luke and I raced out of there. First thing that happened was we stumbled on some Black Magick books and one of Carolyn's trunks." Abigail shook her head. "I packed two trunks in New York. The third one was locked and ready to go. It never occurred to me to check it, so I didn't, and I'm sorry. Anyway, that trunk was spelled, which was why we didn't know what was inside. We discovered later it was chockfull of books just as hideous as the ones we found."

"So dark agents pulled the trunk off the coach—" Don leaned forward, his lips set into a thin line "—and made off with the books, or most of them."

"Yes, sir," Abigail said.

"What happened then?" Breana asked.

Luke started talking again. "I borrowed a couple of horses from a nearby farm and Abigail and I took off after the books, figuring whoever had them had your daughter too. By then, I'd put out a distress call for other enforcers."

"Luke got quite a bit ahead of me," Abigail said. "A mad wolf jumped me and shoved me out of the saddle. I killed it. By the time I got to my feet and called my horse, which had bolted, Carolyn walked out of the woods." Abigail clasped her hands together so hard, her knuckles whitened. "Except by then, her body had been taken over by Sarah Osborne."

"Goddammit all to hell." Don lurched to his feet and pounded his fist into the porch railing. It must have hurt like hell, but he didn't even grunt. "That bitch has been after those books ever since we agreed to barricade them in our basement."

"It's actually a little worse than that." Abigail forged ahead. "She told me she was The Promised and that she was gathering power."

Don hissed and curved his fingers in the sigil against evil. "Keep talking," he rasped.

A low, keening sound rose from Breana. She looked so distraught, Luke wanted to go to her, but didn't. Comforting her was Don's job, not his.

Luke swallowed past a thickening at the back of his throat. "By then, I figured something must've happened to Abigail, so I doubled back. I came across Carolyn and her facing off. I'll never know quite what tipped me off, but I stayed in the shadows, cloaked myself, and listened for long enough to figure out what was going on. When Sarah said she was going to kill Abigail, I shot her, with silver and iron."

"It would have been awful enough if that had been the end of it," Abigail said in a low voice, "but Sarah jumped ship at the last possible moment and possessed me."

Don stalked in front of her and barked, "Stand up."

Abigail got to her feet and faced him with her shoulders squared. Luke felt a truth spell drop around her.

"You must have let her in." Don enunciated each word painfully clearly, his gaze never leaving Abigail's face.

"No, I didn't," Abigail said, raising her voice just a little. "She used compulsion on me, but I fought against it, even though my only other option was death. Somewhere in the midst of all that, Luke's gun went off and the Salem witch, or The Promised, took matters into her own hands and slipped inside me. She blew past my wards like they weren't even there. Right after that, a bunch of enforcers showed up. Not this crew, but half a dozen other ones, and they burned your daughter's body with mage fire." Abigail gritted her teeth. "I knew they didn't have to do that, but I couldn't tell them. Sarah wouldn't have let me."

The spell frittered away.

"Thank Christ you told me the truth." Don's voice shook. "If you'd lied, I'd have killed you myself."

"Oh, Don." Breana stumbled to her feet and moved to Abigail's side. "Two wrongs wouldn't have brought our baby back." She focused her ice blue eyes on Abigail. "I don't sense evil in you now. What happened?"

The four enforcers came close and told their story. At the end of it, Breana laid a hand on Abigail's arm. "I'm grateful you're still on our side and didn't succumb to the dark."

"If it was really The Promised you immolated in mage fire, it was a good day's work," Don growled, glancing from one enforcer to the next.

"Doubtful," Luke murmured. "If a Dark Messiah actually exists outside of legend, I suspect it would be far harder to annihilate than that."

"Never mind about The Promised right now." Tears sheened Abigail's eyes. "I'm so sorry about your little girl."

"Thank you. I believe I'll go inside." Breana turned and walked unsteadily up the porch steps.

"Feel free to stay," Don said hoarsely. "My wife needs me."

"Oh no, I don't," Breana said just before she slammed the front door behind her.

"Would you like me to cook something?" Abigail asked Don.

"Sure. That would be nice. Don't think I'll ever feel like eating again, but I've got to find my way past this." His voice trembled and he plodded after his wife.

"Let's take a walk," Joshua suggested.

"Good idea," Sam agreed. "That was pretty intense and I'd like to clear my head."

"I'll unhook the team from the wagon and get them settled in the barn with water and some feed," Luke said. "I'll find you once I'm done."

"Do you need help?" Abigail asked.

She looked almost as ravaged as the Girauds. Luke wanted to hold her, but there'd be time for that later. They'd gotten past this first hurdle with the Girauds, but had yet to settle which side they were really on. It was abundantly clear that Breana wanted nothing to do with Don.

The question was why.

Luke walked to Abigail and kissed her forehead. Placing his hands on her shoulders, he stepped back far enough to look at her and said, "It's pretty much a one-man job. Why don't you go with the boys? Moving around will help chase those *I should have done more* demons out of that pretty head of yours."

ABIGAIL PUMPED water at the sink to cool off the boiling cauldron she'd dragged over from the woodstove. Once it was a workable temperature, she added lye soap and rinsed her cook pot and the dishes they'd used. Luke and the other three men were out on the front porch. The low hum of their voices reached her from time to time. Neither Giraud had emerged from their upstairs bedroom.

When supper, a venison stew with vegetables from the garden out back, was ready, she'd sent Luke to knock on their door. He'd been gone for a long while. When he returned, he'd shaken his head and said, "Maybe tomorrow. Don made a sleeping draught for Breana."

She'd had her doubts about the enforcers' plan to omit some of what had happened, but now she was grateful they'd been able to spare the Girauds even more gritty details about what their daughter had turned into. The tale they'd told was bad enough. Reliving it chilled her blood and made her glad for the warmth of the cook stove.

Maybe Don and Breana would be better able to talk and make some decisions in the morning. Abigail hoped he'd had the good sense to take a little of whatever he mixed up for his wife. Not having a body, or a grave, would underscore their loss, but there was nothing to be done about that other than accept it.

Abigail dumped her dirty water down the sink and switched from washing to drying. Like she'd told Don, they could have spared Carolyn's body from mage fire, but none of them knew it at the time except her and she hadn't been in a position to tell. If she'd tried, Sarah would have silenced her. Abigail remembered Carolyn's outraged squawks when she'd finally truly understood the Salem witch could murder her and walk away without the slightest remorse.

That poor child. What a horrible way to spend her last moments...

Abigail hung her dishtowel on a hook and sat at the table, resting her chin on an upraised hand. She pulled the pins from her hair, shaking it out once it was loose, and reaching under it to massage places the pins had left sore spots. She couldn't think of anything else that needed doing, but she wasn't ready to face the men quite yet.

Joshua's earlier suggestion for them to take a walk had been wise. They'd each said what they needed to about Carolyn's loss and how it might impact the Girauds' ability to continue in a key role in the Coven. They'd also touched on the necessity of determining if the couple had been turned. One thing was certain. They couldn't leave the Girauds alone. In their current state, they'd be prime targets for an attack from the other side. If they were already part of that side, whatever warped loyalty kept them from turning their magic against the Coven might disintegrate in the face of their daughter's death. Don would bristle at the idea he needed protection, but Luke, Joshua, Chris, and Sam weren't going to take *go away* for an answer.

She'd never realized the true scope of enforcer powers. They could make decisions independent of Coven government. If a quorum, which happened to be four, all agreed, it was as if the thing were carved into stone tablets.

Her thoughts turned to Luke. Though he'd been unobtrusive, she'd felt him watching her throughout the long evening, his gaze earnest and kindhearted. She knew he was worried about her. Normally, that kind of overarching concern grated, but she welcomed it from him. Abigail stood. If she was thinking about Luke, maybe it was time to hunt him down. She reached for a shawl Breana kept draped over a peg near the door. It had to be past midnight, and it was cold outside.

She pushed the door open to a chorus of, "There she is."

"I was about to go inside and see if you needed any help." Luke held out his arms, and she sat in his lap, welcoming the warmth of his embrace.

"I finished a little bit ago," she said. "I've been sitting at the kitchen table, thinking."

"What about?" Sam asked.

She shrugged. "A little of this and a little of that. Mostly, I just feel so bad for Breana and Don. They didn't deserve to have something this rotten happen to them."

"That's usually the way of it," Chris rumbled. He tipped a

whiskey bottle to his mouth, leaned across the table, and handed it to her.

Abigail drank. The spirits burned a track down her throat all the way to her stomach. It hurt, but it felt good too, and served as a reminder she was still alive. "Thanks." She wiped her mouth with the back of her hand, and Sam took the bottle from her.

"Guess we could all bunk down for the night," Joshua said.

"Good idea." Sam stretched his arms over his head and rotated his torso. "Little enough night left as it is. Who wants first watch? I figure we'll do two hour stints."

"I'll go first," Joshua said and winked at Luke and Abigail. "I'm not very sleepy, and I suspect those two might want a little time together."

Abigail's face heated, but it was dark enough no one probably saw her blush. "Um, any idea where we can sleep?" she asked.

"I scouted us out a nice hay rick in the barn," Luke replied. "We'll be up in the loft. These three sapskulls picked downstairs."

"Sapskulls?" Sam slugged him in the arm. "So that's how it is now?"

"Aw, hell." Luke slugged him back. "We're all ninnies from time to time."

"Speak for yourself." Abigail laughed. "I think you're all amazing—daring and strong and courageous."

Joshua snorted. "Stop. These other three will become insufferable."

"And you won't?" Sam arched a brow, but Joshua just laughed.

Luke tilted her to her feet and got to his. He fired his mage light, tucked her hand beneath his arm, and led the way across a broad yard and into the barn. It was warm from horses, two cows, and a few goats, and it smelled sweet, like the hay that was stacked in bales off to one side. Luke pointed to a ladder and she climbed into the loft. It was a cozy space tucked under the eaves, but there wasn't space to stand, so she crawled to a place he'd obviously opened a hay bale and arranged clothing and blankets over it to make them a bed.

He hovered, balanced on one of the ladder's upper rungs, mage light bobbing to one side. "Will this be all right for you?"

She cocked her head to one side. "No, but it might be all right for *us*." She unlaced her boots and tugged them off, never taking her eyes off him.

His solemn face lit with a smile. "I didn't want to presume anything." He slithered up the rest of the rungs, worked his way over to her, and opened his arms. She snuggled against him and he drew a blanket over the top of them. His breath was warm against her hair, his hands sure where he rubbed her shoulders and back.

"That feels really good," she murmured against his chest. "I knew I was exhausted, but I didn't realize how tense I was."

"You have every reason to be both. Telling a person someone they love won't ever put their arms around them again has to be one of the hardest things to do. You want to be sensitive and compassionate, but you need to get the job done."

She nodded. "I did a lot of midwifing with Gran. Sometimes the babies didn't make it. Sometimes the women didn't. The worst was when we saved the babe, but the woman died. Mostly the men were in such bad shape over losing their wife, last thing they wanted was a little one."

"I'll bet not." Luke stroked her hair. "Most of us fellows don't have the first idea of how to take care of babies."

He kissed her forehead and strung kisses down the side of her face. Abigail turned her head, seeking his mouth with her own. Luke kissed her, soft and tender at first, but with increasing intensity as she flung her leg over his hip and wound her arms around him.

She opened her mouth, welcoming his tongue. Her heart slammed into a heady rhythm with wanting him, and her nipples pebbled where they pressed against his chest. He groaned and thrust his tongue deeper into her mouth, and then withdrew and nibbled her lower lip with little nipping kisses. His cock swelled and pressed into her belly. Abigail reached between them and curved her fingers around it.

He broke their kiss and moved back enough to look at her. His green gaze was intense, and heat flickered in the depths of his eyes, along with yearning. "Are you sure?"

She smiled. "I've never been surer of anything. We're both well past exhausted, but I want you to make love with me. It will help me move past the filth Sarah spread inside me."

"You're so beautiful." He wound a strand of her hair around one of his fingers. "Maybe instead of that dinner, we could ask Don to marry us. Or Sam, since he's got preacher credentials, and something about Don doesn't feel quite right. And then we could go out to celebrate afterward." He grinned and it made him look young and carefree.

Abigail laughed. "Why don't we get past the bedding part before we make any long-range commitments?"

"Spoken like a true modern woman." He pressed his cock deeper into her hand. "Ready whenever you are, love."

CHAPTER 11

*L*uke's soul took flight. Abigail wanted him, as desperately as he wanted her from the looks of things. His cock jumped against her probing fingers, aching for release. He wanted to free himself, push her skirts out of the way, and take her, but he wanted to gaze at her body too, drink in her loveliness. If he was patient, he could have it all. Reluctantly, he uncurled her hand from around his erection. She mewled in protest and made another grab for him.

"I love it that you can't wait. It's hard for me too, but let me make this a little nicer for us. I can use magic to create walls and heat so we can actually take our clothes off." Even as he spoke, he summoned a casting and wove the air currents around them together until they were dense enough to hold warmth. Before he got around to the next part of the spell, the air heated around them. He'd never taken his gaze from Abigail's lovely face, but now he quirked a brow.

A corner of her mouth turned up in a wry grin. "You didn't say I couldn't help. Besides, we already know our magic works well together." She propped herself on an elbow and tugged at the laces holding his leather shirt closed. "What happened to the ammo belts?"

"Left 'em with my guns. Don't worry. They're close by, just the other side of our bed."

She tried to pull his shirt off, but didn't have the angle right. "Sit up so I can get this off you. Um, if your guns were close, you were planning to sleep here all along."

"Not necessarily. If you hadn't wanted me, I'd have slept over there." He jerked his chin toward the right. "There's another, smaller nest I put together."

She slipped his shirt off and ran her hands down his chest. Her touch was electric and took his breath away.

"Ready for anything, huh?" she teased just before tilting her head and licking one of his nipples.

He grunted with pleasure. "All part of those years of enforcer training. They teach us to have plans and backup plans." It was hard to talk with her hot mouth and wicked tongue moving from nipple to nipple. Goosebumps raised along his arms, and his cock was so hard he was afraid he'd come before he got anywhere near her pussy.

Luke took hold of her arms and pulled her gently away from him and into a sit so he could unbutton her dress. Sliding his hands under the fabric, he found a silky chemise, but no stays. He was just thinking what the best way to get her dress off would be when she tugged it out from under her and whipped it over her head. Her skin gleamed alabaster in the glow from his mage light, with her erect nipples clearly visible through the thin fabric of her undergarment.

He had to remind himself to breathe. She was so lovely with her dark red hair falling around her strongly muscled shoulders and her cat-like hazel eyes. With hands that only shook a little, he tugged the ends of her chemise out of her petticoats and lifted the delicate garment over her head. If breathing had been a problem before, it was doubly so now. She had the most beautiful breasts. Full and tipped with copper-colored nipples, they rode high on her sculpted ribcage.

Abigail laughed low, almost like a throaty growl. "You can touch," she said. "I won't shatter."

The sound of her voice broke into his trance. He found he could move, pushed her gently onto her back, and closed his mouth over one of her nipples. He twirled and teased the other one with his fingers. Abigail arched her back under him and moaned softly when he moved from one breast to the other, trading mouth for fingers and back again. She thrust her hips upward in obvious invitation, so he wriggled a hand under her petticoats and came across drawers with what felt like a drawstring.

He raised his mouth from her breasts for long enough to grin and say, "Women. I swear you wear more layers of coverings." Luke shifted and untied her petticoats and drawers so he could slide them down her hips.

"It's to ensure our virtue stays intact," she informed him roguishly and twisted her hips to help.

"Oh, is that it? I'd always wondered." As long as he was sitting, he toed off his boots and pushed his leather pants down his legs.

"Oooooh." She vaulted to a sit and wrapped both her hands around his exposed cock. "It's beautiful, long, and thick and amazing." She raised her gaze to his face. "The rest of you is beautiful too. Perfect man." She let go of his cock and traced her hands down his face. "Look at you. Between those emerald eyes and high cheekbones, you could pass for a god. Never mind your shoulders." She moved her hands lower and grazed his arms with her fingertips. Gliding across his stomach, she took his cock in her hands again.

Luke wanted to tell her that no, she was the beautiful one with her lush curves, thick tresses, and alluring eyes, but words wouldn't come. It was hard to think of anything but the beautiful woman before him. Her scent was intoxicating. Jasmine, vanilla, and the musk of her need filled him with longing.

He wrapped her in his arms and lay back down, glorying in the feel of her, skin-to-skin against him. She ended up laying half atop him and closed her mouth over his. The kiss was urgent, telling him her need rivaled his own. He ran his hands down her silken back and curved them around the firm globes of her ass. Painfully aware of his erection sandwiched between them, he thrust against her stomach and then rolled her onto her back.

Breaking their kiss, he knelt before her and pressed the tip of his cock against the sensitive nub between her legs. Tight red curls glistened with her juices. He gripped his cock with one hand and rubbed it in small circles around her sex. She spread her legs and brought her knees up, opening herself for him.

He hoped she was ready, because he wouldn't last long, not this first time. Maybe he should bring her to orgasm with his mouth or fingers first. He hunted for the words to ask, since talking about sex didn't come easy, but Abigail circled his body with her legs and pulled, her intent obvious. Color splotched her face and breasts, and her chest heaved as she panted, breathless.

Luke gave himself to the moment. He couldn't talk, didn't want to. The only thing that mattered was how inexorably he was drawn to the woman beneath him. He moved his cockhead back until it seated against the opening to her body. She writhed and twisted, trying to get him inside. Unable to resist, he sank slowly into her, delighted by the heat of her surrounding him, and giving her time to stretch around his girth. She wasn't a maid, but he didn't want to hurt her. Once he hit bottom, he stopped and wrapped strands of magic around his crumbling control. He wanted to at least last long enough to make her come. His entire body vibrated with sexual tension, and his balls were about to explode.

She drove her hips upward and gripped his hips. "Move, goddammit." Her voice was thick, raspy with passion.

He withdrew, almost all the way out, and plumbed her again. After half a dozen long, slow strokes, he couldn't stand it anymore and slammed his body into hers again and again. Her pussy dissolved around him, slippery and scorching. She cried out and he felt the rhythmic contractions of her release. For the barest moment, he nurtured the illusion he could ride herd on his own orgasm, but it was a losing battle. With a groan, he pulled out of her wonderful warmth, gripped his shaft, and spilled his seed on her belly. His cock jerked for a long time as he straddled her, breathing hard.

Luke's legs were shaking. He straightened them from where he'd been kneeling over Abigail, and lay next to her. Emotion thrummed through him. Sex had never felt so right before. It had moved from the physical realm to a spiritual experience. He and Abigail were bound now, body and soul, forever. At least he felt that way, and so strongly, he couldn't imagine she didn't share the wonder of what had just passed between them. He enclosed her in his arms and felt hers wrap around him. They rocked against each other for long moments, breathing each other in.

"You could have come inside me," she murmured. "Even if I got pregnant, I know how to fix things like that."

"We're going to do this right." Luke's vehemence surprised

him, but he kept talking anyway. "We're going to get married before the young 'uns start coming." Protectiveness roared through him, and he tightened his hold on her. Nothing would ever harm Abigail. His Abigail. Ever.

"Sure you don't want to, um, practice a little more before you extend that marriage proposal?" She bucked her hips against him. "If you keep asking, one of these times, I'm going to say yes, and you'll be stuck. Not that I've still got a daddy who'd come after you with a shotgun for reneging on a promise, but still…"

He shifted a hand between her legs and inscribed small circles around her nub. When she pressed against him, he rubbed harder. It felt like she was close again from the quickening motion of her pelvis, so he inserted a finger inside her and pressed down on her sex with his palm. She swayed against him, captured between his finger and his hand, until her muscles tensed and released around him.

"Yes, love," he murmured. "Sweet, love. Come for me."

Gasping with pleasure, she relaxed in his arms and curled her fingers around his still half-hard penis. "We could do this some more. I could take you in my mouth, or I could roll you over and straddle you."

"I can't remember when I had a more attractive offer, but we need to sleep a little. Those two-hour watch cycles go quick, and I should close my eyes for a bit before it's my turn."

She fitted her body against his. "I guess I'm sleepy too, but what we just shared feels magical and I don't want it to end."

His chest swelled with love. "It never has to end. About that marriage proposal…"

"I accept."

Luke crushed her to him. "We'll definitely see about having Don marry us in the traditional Coven ceremony first thing tomorrow."

"Do you think that's wise? Given he's just lost his daughter—and we're not sure about him in other ways."

"Humph. Good point, at least the second one. I'll talk with Sam tomorrow. He might be a better choice, anyway."

Abigail didn't answer, probably because she'd fallen asleep. He settled the blanket around them and withdrew magic from his spell. Even though the temperature dropped rapidly once his magical tenting dissipated, an inner fire raged through him. Two parts love, one part vigilance, he swore he'd devote his life to being worthy of Abigail's trust in him.

They hadn't exchanged love words, not yet, but they would, given time. The groundwork was there, and he'd do whatever he could to ensure their lives blended seamlessly.

Abigail wasn't quite sure what woke her, but when she reached for Luke, he wasn't there. She fired her mage light in time to see him fully dressed and strapping his ammo belts around his shoulders. "What—?" she began sleepily.

"You stay here. Sam roused me. Looks like we may have trouble."

Abigail struggled against her sleep-fuzzed brain and pushed to a sit. "If there's trouble, I can help."

He stopped what he was doing long enough to crawl over to her. "If it comes to that, I'll let you know." He wrapped an arm around her in an awkward hug. "I'm falling in love with you, Abigail. I don't have any idea what's going on. Until I know more, I want you up here. I'll spell the barn when I leave to protect you."

She'd stopped listening after *falling in love*. The words were so sweet and so unexpected they seared her soul. Sure, he'd asked to marry her, but love wasn't necessarily anywhere in the marital equation. People coupled up for lots of reasons. If they liked one another, it was a plus. Love was icing on the cake, and exceedingly rare.

"Abby." He shook her gently, probably aware she was off on a mental tangent. "I have to go. Promise me you'll stay here."

"Sure."

She still wasn't all the way awake. She lay quietly until the sound of his footsteps descending the ladder and leaving the barn faded. Abigail extinguished her mage light and shut her eyes to encourage them to dark adapt again. When she opened them, tendrils of dawn showed through chinks between the barn's boards.

It was probably a good idea to get dressed. If the enforcers needed her, she couldn't do much buck naked. It took a while to sort out her underthings, dress, and Breana's shawl from the tangle of clothes beneath her. The last thing she did was put on her stockings and lace up her boots. She'd kept half an ear cocked, but it was ominously silent outside.

Let's be smart about this.

Abigail fanned a subtle stream of magic outward in a full circle, and dragged it back in a hurry. *Crap!* They were surrounded. Mad wolves, wraiths, men turned by evil. How the hell had they found out about the Girauds' vulnerability so soon?

Truth cascaded down her spine in an icy sheet. The other side must've known about Sarah and Carolyn—likely because the Girauds were already in cahoots with them. Sarah meeting her end in mage fire provided more than ample reason to plot revenge. A group of sorcerers had probably been biding their time, just waiting for her and the enforcers to show up.

Stupid. We were stupid not to think of that...

The Girauds weren't looking all that innocent right about

now. She ran options through her mind and, in a burst of bravery, sent magic their way wondering how they'd respond to a direct confrontation. Whatever happened, it would tell her a lot.

After enough time passed that she feared the worst, Don's mind voice answered. *"Yes, Abigail. What is it?"*

"A dark host is massing not far from the house. I have no idea how many. The men are outside somewhere, planning something to deal with it."

He growled, a ripping, tearing sound that filled her head with awful noise. She would have shuttered her mind, but she needed to talk with him. *"Don."* She screamed his name.

"I'm fine, but damn it all, Breana's barely breathing. I can't rouse her. She wasn't like this before I finally fell asleep. Get in here, Abigail. You've got some healing talent. Use it. I'll join forces with the men."

"On my way."

"Do not let her die," he grated. *"I couldn't stand to lose her. What's already happened is bad enough."*

"I'll do my best."

Abigail's heart stuttered, and her mouth flooded with the acrid taste of fear. Maybe she'd misjudged the Girauds after all. Don sounded genuinely distressed. Luke had told her to stay put, but Don's orders trumped his. She started to call Luke, but reined her mind voice in. If he was hard-pressed, the last thing she wanted to do was distract him.

Grateful she was already dressed, she worked her way down the ladder in the pale light of dawn filtering into the barn. Before opening the door, she summoned magic to render herself invisible. It might not work—the enemy she sensed outside was strong enough to see right through her spell—but it was the best she could do.

She slid the door back just far enough to slither out,

masking her movements. Abigail sucked in a tense breath and eyed the stretch of open yard between her and the house. Maybe fifty yards. Behind her, a horse whinnied nervously. Picking up on the horse's tension, the goats *baahed* and the cows *mooed.*

No time like now.

Abigail forced herself to hold a moderate pace. Moving quickly would make her invisibility cloak much less effective. The air felt still and heavy and wrong. It settled in her lungs like a stone and, for one horrid moment, she wondered if it was poisoned. Despite the chill, frosty morning, sweat dripped down her sides. She kept her hands raised, power balanced between them in case she had to defend herself.

She stumbled, and almost fell as a familiar reek tickled her nostrils. The books. The fucking, goddess-blasted books were close. She'd know their rotten stench anywhere. How the hell had the books gotten to the Girauds' house?

Abigail grimaced.

She didn't like any of the answers that jumped into her mind. It took a lot to force herself to keep moving toward the house. What she wanted to do was disappear back into the barn, curl into a ball, and shudder in horror at the depth of the Girauds' treachery.

Tension carved deep, making it hard to breathe. Her muscles felt like rocks, and pebbles rolling beneath her boot soles threatened to send her sprawling. Though she kept her gaze straight ahead, she gathered information from where she couldn't see with tiny blasts of magic. Not too much. She didn't want to give away her position.

Even though she tried not to think about them, her mind boomeranged back to the books over and over. Black Magick must've transported them here. There wasn't any other explanation. Was it just Don who was corrupt? Or was it both him and Breana?

Fury lent her badly needed energy. How dare the Girauds denigrate Coven leadership by parlaying with the dark behind everyone's back?

Finally, when she was so frazzled it took a huge effort not to scream at the bastards to just show themselves, goddammit, she reached the steps leading to the kitchen door. Abigail took them two at a time, but slowed once she got to the door and eased her way inside. The sense of wrongness was worse in here. Much worse. Maybe that was why she hadn't run into the enemy outside. But her sense of the books' nearness receded, which meant they had to be somewhere outside.

She bit down on her lower lip. If she trusted her magic, and she had no reason not to, it suggested hundreds of dark spirits were congregated in the house. Where had they come from? More importantly, where were they hiding? Abigail slid her gaze from side to side, and clenched her jaw to keep her teeth from chattering. Where were Luke and the other enforcers? They'd done a stellar job masking themselves since she hadn't caught the slightest whiff of their magic outside. Unfortunately, they didn't appear to be in the house, either.

She scented the air, stifling a cough. Breathing too deeply wasn't wise since wraith stench could make her ill. She sent magic out, scanning, and quickly sheathed her power. Breana was upstairs. Don wasn't. Presumably, he'd carried through on his promise to join up with the enforcers. Or maybe he was outside with the books. Wraith energy closed in. She couldn't see them, but she could feel their foulness and smell their rotten meat stench.

Abigail gathered her courage. Don said Breana was unconscious. Maybe it was a lie to lure her into the house, but she had to look for herself, and she'd never be able to sneak her way up the stairs. Her invisibility spell drained power. Time to let it go. In a burst of boldness, she funneled everything she had into deploying a defensive perimeter and loped up the staircase. Wraiths lined the top of the stairs. She blasted through them, watched a dozen fold in on themselves, only to be replaced by a dozen more.

Her fear shrank to manageability now that she had something to do. Kill or be killed. Abigail understood this game. She felt evil behind her, and knew they planned to pen her in. So much for staying a safe distance from the bunch above her. With a wild war whoop, she charged the wraiths that were spewing Black Magick from the balcony. They fell before her as she topped the stairs and raced down the hallway.

Breana had to be behind the closed door. Abigail rattled the knob. Locked.

Shit!

She turned, pressed her back against the door, and sprayed the wave of wraiths closing in on her with the unmaking spell. That wasn't the sort of magic she could call on for very long because it was a real power hog, but she hoped it might intimidate the rest of the wraiths and give her a few moments' respite.

While she fought, she trickled magic behind her seeking the right touch to unlock the door. The tiniest of *snicks* thrilled her as the bolt drew back. Damn if the door wasn't open. With a final volley aimed at her tormentors, she slipped into the room and threw the bolt back into place. By the time she was certain the door was secure, Abigail was doing more than panting. She gasped for something to breathe in a space where decent air had departed. Maybe her breathless state was a result of sharing the hallway with so many wraiths they'd polluted her lungs, but it felt as if someone had sucked most of the oxygen out of the room.

No wonder Breana was unconscious.

Abigail wrapped the door in a *you will not enter* spell and turned to the comatose woman sprawled on the bed. Her first glance twisted her gut into a knot. Breana's face was the color of her pillowcase, and she lay so still, it was unnerving.

Maybe it's better this way. I don't trust her as far as I can see her.

Abigail raced to the room's only window and peered outside. No wraiths. She took a chance and shoved the sash up to pull better air into the room. After a deep, cleansing breath, she hastened back to the bed, bent over Breana, and placed a finger beneath her nose. When she felt a faint puff of breath, she was so relieved, tears threatened.

No time for that. If I make it through this, I can fall apart later. Besides, maybe it's a huge mistake to wake her. At least this way, she's not trying to claw my eyes out.

Abigail sent magic into Breana, assessing what was wrong, what she could fix. Though she searched for wraith-taint, she didn't find any. Breana had withdrawn deep into her mind, barricaded herself in. Maybe it was her reaction to losing her daughter. Maybe her husband had done this to her on purpose. Regardless, it was only a matter of time before wraiths stormed them, and Breana was helpless in her current state.

What had Don said? Something about her not being like this earlier, not that his words carried much weight.

Abigail debated what to do. Fight the dark on her own, call Luke, or try to get Breana awake enough to help. The latter was definitely a two-edged sword, given Abigail wasn't at all certain just where Breana's allegiance lay. Noise escalated in the hallway, loud enough to drive ice picks into her brain. The certainty of an upcoming battle—of things that wanted her dead—decided her.

She cradled the other woman's head between her hands and sent energy pulsing into her.

"You have to come back."

She repeated the phrase over and over, upping the volume until the unconscious woman squinched her eyes shut tighter. *Good!* It meant she'd reached her.

"You have to come back now," she repeated.

"Can't. Hurts too much." Breana's mind voice was weak, wispy.

"I know it hurts. Losing a child is the worst thing a mother can live through, but we're all in danger. Your husband is outside fighting for his life. We need your magic."

"I don't give a shit about him. Death's too good for that bastard. Just leave me alone and let me die."

Abigail hoped Breana's words about her husband were true. Assuming they were, waking the woman was even more critical because she could help fight the dark horde massing both outside and within the house.

Abigail considered slapping her, but focused her desperation and let it spark through her next words. *"Yes, you're hurting, but you scarcely have a corner on that market. We've all lost a lot. Luke lost his sister. He's not curled up in a ball with his head up his ass. I almost lost my life for chrissakes. We need you, Breana, so long as you fight on the right side. You can sink yourself in self-pity once we're safe. We're badly outnumbered."*

Abigail ran out of words and inhaled sharply. She didn't know what else to say, so she just whispered, *"Please,"* and held onto Breana, hoping against hope she'd gotten through.

Something crashed against the bedroom door. Not wraiths. They weren't corporeal enough to pound that hard. Must mean humans had joined their ranks. Because she was frantic and didn't know what else to do, she sent out a call to the enforcers and hoped to hell they didn't die trying to save her and Breana.

The woman stirred beneath her hands and wrenched herself away from Abigail. She opened her eyes and her face twisted into a grimace, distorting her beauty.

"Right now I hate you," she said, her words slurred and harsh.

Abigail cracked a grim smile. "We all hate duty when she calls us. Pull your magic together. It's only a matter of time before the bastards break down your door. We need to be ready."

"You don't understand."

"Try me." Abigail kept one eye on the door, watching it shudder. "But hurry."

Breana whipped her bloodshot gaze to the door and barked a word in demonspeak. She curled her lips back from her teeth. "Yes," she hissed. "I know their language and for the best of reasons. Don made a deal with them, but it cost me my daughter." Fury blazed from her like a white-hot tide. "I tried to kill him last night, which is why he buried me in spells."

The door splintered and a two-inch long crack opened. Abigail took a chance.

"Will you swear on whatever you hold true that you'll help me?"

"If I won't?"

Abigail gathered killing magic, let it hover in the air between them. "Then you'll get your wish about dying." She gritted her teeth together. "I'd kill you right this minute because you admitted a cardinal sin in knowing the demons' tongue, but I need your help. Keep in mind I have no power to offer anything, but if you do the right thing now, the Coven may spare your life."

Breana clacked her jaws together. "I'll help you on one condition."

Abigail quirked a brow. The door splintered again, about to fall in. "You're scarcely in a position to bargain. What?"

"If Don's not dead by the time we get out of here, you'll help me kill him."

"Done."

"I'll hold you to that." Breana lurched upright and joined Abigail.

They clasped hands and lobbed power at whoever stood on the far side of the door. Breana was amazingly strong, dazzlingly so. Abigail concentrated on doing whatever she had to, so both of them got out of the house alive. There'd be time to unravel the Girauds' sad tale after that—and burn the rest of those blasted books.

The door blew inward with a wrenching, tearing *thud*. Abigail jumped out of the way just as a tall man with tawny hair, jauntily dressed in white buckskin, strode through followed by a nondescript dark-haired fellow. The second man radiated danger with hard, dark eyes and deep furrows in his face. A black shirt and leather pants hugged his spare frame. By contrast, the first man looked as if he'd been invited to a social event.

"Top of the morning, ladies." The man in white grinned, his blue eyes glittering mischievously.

"The hell it is," Breana spat. "No morning that has you in it could possibly be good, Alistair." Power flew from her hands, but it sputtered and died before it reached either man.

"They're warded." Abigail grimaced because she should've known.

Alistair shrugged. "So are you, witch. Why would you expect less of me?"

Her stomach clenched with fury, but she forced herself to conserve her power. No point in bombarding the men if nothing she sent had any impact. "What do you want?"

"Trouble," Breana said succinctly. "It's what he feeds on."

"Oh, come now. I've told you if you ever tire of that husband of yours—"

"Shut up!" Breana howled. "You killed my daughter."

"No. Sarah killed her. I swear, that woman never had any sense."

Breana's features distorted into pain laced with fury. "That isn't what you said when you talked Don into letting her travel inside Carolyn."

"My clairvoyant skills must've been taking a holiday." Alistair shrugged.

Breana snarled low in her throat and lunged toward him, but Abigail dragged her back. "He's baiting you," she snapped. "Ignore him."

Breana opened her mouth, and then clacked her jaws shut. Rage sparked from her blue eyes.

Abigail eyed the tableau in front of her and tried to see what she could possibly do to pound her way through the shielding around the men. Magic bubbled in the air around her as she experimented with different combinations of elements. No reason to be stealthy since the man, Alistair, apparently saw himself as invincible.

He focused his unsettling gaze on her. "Don't waste your effort, witch. I'll deal with the two of you later." He barked a few words in demonspeak and the doorframe took on a flame-tinged appearance. Darker air wafted where the door had stood.

"What do you want me to do, boss?" the second man asked.

"Make certain the ladies are comfortable." Alistair grinned with all the warmth of a rattlesnake. "No one will be able to get in or out of the door now that I've spelled it."

The dark-haired man grinned ominously. "Comfortable, eh? Sounds like fun."

"Just make sure they don't get away from you." Alistair

narrowed his eyes, loped across the room, and muttering more demonspeak, jumped through the open window.

Abigail ran to it and looked down, not surprised he'd disappeared. "Damn. I was hoping he'd be a splotch on the dirt."

"It takes more than wishes and hopes to hurt him," Breana said bitterly. "I've wanted that bastard of a dark sorcerer dead for years."

"Hey now!" The dark-haired man walked briskly to her side. "I'll not have you talking disrespectfully about our lord and master."

Breana twisted away from the man and screeched, "Blast him, Abby. He's not as strong with Alistair gone."

Abigail focused the magic still thrumming around her at the man in black. It shimmered and crackled when it ran up against his wards. He sent blows her way and Breana's, but she and the other witch stayed on opposite sides, forcing him to split his attention. Even so, he was strong enough they barely felt evenly matched. She ran Alistair's name through her mind, paired with their opponent calling him *lord and master*, and an unsettling thought intruded.

"What's Alistair's last name?" she panted, almost sure she already knew.

"MacDuff." Breana spat the word out.

God damn son of a bitch. The head of The Alchemical Council.

Fear threatened to immobilize her. For the barest moment, she began walking toward the spelled doorframe, knowing intuitively its power would kill her, but unable to stop herself.

"Stop!" Breana cried. "He wove coercion into the spell. But it's a compulsion that feeds off hopelessness. Get hold of yourself."

Abigail froze in her tracks and tore her gaze from the mesmerizing black light flaring around the doorframe. "Thanks," she said shakily. She took a steadying breath, turned, and lobbed more magic at the man leering at her. The simple act of fighting back went a long way toward clearing her head.

Alistair's not here now.

Breana's still on the right side of things. Probably.

If we can kill this guy, whoever he is, it will be one less soldier in Black Magick's army.

CHAPTER 12

$\mathcal{L}$uke started when he heard Abigail's voice in his mind. He'd left her safe in the barn, goddammit, layered in protection spells. He and the other enforcers—and Don —were scattered in a rough formation, blasting the living shit out of mad wolves and humans who'd been turned. So far, they'd dealt death handily, and all of them were still alive.

Because Sam had been on top of things, the battle was unfolding out by the main road rather than in front of the Girauds' home. Bodies littered the ground, running red with blood. Flies had landed in droves, their buzzing loud and angry. Crows and turkey vultures were just now closing in. It wouldn't take long for the rest of the native cleanup crew to make an appearance.

Luke took a breath and gagged. Between ruptured guts, spilled shit, puke, and the overarching, coppery reek of blood, death always smelled appalling. Someone had to be behind this, probably one of the dark sorcerers. Luke wondered if other Salem witches were still kicking around, spreading their venom. It was possible a few had copied Sarah and borrowed living bodies to do their dirty work.

Still, there had to be a mastermind behind everything. For the first time in a long time, he longed for Aethelred. The mage kept a level head and was one of the best strategists Luke had ever known.

"Who's going back to help the women?" Sam asked.

A column of mad wolves raced out of thick timber from across the road. Mouths open, tongues lolling, their canines glistened with blood. *Christ!* Who had they killed?

"None of us are going anywhere yet," Luke yelled and focused lethal blows at the pack of wolves. For each one that fell, two more sprang out of the evergreens and aspens, ravenous for victims. His nose twitched and shock registered. It couldn't be, but it was. He smelled the books. Luke glanced at Sam, Chris, and Joshua, wanting to ask if they scented them too. He couldn't use mind speech or Don would hear.

Luke wasn't certain quite how Don had found out they were engaged in a fight, but he'd shown up a while back and simply joined them.

"Let's use our brains," Don suggested, his voice silkily smooth.

The air shimmered menacingly, and Luke felt magic pour from the Coven leader. It took him a moment to understand and then he shifted his power to block him. Rather than taking down individual wolves, Don was merging their power, driving them forward. Luke was impressed. It was the sort of thing Aethelred would have done. Neat, clean, minimal magic for maximum effect.

Too bad Don wasn't fighting on their side.

At least fifty of the new crop of mad wolves rushed them. Luke blocked Don's power in individual wolves until the pack milled about uncertainly. Don nodded his approval and shouted, "Nice work," as if the whole thing had been his idea. As if to create an excuse for his earlier command to attack, Don polished off his spell with an elegant touch: compulsion to return to being forest wolves.

Luke heard the words, subtle and seductive, exhorting the wolves to blame the dark for their misery and have nothing more to do with them. Grateful to finally have a clear path before him, Luke laughed grimly and planted himself in front of Don. "What the hell are you doing?" he demanded.

"Fighting darkness. What else would I be doing?" Don's mouth curved into a parody of a snarl.

"That does it, at least for now." Joshua loped to where Luke stood.

"Oh no, it doesn't," Luke said.

"Luke's right," Don agreed affably, an unreadable expression on his face. "Whoever's masterminding this charade is still out there. I can't feel him all the time, but an occasional twinge of wrongness tipped me off." He pounded a fist into his open palm. "Got to make sure the women are safe."

Luke narrowed his eyes and bit back an accusation that Don was the mysterious unknown masterminding everything. He'd get to that soon enough, but right now, he needed information. "Speaking of women, why's Abigail in the house?"

"Because Breana was out cold. I have no fucking idea what happened. She finally cried herself out and fell asleep in my arms." Don's nostrils flared. "When Abigail woke me to tell me what was going on out here, Breana was sunk so deep I couldn't reach her. I knew you four would need my help, but I couldn't leave my wife. Abigail's got that healing gift, so I ordered her to sit with Breana."

Luke had been listening carefully. Don was smooth, but his words pinged sour off Luke's truth spell. Not very sour. If he hadn't been paying close attention, he might not have noticed. Don turned to leave. "Not so fast." Luke grabbed his arm.

"What?" Sam chugged to his side, followed by Chris.

"Bind him," Luke barked.

Don writhed in his grasp, but Luke held fast and Sam grabbed the man's other arm. "I'll have you dragged before our council for treason," Don snarled. "Unhand me this instant. I outrank all of you."

"Enforcers are independent of Coven government," Chris ground out. "Or did you forget that little fact?"

"Luke's word is good enough for me," Sam said and began to chant.

Joshua, Chris, and Luke joined in. Don mounted a counterattack, calling fire and a hail of small stones, but he was no match for the four enforcers. When mad wolves lumbered out of the forest, Luke targeted one and it exploded, showering its fellows with blood, sinew, and gore. Snarling, snapping, and howling, they took off the way they'd come, but not before they'd grabbed chunks of their dead companion. Meat was meat.

Don sank to the ground, still breathing, but unconscious.

"What should we do with him?" Joshua nudged the body with his boot.

"I'd like to kill him, but we need either him or Breana to tell us the truth," Luke said.

"Fine. Everybody grab something. We'll haul him back to the house and bind him with magic until we make sure the women are okay." Sam took a leg. The others followed suit.

"Abby?" Luke called, worried because it had been at least half an hour since her frantic summons. When she didn't answer, he broke into a run with the other four men flanking him. Don's body flopped between them.

Damn it!

He should've taken off and let the others fight the mad wolves—and corral Don. What the hell was in the house with the women? He threw his magic wide, seeking information.

Wraiths.

Stinking, nasty, undead bastards. Hundreds of them from the feel of it. And the book stench was stronger too. "Books," he panted. "Can you smell 'em?"

"Son of a bitch," Joshua swore. "How the hell did they end up here?"

"Ask a stupid question," Chris snapped.

"Maybe we should forget about finding out the truth," Sam muttered. "We can throw this piece of shit in mage fire along with his precious books."

Luke ran faster. He'd never seen more than a couple dozen of the wretched undead in any one place. Maybe Don had inadvertently disclosed part of the truth about an unseen puppeteer manipulating strings from the sidelines, and there was a second black magician in the vicinity.

"Come out and fight like a man," he muttered. Fury sparred with fear he wouldn't make it back in time to save his love. Guilt over losing Tamra had devastated him. If he lost Abigail, he didn't know how he'd find the heart to go on living.

"Hang on, love. Hang on. We're nearly there."

"Hurry."

Her mind voice was faint, but it lent wings to his feet.

Luke steamed into the yard and dropped Don's arm. Leaving it to the others to wind magic around him, he pounded up the stairs into the house. Wraith stench hit him in the yard, but inside it thickened to a nauseating miasma that threatened to choke him. He coughed helplessly, moved his bandana up to cover his nose, and hoped he wouldn't puke. Wraiths stank, but their dismal reek had never been so overpowering before.

Sam pushed past him and spun, blocking the kitchen door.

Luke raised his brows. "That didn't take long."

"Because we didn't worry about using too much magic and killing him by mistake." Sam shrugged. "If he's gone, good riddance, but I suspect he's only unconscious. Let's finish this."

"Abby's still alive," Luke said. "She just answered me."

"Breana?" Sam asked.

Luke shook his head. "Don't know."

Sam mowed up the stairs, power blazing from his entire body. Luke followed in his wake. It was like plowing through mud—thick, magical mud—but at least it cut the wraith stench. The foul creatures lined the stairs and were packed into the balcony and upper hallway. As Sam cut their connection to whoever was driving them, they faded and flickered.

Luke stared at what was left of the Girauds' bedroom door. Something had splintered it as if it had been matchsticks, not inch-thick oak. Magic sparked across the doorway, black around the edges, and Abby came into view. Burns tracked across her face and arms and her hair was singed, but at least she was on her feet. He started forward.

"Don't touch it," she shrieked. "The magic in the doorway is spelled to kill you."

"Bitch!" sounded from inside the room.

"You shut up or I'll snuff your sorry life out," Breana cried, her voice hoarse and gravelly.

Rage set Luke's insides on fire. What in the goddess's name was in that room with the witches? Joshua pounded up the stairs, joining them.

"Where's Chris?" Luke asked tersely.

"Standing guard over Don. I would've stayed, but he and I thought you might need me up here."

"More firepower never hurt." Luke motioned and Sam and Joshua flanked him, one on either side.

"Let's tackle that spell," Sam muttered.

"Sounds as if the women have things under control." Joshua grinned, but it faded fast as he twirled, facing the staircase. "Shit! Chris might be in trouble. He just told me things are under control, but Don isn't as deeply unconscious as how we left him."

Dread speared Luke. "Goddammit. Don's dangerous." He felt torn. Chris needed them, but Abigail and Breana did too.

"Our spell ought to hold for a few more minutes. I'll see to him just as soon as we've got this door taken care of." Sam gave an encouraging thumbs-up and added, "Hey, Josh, why don't you polish off those wraiths?"

"On my way." He trotted a few paces down the hall, and it lit with targeted blasts of mage fire.

The air flickered where Sam sent exploratory magic toward the doorway. His spell burst into flames. Sam yelped and jumped back. "Shit. Whatever it is has a bite to it."

"That does it for the wraiths. At least it won't stink so bad in here soon." Joshua stalked toward them dusting his palms together. "Next problem, boys?" His face creased into a grim expression. "I heard Breana in there, just as feisty as ever. Abby looks like she's okay too."

"Feisty, is it?" Breana drawled. "You boys always did waste a pile of time jawing. 'Sides, Alistair MacDuff's still about. He kicked down the door, sealed it with magic, and went out through the window. He left us a little consolation prize, but we made short work of him." Breana laughed wryly. "Never underestimate a determined witch."

Luke whistled at the sound of Alistair's name. He'd been head of the Alchemical Council for at least the last fifty years. "So there're three of 'em," he said. "Don, Alistair, and whoever's in the bedroom with the women."

"Eh, this one's been declawed," Breana said. "No need to count him."

Sam snorted. Power tumbled from his raised hands as he attacked the Black Magick around the door again. Instead of running up against MacDuff's working, Sam's spell skirted the edges, tasting, testing. Sparks flashed where his magic touched the dark casting.

"I'm going to go see what happened to Chris." Joshua turned and hustled along the hall. "He's probably fine since I haven't heard back from him, but I'm checking anyway. Besides, you don't need extra magic mucking things up. Seems like that spell needs to be outsmarted, not outgunned," he called over a shoulder.

"Go ahead and kill Don," Luke shouted after him. "Breana can tell us what we need to know."

"You bet I can, sonny," she yelled from inside the bedroom. "I'd ask you to save his sorry hide for me to kill, but the sooner he's gone, the safer we'll be."

"Where are the books?" Sam asked, still working on destabilizing the Black Magick spell.

"In the springhouse. Torch the miserable things," Breana said. An outraged shriek from the male occupant of the bedroom was silenced immediately.

Luke gazed at Abigail. He wanted to power through the barrier, but Joshua was right about the spell needing to be outsmarted. Sam's magic bounced back and nailed him—again. Luke quirked a brow, but Sam shook his head. "Let me get a better feel for it before I do anything else."

"I really am all right." Abigail met his gaze, her hazel eyes warm.

"If you're feeling all that spunky, how about if you spell me for a bit?" Breana groused.

"Who's in there with you?" Luke craned his neck, but couldn't see past the magic blocking the door.

"One of Alistair and Don's sidekicks," Abigail said.

"He got a name?" Sam asked.

A muffled grunt and cursing followed. "You heard the nice man," Breana prodded. "Name."

"Hell's too good for you," a voice gasped. It sounded as if someone was sitting on his larynx.

"How come you didn't finish him off, Breana?" Luke asked. He moved to the side and sent questing magic into the barrier to help Sam.

"Long story. I needed something to make sure I pulled my head out of my ass and kept it there. Playing games with numb nuts here was just the ticket."

"Do you know how to dismantle this ward?" Sam asked.

"No," Breana replied brusquely. "I did learn the underpinnings of Black Magick, but what I know isn't a match for something Alistair crafted."

"Why'd you sully yourself with something so poisonous?" Luke asked, his suspicions ramping up to full alert.

"Don hounded me. Reminded me constantly that it was stronger than ours. I always told him I didn't care. It made me feel dirty whenever I used it. I couldn't imagine running power like that through my body on a regular basis."

"That wasn't an answer. Keep talking," Sam urged.

Breana shook her head. "Later. Not now."

Abigail snorted and Luke wondered what had passed between the women. He was about to troll for details when Joshua screeched from outside, "Shit! Goddamn your sorry ass to hell."

"Go." Abigail made shooing motions with both hands. "We've got it covered here."

Luke flew down the stairs with Sam on his heels. "If we get lucky and kill Alistair," Sam panted, "it will nullify his magic, including what he slopped around the upstairs bedroom."

Alistair.

Even thinking the name made Luke wince. That had to be who was outside. He and Don were all that was left, since the wraiths and mad wolves had deserted. Four of them against one —maybe two if Don had chewed holes in their spell—shouldn't be much of a contest, but he'd learned not to underestimate dark sorcerers. They tapped into demon-fueled power. It *was* more potent than theirs, but there was a price to be paid. You had to sign your immortal soul over to the Dark Angel and promise allegiance, even after death.

Luke shivered. All his other confrontations with evil paled in comparison with what he was about to face. He girded himself for the worst. Maybe Chris was already dead, or worse, he'd succumbed to inducements from the other side, which would mean they'd have to kill him, not a pleasant prospect.

Thank God, Abby was safe. He could face damn near anything so long as he knew he'd be able to wrap his arms around her when all this was over.

He pushed into the yard, jaws clenched, ready for anything.

"Top of the morning to you boys." A tall, strikingly handsome man with shoulder length tawny curls grinned invitingly. He was dressed in white buckskin and had silver and turquoise Navajo jewelry draped around his neck and on his fingers. His blue eyes twinkled merrily, as if he was having the best of times.

Luke scanned the yard. Joshua stood over a body that lay in the dirt. It had to be Chris, but Joshua had wrapped magic around him, so all Luke saw were hazy edges. He tipped his chin up in question. Joshua shook his head slightly, and Luke gritted his teeth in frustration. That headshake could mean anything. Where was Don? He wanted to ask, but he couldn't divert his attention.

"This has been entertaining," Alistair went on, "but I know when I'm bested. Think I'll get out of your hair now, but I'm sure we'll meet again."

"Hold up a minute." Luke stepped forward.

Alistair curled his mouth into a sneer. "For what, mage? I've been out here listening. You couldn't even figure out how to dismantle a simple spell. You don't have the power to kill me." He snorted. "I didn't bother warding the window. Thought that worthless sack of dung I left guarding the women was better than that. Pfft." He spat in the dirt. "Still can't believe he got run over by a couple of females."

Alistair shook his head in dismay, and then tossed his head back and laughed. Once he got control of himself, he added, "You can always toss the gals a rope, so they can shinny outside. Or you can wait. Once I'm gone, my spell will disperse—in a day or two."

The dark sorcerer's laughter held fey edges and filled Luke with blind fury. He wanted to wrap his hands around the man's neck and kill him, up close and personal.

Alistair's blue gaze settled on him, and he narrowed his eyes to slits. "The feeling is mutual. But if it were me, I'd take your woman right in front of you first. Make you squirm a little. She's a hot little number that one. If you ever get tired of her…"

Luke shrieked a high, feral sound. Anything to shut Alistair up. He gathered himself for a frontal attack, but Sam grabbed his arm. "Stop. He's taunting you. If you get close enough, he can do real damage."

"At least one of you has some brains." Alistair eyed Sam.

"Want to switch sides, buddy? We have better pay, much better hours. All the women you can fuck. Young ones too. Untouched. The finest food—"

"Shut the hell up." Sam spat the words out. "I'd rather be dead than your lackey. Speaking of which, where's Don?"

Alistair shrugged. "Oh, is he missing? I hadn't noticed." The air around him developed a numinous quality.

Luke exchanged glances with Sam. The black magician was leaving and there wasn't a damn thing they could do to stop him —not with magic, anyway. Alistair knew it and mocked their weakness with a supercilious grin.

In a fluid, practiced motion, Luke drew a six-gun and fired again and again, drilling a line of bullets from the magician's groin to his head, each shot perfectly lined up. A shocked expression blossomed on Alistair's face. He clutched his stomach and chest, chanting furiously.

Since his silver and iron ammo at least slowed Alistair down, Luke pulled his other gun and emptied it into the man swaying before him. Sam's chanting rivaled Alistair's as a magical net settled over the black mage and drove him to the ground.

"As long as we can keep him from leaving," Sam ground out, "we'll be in good shape. We can polish off what's left with mage fire."

Luke scanned the yard. Where was Don? And then he thought he knew. In the springhouse protecting his precious books.

Alistair groaned, blood pooled around him. "Lift your spell, mage," he gasped. "I'm rich beyond measure. I'll promise you anything—and make good on it." Blood burbled past his lips, ran down his chin, and added more stains to the rapidly reddening buckskin.

"If I believed that," Sam growled, "I'd deserve a place right next to you in Hell. Die, goddammit."

"How's Chris?" Luke called to Joshua.

"Not good. He faced Alistair in hand-to-hand combat. When I got out here, they were rolling around in the yard and Don was nowhere in sight. Alistair barked some kind of command in demonspeak, and Chris clutched his throat as if he couldn't breathe. That was when I managed to drag him over here and protect him with magic, but I couldn't take my eyes off that putrid slime ball to do anything else."

"You did great," Sam said. "See to Chris. We've got things handled. Alistair needs to be deader than this before we call mage fire to finish him, but he's not going anywhere between now and then."

"Why will it take him so long to die?" Luke asked, confused. "I pumped twelve bullets into him. Christ, he's swimming in his own blood. He ought to be dead now."

Sam shook his head. "He's got Satan on board. It's why I have to be careful just when I call mage fire, else it'll bounce right back at me like his spell did upstairs. Those who've sold their immortal souls linger on this side of the veil." He made a sound between a snort and a grunt. "Maybe it's on account of now that they know what they got themselves into, they're having second thoughts."

"I'm pretty sure I know where Don is," Luke said. "If you can spare me, I'll see if I can't tie off that loose end."

Sam nodded curtly. "You and I came up with the same answer. He's wherever the books are."

"According to his wife, that's the springhouse." Luke loped toward the small structure on the far side of the yard, his hands extended, magic pulsing from them. He didn't care about conversation. Not anymore. He wanted Don engulfed in mage fire and the rest of the books incinerated along with him. He commanded the door to open and shot mage fire through it. Don screeched like a scalded cat and burst through the doorway.

"Stop! I've seen the error of my ways—" He raised his hands and dark fire raced to obey his call. It met Luke's magic in the yard between them, blazing and popping.

"Bullshit." Luke spat the word, called mage fire, and held his breath. Would it be strong enough to power through Don's casting? The fires blazed against each other, one red-orange, the other black-tinged. The ground shook and thunder rocked Luke's stance. He balanced on the balls of his feet and poured magic into his spell, giving it everything he had.

On the other side of the wall of flame separating them, Don was no doubt doing the same thing. Black flames roared up, close to consuming his mage fire. Luke reached deep, summoning recesses within himself he hadn't touched since the night Tamra died. Slowly, inexorably, his mage fire brightened and drove the dark fire toward Don. With a tremendous heave that nearly flattened him, Luke commanded his fire to surround the dark flames. Once that was done, he tightened the inferno around Don. The man shrieked, shrill and terrible, but they were only shrieks, not an incantation.

Luke stepped toward the pyre, his hands and body shaking from the stress of holding everything together, but Don was burning, screaming and burning, goddammit. Luke wanted to cheer, but he couldn't divert his attention. Success was like a balm, though, and it jolted his tired body onward.

Time passed. Maybe minutes, maybe an hour. Just when he was about to call Sam to spell him, Don's body burst within the pillar of flame, spraying the ground with blood and bits of grit and sinew.

Luke dropped his weary arms to his sides, breathing as if he'd just run a race. "Thank you," he gasped over and over, not quite sure who he was thanking for what, but relieved beyond words that the corrupt Coven leader was dead.

When he'd recovered enough to manage the next task, Luke lunged through the springhouse door. He'd known the evil tomes would be there, but he was too exhausted to manage his body's instinctive reaction, and his gut twisted in revulsion. If books could leer, these did, stacked at odd angles in protective formations. Their magic stung, but Luke powered through it and kicked over stack after stack. As soon as their power lessened enough for him to get close, he scooped armfuls and carried the books outside, feeding them into the fire that had reduced Don to a charred lump.

Seven trips later, he was sweating, panting, and nauseated from touching the miserable things, but the job was done. His arms and chest throbbed from where the books had touched his body, but he forced himself back into the springhouse one last time to make certain none of the hideous things had hidden themselves in some dark cranny. Sure enough, he found two, butted behind some shelves. Luke wasn't so tired he didn't relish the satisfaction when he chucked the stragglers into his fire and commanded it to consume everything within it. That done, he staggered over to where Joshua knelt in the dirt next to Chris.

"How is he?" Luke asked.

Joshua shook his head. "Not good. Alistair must have bitten him. He's full of dark poison from his long association with evil."

"Can I help?"

"Nah. Your magic's not any good for healing something this complicated." Joshua pressed his lips together. "Thanks for offering, though."

Abigail and Breana dashed into the yard.

"The spell weakened enough I could blast through it," Breana said. She trotted to Sam's side. "Abby and I killed the one upstairs. Did you kill him?" She nudged Alistair with a toe and he groaned. "Humph. Guess he's not quite dead. Too bad. Where's my husband?" She scanned the yard, her gaze settling on the second pyre. "Never mind." Breana strolled to the second fire and spat onto the dirt. "Burning's too good for him. Mage fire saved him from the life of the damned."

"Yes but it also saved us from him," Sam pointed out.

Normally, Luke would have stayed with Chris, but all he could focus his worn-out mind on was Abigail. He made a beeline for her and wrapped her in his arms.

She sagged against him. "I'm so tired. Thank the goddess this is over," she murmured. "It looks as if we'll get a few days' peace."

"Few days', hell." Luke tightened his hold on her. "After what we've been though, we deserve months, maybe years."

"Abigail." Joshua's voice held an urgent note. "You've got healing ability. Help me."

She scooted out of Luke's arms and joined Joshua in the dusty yard next to Chris' inert form. "My powers are pretty depleted. Do you know what's wrong?"

Joshua nodded. "A whole lot. Like I just told Luke, Alistair must've bitten him. Dark poison has quite a toehold. It's spread all through his body."

Abigail skinned her lips back from her teeth, looking like one of the Furies. "No! We cannot let them have him. If we can't call him back, they'll take him. It's how they turn the unwilling."

"I'm open to suggestions." Joshua looked as disconcerted as Luke had ever seen him. "I'm afraid if I send my magic into him, it will implode or something."

"We don't have a choice. If...If the worst happens and we feel him slipping over, you've got to drown him in mage fire. At least that way, he'll have a clean death." She shook her head. "I hope I'm more help than I think I'll be."

"Pretty tapped out?" Joshua asked. When she nodded, he took hold of her hands.

A surprised look blossomed on Abigail's face. "You're boosting my magic."

"Don't bother to thank me," he said dourly. "It's self-serving on my part because I need your help."

"All right. I won't." She inhaled deeply and pulled her hands away. "It's enough. Let's get started."

Luke joined them. Pain for his friend settled in his gut like jagged glass and cut deep with each breath. "I've got the death part. You two just concentrate on doing everything you can. If you can't save him, just say the word and get out of the way."

Abigail knelt on one side of Chris, Joshua the other. They joined hands and moved them down Chris' body, chanting. Chris screeched, swore, and writhed, but he was caught fast in their spell. When he switched from English to demonspeak, Luke fought a sinking feeling.

They were losing him.

"Oh no, you don't," Breana shouted from where she stood next to Sam.

Luke spun around just in time to see her whip a knife from a sheath on her belt and cut through Alistair's neck from one side to the other. What little blood remained in his body welled against the man's coppery skin. With a cry, she plunged the knife into his heart. Luke felt the air thicken and understood she was exhorting the goddess to make certain the abomination drowning in his own blood was well and truly dead.

"I'll do you one better. He's finally dead enough." Sam dragged Breana upright and called mage fire. It leapt to obey him and enveloped what was left of Alistair in a smoking, stinking pyre.

"Whatever she's doing, it's helping us," Abigail cried.

"Yes." Joshua croaked. "That sneaky bastard must've taken refuge in Chris, riding on the coattails of his poison. It was why he wouldn't die, and why we couldn't call Chris back."

Chris' thrashing slowed, and then stopped. His eyes fluttered open and he sucked air like a farrier bellows. "Gone," he moaned. "That horror's finally gone. Jesus, but I feel dirty, used." His gaze settled on Abigail. "God's teeth woman, how did you manage to have such evil inside you for so long?"

"One minute at a time." Abigail pushed to her feet. "Let me get you some water."

"Nah." Chris flipped over on all fours and lurched upright. "I'll get my own. Good for me to move around." He staggered toward the creek, shucking his gun belt and bandoliers as he went, and threw himself into a deep pool, clothes and all.

Joshua breathed a huge sigh, but didn't make a move to get up. "I didn't think we were going to win that one."

Luke extended a hand and dragged the other man to his feet. "It was close. When Chris started in with demonspeak, I damn near just doused him in mage fire to get it over with."

Sam trudged over from where he'd been standing next to Breana. "Bet he'll be glad you didn't."

"I heard that," Chris called from the creek. "Water's great. I made it warm."

Abigail leaned against Luke. She rolled her eyes and said, "Witches and mages have good ears."

Everyone broke into laughter, but it held a hysterical edge and Luke understood why. They'd all had such a close call, anything to break the tension was welcome.

Once their laughter subsided, Luke glanced toward the creek

and nudged Abigail. "I'll bet we could find a more private bath spot."

"Let's do it. I need to heal my burns and all of us stink."

"We may stink—" Sam skewered her with his blue gaze "—but we're still alive. It's all that counts."

"All but my baby—and my husband," Breana said. Her face grew pinched. "No matter what they turned into at the end, there was a time when I cared deeply for them both."

"I'm sorry about Carolyn." Abigail met Breana's gaze.

"I know." Breana looked as if she wanted to say something.

Abigail shook her head. "Later is plenty of time for us to hear what happened."

"Thanks. Maybe once we've all had a wash and a few hours' rest, we can talk about that, and about what comes next."

Joshua nudged Sam. "Long as we've got the fires going, let's go upstairs and get Alistair and Don's henchman."

"I like it." Sam's dark blue eyes glittered dangerously. "Two for the price of one."

"Actually, we got three—and the rest of the books. A good day's work all in all." Luke grinned. Recognizing a good exit point, he tucked Abigail's burned hand carefully under his arm, sending soothing magic to cool it, and walked downstream from where Chris lounged.

CHAPTER 13

Abigail accepted Breana's offer of clean clothes and took advantage of the downstairs bedroom to put on a long green skirt and soft, black woolen tunic. Even though the skirt's hem ended several inches above her feet, it still felt good to have something against her skin that didn't reek of evil. The day had mostly passed with her and Luke asleep, wrapped in one another's arms. The hard press of his body against hers felt new and incredible, and the rightest thing in the world. They'd both wanted more of what they'd shared the previous night, but between her dozing off, and him getting up to help one of the enforcers with some of the cleanup work, all they'd managed were a few fervent kisses. In between everything, she'd worked side-by-side with Breana to get dinner going.

She grinned to herself as she bent to smooth clean socks over her feet. Luke kissed like an angel—or maybe a devil, come to think of it. His lips were hard and demanding when he closed his mouth over hers, and she loved how he tangled his hands in her hair and held her head firmly while he sank his tongue into her mouth. Her whole body tingled with eagerness, impatient for the coming night when they'd have hours together.

A breathy sigh shook her because she regretted not telling Luke how much he meant to her. He'd said he was falling in love with her in the barn, but she hadn't said anything. Hadn't even thanked him properly for standing by her once he knew the Salem witch had shanghaied her body. When Alistair MacDuff and the other man burst into the upstairs bedroom, she'd been horribly sure she was about to die.

Dead women couldn't say much of anything.

Well, I'm still here and I can rectify my omission damned soon.

Abigail tried out a few phrases, but none of them sounded quite right. *Like* didn't quite capture the depth of her emotional state, but *love* and *adore* seemed like too much. Feeling foolish, but determined, she told herself she'd figure it out when the time came and wriggled her feet into boots that were still damp from dipping them in the creek to clean them. The well-worn leather would dry from the heat of her feet. If it didn't, she could always boost it with a shot of magic.

Abigail reached over her head and twisted her torso from side to side. She was stiff and sore, despite Luke healing the worst of her injuries from Alistair and his henchman, whose name they'd never discovered. But her discomfort was only on the surface. Inside she felt more vibrant and alive than ever before.

A tap on the door startled her. In a gesture as natural as breathing, she sent magic outward to see who was there and was delighted to discover Luke on the far side. She clapped her hands to her chest in a girlish gesture that made her laugh.

"If there's a joke, I'd like to be in on it." His deep voice set her heart on fire.

She raced to the door and pulled it open. "I'm just happy is all." She waited, expecting him to pull her into his arms, but he just stared at her, slack jawed. "What?" She pirouetted in a circle.

"You're gorgeous. Those clothes, they, er—" his tanned cheeks blazed with sudden color "—fit you better than what I'm used to seeing you in."

She quirked a brow, teasing him. "We can buy me a whole new wardrobe if you want. You can come to the modiste with me and pick the styles and fabrics."

"Is that like a dressmaker?" She nodded, and Luke sucked in a breath. "Guess I could brave one of those bastions of femininity, if it meant you'd look like this all the time."

"Once I have patterns, I can make things myself, but I only have one dress pattern. It's easy, but it turns out those shapeless shirtwaists."

He ran his hands down her sides almost reverently and said, "This is better."

She stepped forward. The few inches between them vanished, and he enclosed her in his arms. God, he smelled heavenly. She inhaled hungrily and threaded her fingers together behind his neck. An obvious erection pushed into her belly, and she butted her hips against it.

His mouth hovered right above hers. He flicked his tongue over her lips, and desire turned her nether regions to a molten pool. "Dinner," he said, except it sounded halfway like a question.

"We could skip it." Her mouth was dry because every drop of moisture in her body had congregated between her legs.

Desire flickered and caught in the depths of his eyes. "I'd love to, but we can't. Skip dinner, that is. All of us need to talk."

Her nipples ached, and her sex throbbed. All she wanted was to strip Luke's clothes off and bury him in every orifice of her body. Not in any particular order, but she had yet to taste him, or do a whole bunch of other things.

He pushed her back inside the room, kicked the door shut, and fumbled with the laces of his breeches. "Pull those skirts out of the way." His voice vibrated with lust as he pulled his cock out of his pants.

Luke sat on the edge of the bed, cock jutting upward. With a moan, she straddled him, knees resting on the mattress, and sank over his waiting erection, glorying in how he stretched her.

Once he was seated inside her, he rasped, "Wrap your legs around me."

The movement did wicked things to her pussy and she clamped down hard on him, so close to coming she was almost there. He reached his hands under her butt to support her and flowed to his feet. She gripped him more tightly with her legs and wrapped her arms around his shoulders. He thrust into her, face buried in her neck. His hot breath and his fingers digging into her ass made her unbearably hot. The rocking motion where he moved in and out of her put his pubic bone in direct contact with her sensitive nub. Because she'd been partway there before he even came into the room, a climax roiled through her. She felt him release moments later, inside her this time, but it would've been almost impossible to withdraw in time.

They clung to one another, gasping and panting. "Think that'll hold you through dinner?" he whispered in her ear.

She squirmed in his grasp and he lifted her off his still-hard cock and set her on the floor. "The question is—" she rubbed her hand over his engorged penis "—whether it will hold you."

"Come on." He swatted her behind and started putting himself back in order. "Everyone's waiting for us."

She pulled a hand towel off the stand that sported a pitcher and basin and dabbed at herself. Maybe no pantalets had been a good idea. At least there hadn't been anything to slow them down. A thought struck her. "If everyone's waiting for us, they'll figure out what we were up to."

"Probably. Especially when they catch a gander of you. Your cheeks are all rosy and you have that fallen woman look."

She laughed and pulled her skirts and petticoat back down. "How come no one ever refers to fallen men?"

He shrugged. "Masculine privilege. Come on, sweetheart. I'm hungry."

"Thought I just fed you."

"Aw, love." He laid a hand tenderly on the side of her face. "We fed each other."

She leaned into him, and they walked toward the sound of voices and the rich smell of a dinner she and Breana had worked on in the early part of the afternoon. As soon as they rounded the corner and came into view, everyone burst into applause.

Abigail's face flamed, but she gathered dignity around her. "Just because witches and mages have good ears doesn't mean you have to listen."

"Oh, but we like to live vicariously." Sam grinned lasciviously.

"Yup. It's not like we've got women of our own hanging about." Joshua set his mug on the table.

"Now if you'd put this place a wee bit closer to town—" Chris shot Breana a meaningful look "—there'd at least be the possibility of a fancy woman or two."

"If there'd been *fancy men*—" Breana mimicked his inflection "—I might've been tempted to do just that." She crooked two fingers at Abigail and Luke. "Sit, both of you."

"Do we have everything?" Abigail scanned the table. "As long as I'm up, I could bring whatever's left back in the kitchen."

"We've got plenty to get started. Besides, judging from what we weren't supposed to overhear, you need to get some food into you. Night's young." Breana winked suggestively. "You'll need fuel for later."

"Why is everyone so interested in my, um, personal life?" Abigail scooted into the chair Luke held for her.

"Because we're magical." Chris leered. "Sex is where we live, when we're not conjuring enchantments to fight for our lives."

Platters made their way around the table. Abigail tasted the venison and roast chicken, pleased by how they'd come out. Fresh greens from the garden, fried with potatoes and lard, made a succulent side dish, and the hot biscuits she and Breana had rolled and baked were perfect. Flaky and tender.

Abigail looked up from her plate, realizing she'd been so intent on eating, she hadn't been following the conversation. "I'm sorry. If someone could sort of catch me up, I'd appreciate it."

"Breana was telling us what happened this morning." Sam's tone was somber. "Thank you for hounding her, for calling her back."

Abigail took a deep draught from her mug of home-brewed ale and met Sam's gaze over its rim. "Didn't have much choice. I wasn't certain who was outside the door, but I knew it had to be one of the dark sorcerers, and I needed her help. Breana's a hell of a strong witch."

"So are you." Breana raised her glass.

Abigail clinked it with hers, and said, "Here's to witches."

A chorus of, *I'll drink to that*, ran around the table.

Abigail sucked in a breath. They needed to get this next part over with. She looked at Breana. "You have more to tell us than how I dragged you back from Don's spell this morning. Thank the goddess he bound you with our magic. If he'd used Black Magick, I'd never have been able to reach you."

The other woman nodded. "Yes, I have more to say. If someone wants to set a truth spell, I wouldn't be offended."

"Done." Joshua steepled his fingers together and rested his chin on them.

"I'm not certain just when Don got sucked over to the other side," Breana began. "It could've been two years ago when I caught him in the basement with those horrid books, or it might've been a long while before then. He never would tell me."

She drew her brows together. "The day I found out about it, I felt something…wrong and tracked it to the basement. He was in the old wine cellar with Carolyn on his lap, reading to her out of one of those books." Breana's voice broke. "It was the worst moment of my life, to see my little girl with her eyes full of lust for dark knowledge. I confronted Don later when we were alone, but he told me I was overreacting, being foolish. He said he was ensuring Carolyn's magical future. I almost turned him in to Coven authorities—several times—but he always figured out what I was up to and bound me with magic.

"Once I came very close to dying from dehydration. If one of the maids hadn't stumbled into an unused part of our home, I would have. Other times he'd bind me with magic and do something that made it feel as if my skin was being flayed from my body. Between that and the guests from the other side that he insisted on entertaining, it took most of my own magic to present a pleasant demeanor to the servants and on my rare trips to Coven headquarters. I guess because I'd stopped complaining, Don forced me into a sexual liaison with dark spirits one night."

Breana's lips trembled, and she pressed them together. "I think I did die that night, at least I joined the world of the damned for a time. I came to in my upstairs bedroom covered in welts and blood. It took months before I stopped having nightmares and felt halfway whole again…"

Breana took a swallow from her glass, and then another. "I was more careful after that, around both my husband and child. It was hard keeping myself warded all the time. Drained me. Anything I said to Carolyn got right back to Don, and I became a prisoner in my own house. In the meantime, their practice of Black Magick accelerated. I tried to run away a few times, but Don always tracked me, hauled me back, and punished me." Tears welled, but she blinked them away. "I can't begin to describe how horrible some of what he did was."

"Did you know about Sarah?" Abigail asked.

Breana nodded. A tear slipped down one cheek. "That was when I knew my baby was lost. Don and Carolyn insisted Sarah would be a great boon to my girl, would protect her on the journey, but I knew different. As devastated as I was when your stage pulled in and you told me she'd died, I was relieved too, especially once I found out she'd met her death in mage fire. At least the dark didn't get her in the end."

Breana took a drink, staring into lantern light. "One last thing, and then I'll be done. I finally forced my antipathy to back down, and I learned how to manipulate Black Magick, blending it with my own power." She tilted her chin defiantly. "The only reason I did that was so I'd have something I could use to kill Don. Never did get the chance I practiced for, though."

She tipped her glass, emptied it, and met each of their gazes in turn. "I accept whatever you decide to do with me. I know it was wrong not to turn Don—and my daughter—in to the enforcers to face Coven justice. The God's truth is I could have turned him in, but not her." Breana folded her hands in her lap. "It feels good to finally tell someone. This has been like a poison. It's been eating me from the inside out for far too long."

Luke exchanged glances with Chris, Joshua, and Sam and then got to his feet. "You passed Joshua's truth spell with flying colors. You've suffered enough, Breana. Try to make a life for yourself."

"Really?" Her face crumpled in on itself. Sobs wracked her and she croaked, "It's more than I deserve."

Abigail went to her and wrapped her arms around the other woman. "No, it's not. You've lived through hell." She kissed her forehead. "I hope you find peace."

"Thank you." Breana smiled sadly through her tears. "I wish the same for you. It can't have been easy playing host to Sarah. That woman was deceitful, self-absorbed, and steeped in wickedness. I'll be all right. You go back and sit next to your fellow."

"Thanks. I will." Abigail patted her arm and found her way back to her seat.

"We were thinking we might stay a while." Joshua crossed his arms over his leather-clad chest.

Maybe in reaction to Breana's dismissive wave as she wiped her face with a linen napkin, Chris cut in, "Just till we're certain the danger's past."

"Maybe two of you," Breana conceded after a pause. "I could use help figuring out how to manage the farm on my own." Her forehead furrowed. "I just thought of something. Gosh, but I hope enough folk at the station didn't notice Sam and Luke to blow their undercover status. Actually—" she eyed the two men "—not that I have Don's power to grant anything, but how about if both of you take a couple of months off? You could go to ground, lay low. Stop tempting trouble—if that's even possible."

Luke leaned into Abigail and draped an arm around her shoulder. "Did you hear that? She's giving us a wedding present."

"Wedding?" Breana's mouth fell open. She jumped to her feet, scooted behind Luke and Abigail, and hugged them both. "I'm deeply pleased." She kissed Luke's cheek, and then Abigail's.

"You'll have to let me plan something special for the ceremony. It will be good for me to have something uplifting to occupy myself."

Abigail tried for words, but they wouldn't come. Luke and she had talked about getting married, but somehow she'd thought it would happen a long time from now, like maybe in a year or two, once he'd assured himself she was free from Sarah's evil.

And once I'd convinced myself of the same thing, a voice of reason intruded.

"Let me make this official." Luke disentangled himself from Breana and pushed his chair out of the way. He knelt in front of Abigail and took one of her hands between both of his. "Would you do me the honor of becoming my wife?" His green eyes glowed with tenderness and unspoken promises he'd care for her always.

Tears threatened. She blinked most of them back, all but a couple of renegades that dripped down her cheeks. "The honor would be all mine." A shy smile mingled with her tears. Somehow, he was on his feet and she was in his arms, and everyone was gathered close clapping them on the back and wishing them well.

Breana clattered out of the dining room. When she returned, she held a dark amber bottle aloft. "Fifty-year-old brandy," she announced proudly. "I was saving it for something special." She pulled a pocketknife from a skirt pocket and scored the wax seal.

Sam rustled through the sideboard, found shot glasses, and poured everyone a drink. Once they'd been handed around, he raised his glass. "To a long and happy life for Luke and Abigail." Voices echoed his toast and everyone drank.

"So, brother." Luke made his way to Sam's side. "Will you do the honors?"

"It would be a privilege." Sam grinned broadly and clapped Luke on the back.

"If you're asking him to marry you," Breana cut in, "I can do that. Actually, I'd love to. There's a positive energy with the wedding ceremony that would go a long way toward healing my scars."

Abigail glanced at Luke and saw him nod. She went to Breana, hugged her, and said, "We'd like that."

"Thank you." Tears sparkled in Breana's eyes. "You've just made me very happy."

Abigail let go of Breana, but felt the other woman's gaze on her. "I know what you're going to ask," she said, "and we can do that."

Luke shook his head. "You lost me."

Breana squared her shoulders. "You don't have to do this, but if you could see your way to naming a daughter, assuming you have one, after Carolyn, it would mean a lot to me." She inhaled raggedly. "In some small way, it would mean my girl will keep on living somewhere other than here." She tapped her breast. "Carolyn wasn't always wicked. And she wouldn't have been at all, if Don hadn't tempted her with unnatural power."

It wasn't the most delicate question, but Abigail asked anyway. "How come you never had other children?"

"I had a hard time," Breana said. "Got torn up inside and Don didn't want to chance losing me, even though our healers fixed the damage." Her face twisted into a wry expression. "That was before he got seduced by the other side. After that, he'd have been glad enough to get rid of me, but by then the last thing we were talking about was having other babies."

Abigail looked away, willing the woman a private moment in the midst of them. She gestured to Luke and the other men to help her carry dishes into the kitchen. By the time they'd cleared the table of the main course and brought in the apple pies, Breana had taken her place at the head of the table again.

"Is there coffee?" Luke asked.

Abigail nodded. "I have to grind the beans, but there's hot water on the stove."

"Strainer's hanging on the wall," Breana said.

Sam laughed heartily. "We can just pick the grounds out of our teeth. We are men, after all. Try to make us too civilized and I guarantee you won't like the result."

Chris slugged him in the arm. "Couldn't have said it better myself."

Joshua just snorted.

After pie had been served, Abigail brought a steaming pot of very strong coffee to the table, along with the sugar bowl and a pitcher of cream. Breana clinked her fork against her cup. Amiable chatter quieted and she shifted her gaze from Abigail to Luke. "Are you certain you wish to marry?"

"Yes." Luke bent toward Abigail and brushed his lips across her cheek.

"Yes for me too." Abigail smiled softly.

"Let me get the Tarot cards." Breana planted her palms against the tabletop and rose. "I'll cast a spread while we finish eating, and we can pick the most auspicious date."

"If you really get a few weeks off—" Abigail turned to Luke "— we could go to San Francisco and visit Gran and Pop. She nagged me for years about my single status. She'll be ever so pleased to meet you. Pop is old and ill. It'll make him a joyful man to leave this world knowing I have someone who'll love me as much as he loved Gran."

Breana shoved a Tarot deck into her hands. Abigail shuffled and handed them to Luke to cut. Breana took the deck and retreated to her seat.

Luke smiled. "It's a long way across the country, but I was hoping you'd want to come back to the village where I grew up. I know we'll have already been wed and blessed by the Coven, but I'd like Aethelred to consecrate our marriage too. And my sisters will want to see who finally snagged me." He chortled. "They couldn't have been any pushier than your gran about telling me I needed a wife."

The gentle slap of cards against the table continued while they ate and talked. After a time, Breana glanced up, a broad smile wreathing her face. "You're in luck. We'll have us a wedding tomorrow at sunrise. After all, you wouldn't want to keep living in sin if you don't have to."

"What?" Abigail inhaled sharply and choked on a flake of piecrust. Luke clapped her on the back. When she could talk again, she sputtered, "I have nothing to wear and no time to sew anything." Her face heated and she knew she was blushing. "Not that I've spent hours mooning over what kind of bride I'd be, but..."

"It's you I want, not a dress," Luke said softly.

"We can come up with something out of my trunks." Breana gathered her cards together and tied a satin ribbon around them. "I brought a lot of things from New York that I realized were foolish once I saw just how primitive it is here."

"If you're sure it wouldn't be an imposition," Abigail murmured. "Like Luke says, it's the words that will pass between us, and the goddess's blessing, that are important, not what I'm wearing."

"It would be good for someone to get a little more wear out of my fancy duds before the moths finish them off." Breana rubbed her hands together, eyes gleaming with anticipation. "Come with me, dear. We'll make you the most luscious bride. So delectable, your groom will have a hell of a time not ravishing you before the ceremony's over."

Sam drained his coffee and got to his feet. He shot knowing glances at the other men. "We're going to have us a bachelor party."

"Huzzah!" Joshua jumped up and grabbed his sheepskin coat off a hook near the door.

"We going into town?" Chris asked.

"You betcha." Sam grinned.

"What if I don't want to leave here?" Luke looked from one enforcer to the other.

"Rubbish." Sam got up, came around the table, and dragged Luke to his feet. "This is your last night as a single man. Least you can do is get roaring drunk."

"Come on, Abby. All this male talk is about to choke me." Breana stood and headed into the kitchen.

Abigail stared after her. She opened her mouth to tell Luke he could drink all he wanted, but to keep his hands off the fancy women, but changed her mind. Part of the cement in any marriage was trust. If she couldn't trust him to leave her side, she oughtn't to be marrying him.

"*Good call.*" Luke's voice rang in her head, and he winked at her just before the other men swept him out of the house.

"Coming?" Breana called.

"Yup." Abigail grinned. "I'll bring the pie things back to the kitchen on my way."

CHAPTER 14

The December morning dawned cold, and clear. Luke woke to pale, gray light filtering into the barn, with the other men sleeping nearby. He'd wanted to hunt Abigail down the previous night, but the others hadn't let him anywhere near her when they'd returned past three a.m., far more drunk than sober.

He had a headache and he could still taste the whiskey the boys had poured down him. They'd had a grand time playing cards and teasing the ladies of the night, who'd offered to take him upstairs and show him the time of his life—once they realized he was getting married the next day. Luke had sent Sam, Joshua, and Chris in his stead. They'd stayed gone for the better part of an hour and returned with huge smiles and rouge smears on their faces.

He'd played poker and drank to while away the time. It had given him a chance to replay everything that happened and put it into perspective. Luke was used to having long hours alone in the saddle to process things, and there'd been precious little of that in quite a while. He'd just been marveling over his luck at finding Abigail when the other three enforcers tromped down the stairs, raving about the fancy women and their prowess. After that, the conversation shifted to pleasantries and future plans. The ride home in clean, white moonlight had been invigorating and helped clear his head. Otherwise, his headache would be far worse.

Luke thought about Abigail and smiled in the semi-gloom of the barn. Joy trod so close to the surface, he was surprised it didn't spill out in rainbow colors. Today was his wedding day. The thought galvanized him into action. He focused magic to soothe his throbbing temples and got to his feet, brushing straw out of his hair and clothes. None of them had bothered to undress last night.

"Ergh. Morning already?" Joshua mumbled and groaned piteously.

"Not only is it morning," Sam said brightly. "We have to get the groom ready."

"And damned fast if the ceremony's at dawn." Chris lurched to his feet and frowned. "Any of you have something halfway clean our hero can wear?"

Sam snorted. "Real men don't need clean clothes." He got up too, and pulled Joshua upright, still groaning.

"I have clean leathers in my saddlebags," Luke said. "First, though, I'm going to take a quick dip in the creek. I still smell like booze and cigars. Anybody want to join me?"

"Maybe if we make the water warm," Joshua muttered.

"Coward." Sam slugged him in the arm and led the way out of the barn and into the beginning of daybreak.

Breana was already fussing over a table she'd dragged down from the porch. "Ten minutes, boys," she called over one shoulder.

"Crap!" Luke sprinted for the creek, loosening clothes as he went. He dropped them in an untidy heap, and was already up to his waist in water cold enough to make his teeth chatter, when the other enforcers jumped in.

"Christ! You're a fucking masochist." Sam squatted in the shallows and sluiced water over his head.

"Now who's the coward?" Luke pushed his long, wet hair out of his eyes and wrung water out of it. "Not so bad once you're in here for a bit."

"That's because your circulation starts shutting down," Joshua said, followed by, "Aw, what the hell," as he dunked himself and came up sputtering.

Luke lumbered out of the creek. "No point in dressing twice," he told the others. "If one of you could gather up my clothes and bring them into the barn, I'd appreciate it."

"Sure." Sam joined him on the riverbank. The air around him thickened where he drew magic to dry himself.

Luke scooped up his boots and loped toward the barn. Breana whistled and clapped from her vantage point. "I can see why Abby's so taken with you," she called after him, followed by, "Wow! Just look at all you men."

His face heated. Female witches were a randy bunch. It wasn't that he'd totally steered clear of them during festivals, when sex was always a given, but he preferred his dalliances private. Now that Abigail had hold of his heart, he was glad he'd been selective about the few partners he'd bedded. He could come to his true love with a clear conscience, knowing he'd never taken advantage of any woman, or engaged in the bawdier, group romps.

He rummaged in his saddlebags and drew out a pair of pale, buckskin leggings and a bright blue shirt, embellished with Native beadwork. He'd always loved the shirt, but had worn it very little, concerned he'd ruin it. Dyes that bright never held up very well. Once he'd laced up his pants and shirt, he stepped into soft sheepskin moccasins he also kept in his saddlebags. He ran a comb through his hair and considered braiding it, but in the end, he left it loose. Breana had said ten minutes, and it must be very nearly that now.

He strode from the barn and met the other enforcers on their way inside to leave the clothes he'd dropped next to the river, plus a few things of their own. "Meet you in front of the house," he said.

"We'll be along directly." Sam nodded.

"You bet. Wouldn't miss any of this for the world." Joshua cast a warm smile his way.

"Married," Chris muttered and shook his wet, brown hair. "Never would've believed it."

"Why not?" Luke spared a moment to meet Chris' gaze.

He shrugged. "You always seemed so...standoffish and independent."

"Maybe it's because I never met the right woman before." Luke grinned and hurried to where Breana stood.

She cocked her head to one side when he walked up to her, cast an appraising glance his way, and smiled softly. "You look very handsome, but just wait till you see your bride."

Luke's smile broadened. "I wanted to see her last night, but the boys weren't having any of it."

"Of course not." She shook a finger at him in mock anger. "It's bad luck to lay eyes on your bride right before the wedding."

"Who came up with that stupid custom?" he muttered just as Sam, Chris, and Joshua joined them.

Breana shrugged. "Does it matter? Some things, we just take on faith." She turned to face the east, where the sky was turning a pearlescent pink. "It's time."

Luke glanced expectantly at the front door of the house. It

opened and Abigail stepped out. Chris trotted up the porch steps, joined her, and she took his arm. In a flash of understanding that thickened his throat with emotion, Luke knew Chris was going to stand in for Abigail's absent father. Since neither of her parents had been witches, and were long since dead, it was kind of him.

She and Chris strolled from the porch's deep shadows and made their way toward the front steps. Luke's eyes widened. Abigail was barefoot and swathed in a cream-colored lace top and long, shimmery white skirt. Her red hair fell in curls to her waist and someone had woven flowers into it.

She met his gaze, her hazel eyes uncertain. "It seemed like a little much—" she began.

"It's not," he cut in. "You're the most beautiful woman I've ever laid eyes on. I can scarcely believe you agreed to marry me." Luke swallowed hard, overwhelmed by her loveliness.

"If she has a last minute change of heart—" Sam walked to his side, flanked by Joshua "—I'm sure one of us would be glad to fill in."

"Nice try." Abigail grinned. "But I'm spoken for."

Breana glanced at Luke's feet. "Take your shoes off. We draw our magic from Mother Earth. Both of you must be in contact with Her so She can bless your union."

Luke toed off his moccasins, grateful he hadn't bothered with socks. He held out his hands for Abigail, but Breana batted them away and said, "Not yet." She turned to face the east. Wisps of sunlight curled about the horizon as she began a Gaelic chant requesting that the four seasons and four directions bless him and Abigail. Breana asked who wished to see Abigail wed this day. Chris answered in Gaelic that he gave her into matrimony. Obviously familiar with the ceremony, Abigail let go of Chris and took a few steps to stand beside Luke.

His heart filled with elation and cracked wide open as he threaded his fingers through hers. His woman. She would be his forever. Time seemed to stand still. He promised to care for Abigail always, to love and cherish her. She promised the same, even promised to obey him, but he would never hold her to it. They'd be equals in all things.

The air about them took on a shimmery hue, and he felt Breana wrap tendrils of magic around them. She pulled a knife from her skirts and took his right hand. The blade flashed and she cut an inch-long gash in the meaty part of his thumb, and then did the same to Abigail's right hand. She pressed their cut flesh together, drew a strand of linen from a pocket and bound it around their joined hands, chanting all the while. Chris joined the Gaelic chant. After a brief hesitation, so did Joshua, and Sam.

Luke sent his magic into Abigail and felt hers enter him. Her power was different from his, more subtle, yet not any less potent. Breana straightened and unwound the bloodstained linen. "It is done," she said and smiled softly. "Go ahead, kiss the bride."

Luke bent toward Abigail, seeking the taste of her soft lips, when Breana said, "Oops, one more thing."

Luke glanced her way. "This better be good. She's my wife now, and you're standing in the way of me kissing her."

"Indeed she is," Breana concurred and tapped his chest with her index finger. "You're a mage, so you may not know all our customs. Witch marriages are forever. You're bound now, with blood and magic."

Luke cocked his head to one side. "Is that all? For a minute I thought you were going to tell me something I didn't know."

She nodded and pressed the bloodstained cloth into his hands. "Bury that deep and say a prayer over it. Now let's get that kiss over with. I was up most of the night making a wedding breakfast. It'd be good to eat it before everything gets cold."

Luke spun Abigail to face him and enclosed her in his arms. When he kissed her, he was surprised the heavens didn't open with a bevy of angels singing. He felt buoyant, ecstatic, on top of the world as she melted into his kiss and wrapped her arms around him. Clapping and cheering rose around them, but Luke almost didn't hear it because he was so focused on the woman pressed against him. Her scent blended with the tiny flowers in her hair. He tangled his fingers in her locks and deepened their kiss, wanting to be just as close as he could be.

"Enough already," Sam's voice boomed. Hands settled around Luke's arms and tugged on him.

Luke felt lightheaded, like he'd emerged from a dream. "What?" he sputtered. "We're married now; I can kiss her all I want."

"You have duties," Sam informed him archly.

"Responsibilities," Chris concurred. "There's a spread of food inside, and we're all anxious to get in there and sample it. Breana's a mighty fine cook."

"Why thank you." She mock bowed. "Abby helped me. Once we decided what she'd wear, we settled down to cooking."

Abigail wormed out of his arms, but latched a hand under his elbow. "Come on," she urged. "I made the cake. Can't wait for you to see it."

"In a minute." He made shooing motions with both hands. "The rest of you go on inside. I promise we'll be along, but I want a private moment with my bride." When he said the word *bride*, he nearly burst with delight.

As soon as the front door shut, he scooped Abigail into his arms and crushed her close. "I love you," he said into her hair.

"I'll care for you and protect you always. You'll never want for anything."

She pushed back so she could meet his gaze. "Silly. The only thing I want is you. I'm falling in love with you too." She shook her head and her eyes filled with tears. "Damn it!" She swiped them away. "I swore I wouldn't cry, and just look at me. I'm the happiest woman alive today. Thank you for believing in me and for wanting me—in spite of everything."

"Thank you for being you." He brushed his lips over hers. "Now I suppose we ought to get inside. It was kind and thoughtful of Breana to do all this for us."

Abigail nodded. "It was good for her too. A reminder life goes on after we lose things that are precious to us." She took his hand and tugged him toward the steps. "Come on. Everyone wants to share our joy."

Luke followed her into the house. No matter what happened next, he vowed he'd do his damnedest to be a good husband.

Abigail turned to him just inside the door. "We'll be good to each other," she murmured.

"You were inside my head."

"Of course. Shameless of me, but I want to get to know all of you."

"Hey, you two lovebirds. Get in here," Sam shouted. "Food's getting cold."

ABIGAIL ATE and drank until she couldn't hold another crumb. Luke's energy warmed her and filled her with hope for their future. The harsh planes in his face had relaxed. He looked positively boyish, and so stunning he stole her breath. She'd never seriously considered sharing her life with anyone, not for any particular reason, but she'd never met a man who felt right before. In a moment of honesty, she understood she'd quit looking for a life partner ages ago, and had done an extraordinarily thorough job erecting protective walls around her heart. If it hadn't been for Sarah, she might not have dropped her barriers long enough to truly appreciate Luke.

Guess the goddess was watching out for me.

Feeling the intensity of Breana's gaze, Abigail glanced up. "Thank you," she told her. "For everything."

"You needn't thank me." Breana nodded knowingly. "Seems like there's plenty of gratitude on both sides."

"What's next for everyone?" Abigail scanned the room.

"Josh and me, we're staying right here," Chris said and grinned. "We'll hook up with the enforcers that are already here and make certain there isn't any more trouble."

"We'll help Bree figure out how to manage this spread," Joshua said, and then added, "She'll be able to utilize magic to do a lot of the chores, but when that doesn't work, it might be useful to have some muscle-power close to hand."

Sam blew out a breath. "I've been thinking about what's next for me." The corners of his mouth curved into a wry smile. "Don't know as I've had any time off from anything in quite a while. Anyway, I'm heading for New Orleans. Left a special gal there a long time ago and I thought I'd look her up." He nudged Luke. "Maybe you're an inspiration."

"If I am," Luke said, "don't go getting married without me as your best man."

Sam snorted. "If she hasn't latched onto someone else and produced a brood, it will be a miracle. I haven't seen her for five years."

"I'll keep my fingers crossed for you, brother." Luke put out his hand and Sam grasped it.

"We're going to San Francisco," Abigail told the group. "I want to see my grandfather again before he dies."

"Give my best to your gran," Breana said. "Hester's a fine witch, one of my mentors from back in the Old Country. You be sure and tell her I'd be glad to make her a place here with me. And of course your granddad too, if his health improves enough for them to travel."

"I'll let her know." Abigail smiled her thanks. "You never know. She just may take you up on that."

"Once we're done in California—" Luke ran a finger through a bit of frosting on the edge of his plate and ate it "—we'll head for my childhood home west of Boston."

"Be sure to check in with Coven headquarters in New York on your way through," Joshua said. "That way if anything's come up, we'll have a way to let you know."

"Sure." Luke grinned. "No problem." He quirked a brow. "We seem to have the eating and drinking and visiting parts out of the way. Would anyone object if I spirited my bride off somewhere a bit more private?"

Amidst whistles and catcalls, he hustled Abigail outside into a clear, sunny day and hugged her close. "What would you like, love?"

"What are my choices?" Her hazel eyes twinkled.

"We could ride into town, and I could book us the very best room in Salt Lake. It's a big enough town, I'm sure there's a honeymoon suite somewhere."

"Or?"

"We could retreat to the barn, or the downstairs bedroom inside, 'cept that might be a little close."

Abigail laughed. "Witches have very good ears."

"Yes, mages do also. Funny how that's come up a time or two."

"I have a fourth suggestion."

Luke drew her tighter against him. "Whatever you want, my love."

"There's a wonderful glade on the far side of the creek not far from here. I found it last night when Breana needed wild onions and watercress for what we were cooking. If you could make one of those magical tent things like you did in the barn…" She gazed up at him through lowered lashes, so desperate to have him it was a struggle not to push him down into the dust of the yard.

Luke glanced at her still-bare feet. He'd put his moccasins back on before they'd gone inside the house. "Don't you need shoes?"

"Probably. Let me run inside and get something."

It took a few minutes longer than she would have liked what with everyone inquiring where the secret marital bed would be, but she escaped into Luke's arms and led the way to the wonderful glade she'd found. A few late season wildflowers grew there in defiance to winter's chill, and the grass would make a soft bed. She wanted to make love outdoors to pay homage to the goddess. That it would put a little distance between them and the voyeuristic crew in the house helped too. Abigail cared about Breana and Chris and Joshua and Sam, but what would soon pass between her and Luke felt sacred, not something to be shared in any way, with anyone else.

*L*uke ducked under evergreen boughs and into the sheltered, sylvan glen she'd picked. The secluded patch of greenery looked inviting, as if it had been created just for them. "This is perfect." He plucked a tiny blossom from a grassy knoll and added it to the flowers already in her hair.

"No. You're perfect." She was in one of those places where words didn't come easily, so she just gazed at him, letting her deep need for him spill through her eyes.

"I hope you're still saying that ten years from now."

"If we take care of each other every day," she said, feeling suddenly solemn, "the years will take care of themselves."

"I knew there was a reason I loved you, beyond your considerable charms. You're wise as well as beautiful." He captured her hand in his and glanced about. "Where would you like us to be and I'll build us a warm nest."

"I'd thought over there." She pointed to a grove of fragrant juniper trees growing in a half circle and tugged gently on his hand.

He hunkered where she'd indicated and summoned magic.

The air glowed so enthusiastically, it was as if it were blessing their union too. Abigail started to sit, and then worried about her borrowed finery. Breana had been more than kind. It wouldn't do to return her clothing with grass and dirt stains. While Luke put the finishing touches on his spell, she took off the cloak she'd tossed around her shoulders on her way out of the house, thinking it might be something they could lie on, and set it down. With fingers that shook a little, she unbuttoned her skirt and stepped out of it. Next, she removed her borrowed top. She hung the skirt and tunic over a tree limb to keep them out of the grass, and slipped out of her chemise, petticoat, and pantalets.

"It's been wonderful watching you undress—" Luke's voice held a husky note "—but I'd planned to do that."

She sank to the ground next to him and pushed off Breana's scuffed house shoes. "If I'd been rational, I'd have changed clothes, but all I could think about was getting off alone with you."

Luke laughed. "Funny, that's all I could think about too." His gaze roved over her naked body. He licked his lips appreciatively and said, "I'm feeling overdressed all of a sudden."

"How about if we do something about that?" She reached for the laces of his shirt. "This is really beautiful. Navajo?"

"Cree. Thank you. It was an indulgence when I bought it, but I fell in love with the color and the beadwork." He shrugged self-consciously. "Guess I'm not as unremittingly masculine as I like to think."

"You're way more than enough male for me." She chuckled. "Besides, if you weren't a sucker for pretty things, you might not have noticed me."

"Oh, I'd have noticed all right. A man would have to be dead not to." He brushed his fingertips over her breasts and her nipples hardened, tingling in anticipation.

She reached beneath the shirt and pushed it upward. He gasped at the touch of her fingers on his bare skin and helped her maneuver the shirt over his head. He started to spread it on the ground, but she shook her head. "It's too pretty. My cloak and your breeches will be plenty."

Her throat was dry when she fumbled with the lacings of his pants. His cock was already hard, its outlines clearly visible beneath the buckskin. She pushed his breeches open, bent her head, and licked the head of his penis. It jerked against her mouth, so she wrapped a hand around him and circled his shaft with her mouth. She loved the taste and feel of him, and how he stretched her mouth as much as he stretched her pussy.

His hips bucked, and he placed a hand on either side of her head to show her the rhythm he liked. The more she licked and sucked, the hotter she got. Abigail rubbed her thighs together, the friction almost enough to make her come.

Luke pulled out of her mouth, breath coming fast, his tanned face rose-tinged with passion. "If you keep that up, I'll come."

She grinned at him with a smile that might've done Aphrodite proud. "That's the general idea."

"Except I want this first orgasm after we're married to be something we share." He grinned back. "I promise you'll have years to..." his face reddened even further "...to do what you were doing."

She crawled up his body and laid full length atop him, reveling in how perfectly he fit with her. She kissed him and he threaded his arms around her, hands cupping her ass, while his tongue slid inside her mouth. His chest pressing against her nipples made little zinging sensations shoot straight to her pussy, not that she needed to be any hotter. Sexual tension was so thick it intensified everything, every touch, every murmured endearment, until all she could think about was getting him inside her.

Abigail was just spreading her legs, when he broke their kiss and rolled her onto her back. He knelt over her and traced the lines of her body, pausing to tweak her nipples. He rubbed calloused fingers over her engorged nub before sinking them inside her. She gripped his wrist and tried to tell him she couldn't wait any longer, but the only thing that came out was a chittering moan.

He must've understood because he wrapped a hand around his shaft and guided it inside, trading it for his fingers. She was so wet, he could have entered her easily if he hadn't been so big, but he took his time and let her stretch around him, supporting his weight with his arms. Once he was all the way inside, she wrapped her legs around his waist and placed her hands on his hips. He withdrew a little and pressed himself back inside. Soon the slow half strokes gave way to bigger, faster ones as need drove him.

Abigail's gaze never left his face and body. His muscles bunched beneath his skin as he grew hotter and hotter, and his nipples tightened into hard, little buds. His green eyes blazed with heat as he thrust and retreated. She wanted to extend the moment, make it last forever, but her body betrayed her. A climax began deep in her belly and spiraled outward, almost catching her by surprise, its intensity so profound her vision grayed at the edges.

"You're so beautiful when you come," he gasped. "I could watch you forever." His cock thickened inside her, and his face contorted with ecstasy.

"Stay inside me," she begged. "Bless the goddess and our love." She felt his release start in the base of his cock. It juddered inside her over and over, flooding her with hot semen.

Abigail pulled him down atop her and cradled him in her arms. She didn't realize she was crying until she felt the moisture on her cheeks. Luke repositioned them so they lay facing one another. He traced a finger over her damp cheeks. "Is something wrong?"

"Not at all. Everything is so right it's scary." She laid her head against his chest. "I'm happy. Happier than I've ever been, and it terrifies me."

"Me too." His voice rumbled against her hair. "I think the scariest part is when you love someone, it opens you to the possibility of losing them—sort of like with Breana and her child."

Truth resonated and chagrin at her retreat from emotional commitments filled her. "That's not a reason not to live, though." She propped herself on an elbow. "Even if that's sort of what I did, boxing myself off from anything I might care about, it didn't make it right."

"We have a lot of exploring and growing to do, both of us." He pushed a strand of hair laden with crushed flowers behind her ear. "I can't think of anyone I'd rather do it with."

"That may be the sweetest thing anyone's ever said to me."

He drew her close again. "I want to spoil you, make you feel so loved you can't even remember what it was like to be alone."

Because she didn't have words, she just snuggled against him.

THE SUN WAS WELL PAST its zenith when they woke in each other's arms. "Guess we were pretty tired, huh?" She sat up and stretched.

"We had every right to be. Neither one of us has had much sleep to speak of in days. Before things heat up again, we need to talk about babies." He nailed her with his emerald eyes. "If I come inside you as much as I expect we'll be making love, you'll conceive in no time."

She inhaled raggedly, suddenly anxious, knowing this was the sort of question she should've asked before they got married. "Are you all right with us having children?"

"Sure, but I'm selfish enough, I'd hoped for a few months with just you and me."

Abigail liked the sound of that. In a secret place inside her heart, one she only rarely visited, she longed for babies, a houseful of them. It had seemed so remote, though—since she'd have needed a husband, or some willing partner—she'd buried the idea deep so it wouldn't bother her.

She let out a breath. "I can live with that. Maybe a year or so with just us, and then we can try for a family."

"Sounds perfect." He reached for her and she fitted her body to his, aware of heat growing between her legs. No question about it, Luke made her hot. The more she got of him, the worse she wanted him. Abigail straddled one of his legs and pushed her core against it.

He nuzzled her neck and said, "Let me pleasure you, love. I want you to lay back and tell me what you'd like and what you want more of."

"Sounds decadent."

"I'm hoping it will be."

He strung kisses down her body, suckling her nipples until she arched her back and mewled with delight. He captured her nub between two fingers and worked it while he laved her nipples. A climax blazed through her. Before it was quite done, he lowered his mouth to the magical spot between her legs and began nipping and sucking. He slid two fingers inside her and pressed them against something that made her mad with lust. Even though it had never happened to her before, she came again almost on the heels of her first orgasm. Shaking and crying, she writhed between his mouth and fingers.

When he kept on sucking her, she tugged away. "Please." She had to swallow before she could say anything else. "I need a break."

He raised his mouth from her for long enough to say, "No, you don't. I know you can come again."

He ran his tongue around her sex and pressed harder on that place inside her. Her body spasmed. Hips bucking, her pussy turned to molten heat as another climax spun her around and spit her out.

"No fair," she sputtered. "You used magic. I felt it."

"So?" He quirked a brow. "Since when is that against the rules?"

She slithered out from under him and pushed him onto his back. His cock jutted from his body, as hard as she'd ever seen it. Apparently what he'd been doing to her had heated his blood as much as hers. She knelt over his shaft and licked the length of it. When he groaned and thrust against her, she took him into her mouth and milked him with her hands. He buried his fingers in her hair, steadied her head, and thrust into her mouth. She'd been right about him being aroused. It didn't take long before his cock swelled even harder and semen burst from it.

She swallowed every drop, enjoying the salty tang of him, before laying her head on his belly, with one hand still curled around his penis. Long moments passed while they got their breath back.

He pulled her up his body, kissed her tenderly, and said, "We should go back to the house for a bit. It'll be dark soon, and I don't want any of the rest of them worrying about us."

"Maybe we could bury our binding cloth here where we made love." She looked around for something to dig with and then felt foolish. "Guess we'll have to use magic to make a hole."

"I'll do that before we leave. Glad you remembered it. And you're right; this is a perfect place for it."

She smiled shyly, pleased by his compliment. "I hate to leave here. It's our little, private paradise, but I don't want to worry the others, either. Besides, Breana could use some help. It's a lot of us to cook for." Abigail brushed her lips over his and sat.

"I doubt she had to do much cooking. There was plenty of food left over this morning."

"Well, they've had all day to make inroads on it." She got to her feet, intent on getting dressed, but he flowed upright in one, easy motion and drew her against him.

"I love you, Abigail."

Emotion rocked her to her soul, molten and compelling. "I love you too, Luke. Let's hang onto what we have right this moment."

"We will, love, my sweet love. You'll see, things will only keep getting better."

Abigail forgot about putting her clothes on and melted into his arms.

CHAPTER 16

Three months later

Their horses trotted smartly up a road Luke remembered well. Abigail was an accomplished rider, and he enjoyed watching how she managed her mount. He'd offered to rent a buggy to make the trip from New York, but she'd opted to ride, so long as he didn't mind if she sat astride.

In about a quarter hour, they'd be at Aethelred's. They'd spent longer than planned at Abigail's grandmother's house because Pop truly was dying and they'd stayed until he was gone. After that, they'd traveled up a large inland river to Sacramento and caught a stagecoach to St. Joseph, Missouri. After that, a series of railroad trains brought them to New York. Both of them had checked in with Coven headquarters and been given the okay to make a side trip to Luke's village. After that, they'd be on their way back to Utah in a wagon train with the rest of the Coven's witches.

The Girauds' original intent had been to pave the way. Breana had mailed a full report to Coven headquarters about her husband and daughter. Along with it, she'd sent word for others to follow her west since land was plentiful, and witches could practice their craft undisturbed. Besides, the country was heading toward a war over slavery. The Coven needed to relocate before tensions between the North and the South exploded, making travel difficult.

"How long since you've been here?" Abigail asked.

"I was twenty-five when I left, so twenty years."

"Ooooh." She crinkled her nose at him. "I knew I'd snagged a younger man, but you were practically a child bride."

"Groom," he said, laughing. "That would be groom."

"Bride, groom, what's the difference?"

"Probably not much." He was still chortling. Abigail had a quick wit and a delightful, quirky sense of humor.

"How come you never came back here until now?"

Well, why didn't I?

He took a deep breath. "Truth?"

"Of course, otherwise why bother to answer?" She drew her brows together. "It's on account of your sister, isn't it?"

Luke nodded. "No matter how much everyone said it wasn't my fault, I always felt like I failed her."

"Do you still feel that way?"

"A little. She would've been a mother herself by now. Tamra loved babies, all kinds, human, animal…" Luke hesitated a beat. "There wasn't that much to come back here for. The wraiths got Ma and Pa, and my sisters settled in with our neighbors, the Waverlys. I'd visit them on holidays when I still lived here, but they always stared sidelong at me when they thought I wasn't paying attention, like I was some kind of freak.

"Look around." He waved his arms at the wooded roadway. "It's pretty much a backwater. A lot of the girls don't even go to school, and the boys don't go for very long. Most folk aren't comfortable with magic."

"That's true pretty much everywhere," she said gently.

"It's worse here," he cut in and then shook his head. "That's not accurate. Now that I've spent years traveling the country, I know it isn't, but I've used it as an excuse to stay gone."

"That was a solid insight, but probably a painful one." Abigail reached across the space between their horses and laid a hand on his thigh. "I've found that the lies I tell myself are the hardest ones to get past."

Luke snorted. "Especially when the lie is driven by guilt. You're a good woman, Abby. You keep me honest. Take this next right up the hill. It's not marked, so slow down or you'll ride right past."

Abigail clucked to her horse and guided it onto an overgrown track. "Did you write and tell him we were coming?"

Luke shook his head. "I sat down a couple of times and started letters, but I didn't know quite what to say. It felt awkward."

"It would, because it's been so long."

A warm feeling spread from his belly outward. Abigail understood him and accepted who he was, all of him. He'd tried to tell her how much that meant, but words always felt inadequate.

"My—" she twisted in her saddle, craning her neck this way and that "—these are some old trees."

"They scared the crap out of me when I was a kid. I used to imagine the branches were alive and out to get me."

"I can see how you'd have felt that way. This path is barely even a road, more like a trail, and it's so unkempt it has a bit of an ominous feel, even to me."

"Aethelred did that on purpose," Luke said. "He didn't appreciate casual visitors, so he discouraged them with cheap props like the trees and his raven, though I doubt she's still alive."

"You never know." Abigail glanced at him. "Some of those familiars live a long time."

They crested the hill. A wave of homesickness, poignant and unexpected, twisted Luke's stomach into a knot. The old wizard had been a lot like a father to him, even though he'd never actually admitted it until right now. Before they even crossed the clearing to the rambling stone house with smoke curling from its chimneys, the front door flew open and Aethelred, a little older and a little grayer, hurtled down the steps and burst into the yard.

He clutched a richly carved staff and he wore the same stone pendant he'd loaned Luke that awful night his power had claimed him. "Son!" he cried. "Luke! You came home."

Tears pricked behind his lids, hot and bitter. Luke vaulted from his horse and ran into the old man's arms. "Aethelred." He clasped the old mage close. "I— Christ, but I'm glad you're still alive. It would've been awful if I'd never seen you again."

"Finally realized that did you." The wizard nodded knowingly. "Good thing you didn't wait too long."

"You never did mince words." Luke inhaled the familiar scents of smoke and magic, and the truth of Aethelred's greeting etched into his soul. This was his home. The old wizard had known it all along, but he'd been wise enough to realize Luke had to find his own way back.

"Looks as if you did a fair bit of growing up along the way." Aethelred stepped back and gazed at him from arm's length, his shrewd dark eyes missing nothing, but then they never had.

Abigail dismounted and walked toward them, her face wreathed in smiles. "You must be Aethelred. I'm so very glad to meet you."

"I'd like to introduce my wife, Abigail." Luke said.

Aethelred narrowed his eyes. "Witch, eh?" He nodded as if

something pleased him. "You'll be a good match for my boy."

A huge, black raven winged its way out the open front door, cawing. "Back. You came back. Fool came back."

Luke held out his forearm and the raven landed on it with a solid *thunk*, her talons digging deep. He stroked the bird's shiny, black head. "You were right about me being a fool."

"Fool, fool," the raven cawed sagely. She swiveled her head and stared at Abigail with her beady, avian eyes. "Pretty woman. Too good for fool."

Abigail laughed. "Yup. I tell him that all the time."

"Are you staying for a spell?" Hope flared deep in the old mage's eyes as he looked from Luke to Abigail.

Luke nodded. "For a few days, if you'll have us. I'm hoping you'll bless our marriage."

"I'd be honored, and you staying would be wonderful, just wonderful." Aethelred's smile could have lit a thousand fires. "I've watched you in my scrying pool—and my mirror. And I prayed to the goddess you'd find your way home, but years went by. The longer it was, the less hope I had that I'd ever lay eyes on you again in this life."

Luke swallowed hard, still too close to tears for comfort. The raven's talons digging into his arm helped steady him. Who knew? Maybe that was why the bird was there. It would be very like her to do something like that. She was so canny, he'd often wondered if Aethelred hadn't done something magical to augment to her wisdom.

"It was wrong of me to stay gone so long," he said. Abigail wove an arm around his waist, offering silent support. "A lot happened here that I had a hard time coming to terms with."

"Have you yet?" Aethelred sliced directly to the point, as always.

"Not totally, but I'm closer than I've ever been before."

"Excellent." The wizard smiled warmly. "Let's get those horses taken care of. Then you can come on inside and we'll get a pot of tea going. I want to hear everything you've been up to since you left."

"I thought you watched me in your mirror and your pool."

"Well, it wasn't as if that was the only thing I did." Aethelred rolled his dark eyes. "I looked in on you from time to time is all, so there're some mighty big gaps." He shifted his penetrating gaze to Abigail. "I want to hear all about you too, young lady, though you're not all that young."

"No." She grinned affably. "That I'm not. But I'd be pleased to tell you anything you want to know."

Aethelred rubbed his hands together, a gesture Luke remembered well. It meant he was excited about delving into the heart of something.

"Is that barn still round the back?" Luke asked.

The wizard nodded. "It hasn't fallen down yet. I'll walk with you. Good for me to stretch my legs a bit. I spend entirely too much time sitting in front of the fire."

"Do you still have students?" Luke asked. As soon as the question was out, he became aware of a silence sitting around the old house that answered him better than words.

"Not anymore." Aethelred shook his head sadly. "You'll recall your distrust of magic. Of course you will. You had a healthy enough dose for an army. Well, it's gotten a whole lot worse since the wraiths showed up that time. Folks convinced themselves it was people like me who were a magnet for trouble."

"It didn't seem that bad before I left," Luke murmured.

They reached the barn, and Luke set about unsaddling his horse and removing its bridle. Abigail did the same. Once she was done, she shepherded their horses into the barn.

"The undercurrents were there," Aethelred said, "but you and I didn't leave here that much, so we were spared the brunt of it. Students were thinning out even in your time, though."

Luke thought back. He'd kept to himself so much, he'd scarcely noticed things like that. "How long have you been here by yourself?"

"Better'n ten years, but I haven't been alone." He jerked his chin toward the raven that had moved to Luke's shoulder. "Mollie's been with me and she's good company. Plus, every once in a while, there's a catastrophe in the village, and someone runs to find me." He cracked a grin. "You'll remember. It's much the same thing you did that night."

"I don't know if you'd be interested," Abigail said slowly as she emerged from the barn, "but I've sort of been eavesdropping. After we leave here, Luke and I are headed for Utah Territory with my Coven. I know you're not a witch, but we welcome all magic wielders. Luke's a mage and he's worked for the Coven for a long time. Anyway, we can talk about it, but if you'd like a bit of a change of scenery, maybe you could come with us. We have plenty of room in our wagon. Of course, your bird would be most welcome too." She met his dark eyes and smiled warmly. "It might be better than being here all by yourselves."

"Why that's extremely kind of you to offer."

Aethelred turned away, but not before Luke saw strong emotion distort his craggy features.

"We can talk about it," Luke echoed, hoping the wizard would take Abigail up on her offer.

"I'd like that, son. How about a pot of tea?" Aethelred started for the house, his face still averted.

"I'm right behind you," Luke said.

"Me too," Mollie *quorked* from his shoulder.

"Well, don't forget me." Abigail laughed cheerily and trotted to Luke's side.

He draped an arm around her waist and together they followed Aethelred up the back stairs and into his house. Powered by its own enchantment, the door swung shut behind them. Magic settled around Luke, earthy and familiar, and he hugged Abigail tighter to him, his throat tight with emotion.

She leaned into him. "This truly is your home. I feel it welcoming you."

"Yes, my love. I feel it too."

"We'll use the parlor, rather than the kitchen," Aethelred called from in front of them. "Today is a special occasion."

The raven brushed her shiny beak across Luke's face before launching herself off his shoulder and winging her way deeper into the house.

"Which way?" Abigail asked.

Luke laughed. "Open your magic. The house will show you. Used to scare the crap out of me when I first came to live here, but it's actually convenient. If you take a wrong turn, you'll find out quick enough."

"I'll just hang onto you." She smiled. "It's easier."

Luke steered her through the welter of branching hallways leading to the front room. By the time they got there, a fire blazed bright in the stone fireplace that reached all the way to the ceiling. Aethelred had pulled three padded chairs in front of the fire, and a teapot sat on the hearth.

"Sit. Sit." The mage waved his arms. "Tea needs to steep a bit."

"Maybe yours does," Luke retorted. "Not all of us like it so bitter a spoon will stand upright."

Aethelred laughed long and loud. "Go ahead and pour yourself a cup. Then I want to hear what happened after that devil child got loose in the forest."

Luke poured tea for himself and Abigail, motioning for her to sit. "Why didn't you watch it play out?" he asked his mentor and settled onto his own chair.

"Evil stopped me. Clouded my glass." Aethelred made a forked sign meant to ward off wickedness and leaned close. "Remember I once told you there weren't enough of us to hold the dark at bay?"

Luke nodded solemnly.

"'Tis worse now than it's ever been."

Mollie flew into the room and perched in front of the wizard. "Worse," she quorked. "Worse."

"Not that things aren't bad, but it's possible you interpret them as worse than they are because you've been by yourself for so long," Luke said firmly.

Aethelred opened his mouth, then frowned. "I was going to tell you that you're wrong." He narrowed his eyes. "But you've grown up, traveled widely, and mayhap you see things more clearly than me."

"Come with us to Utah," Abigail urged. "We can learn from your power, and you can learn from ours. Black Magick has a toehold, true enough. It's gotten its claws into many of us. By the goddess, it nearly had me. If Luke wouldn't have been there, I'd be dead right now—or turned, which is worse than dead."

"Worse than dead," Mollie cawed sagely.

"You saved her from the dark?" Aethelred turned his penetrating gaze on Luke.

"I did." Luke sucked in a steadying breath. Whenever he thought about how close he'd come to losing the woman he loved, it chilled him to his soul.

"Tell me," Aethelred demanded and poured himself a cup of tea.

"It was the devil child that you saw," Abigail began. "Her

parents hired me to chaperone her to Utah…"

Night had long since fallen before their tale was told. Somewhere in between, Abigail slipped into the kitchen and cut up bread and cheese to go with pots of tea and some stiff, homemade spirits. Mollie had taken to one of the rafters and had her head tucked beneath one wing.

"Time for sleep," Luke smiled fondly at Aethelred. "We can talk more tomorrow."

Aethelred rose. "Take the guest room on the second floor."

"Not my old room?"

"And where would the both of you sleep, son? That bed was a good size for you—by yourself."

"You're most kind," Abigail stood and hooked her hand over Luke's arm.

"And I can see why my boy fell in love with you." Aethelred nodded slowly. "I'll take you up on your offer. Mayhap not right away. It will take me a bit of time to close things up here, but Mollie and I will meet up with you."

"We'll wait," Luke said.

"And we'll help," Abigail broke in. "Things will go quickly with three of us."

Mollie squawked from the rafters. "Four. Four of us."

Luke laughed until tears ran down his face. "You always were too smart for your own good," he told the bird, but she folded her head back beneath one wing, not deigning to answer him.

This is the end of *Blood and Magic*. Please leave a review. Doesn't have to be fancy. A line or two will do it.

The next book in the Coven Enforcer series, *Blood and Sorcery* is ready for you. It's Breana and Joshua's story. Read on for a sample.

ABOUT THE AUTHOR

Ann Gimpel is a USA Today bestselling author. A lifelong aficionado of the unusual, she began writing speculative fiction a few years ago. Since then her short fiction has appeared in a number of webzines and anthologies. Her longer books run the gamut from urban fantasy to paranormal romance. Once upon a time, she nurtured clients, now she nurtures dark, gritty fantasy stories that push hard against reality. When she's not writing, she's in the backcountry getting down and dirty with her camera. She's published over 70 books to date, with several more planned for 2019 and beyond. A husband, grown children, grandchildren and wolf hybrids round out her family.

Keep up with her at www.anngimpel.com or http://anngimpel.blogspot.com

If you enjoyed what you read, get in line for special offers and pre-release special reads. Sign up for Ann's newsletter on her website or her blog.

BLOOD AND SORCERY, CHAPTER ONE

Salt Lake City, Utah Territory

Breana Giraud bolted upright in her bed, the darkness shattering around her into fire-tinged motes of black. Heart thudding hard against her chest, throat constricted with fear, she reached for power, intent on shrouding herself in a protective spell. Goddamn her husband. He was at it again. It was like him to wait until she was sleeping—and she had to sleep sometime.

Once upon a time, she'd cared about Don—a witch with power to match her own. But he'd been seduced by the dark and become deeply entrenched in Black Magick. Shielding herself against him drained her, but she didn't have any choice. Sucking air around the narrow place that used to be her throat, she sent magic spiraling outward. She didn't sense him near, but the enchantment that just dragged her from a sound sleep had Don's name—and sliminess—stamped all over it.

Her eyes snapped open. Don was dead.

Dead.

What the hell was happening to her?

He couldn't harm her anymore, so why was his stench all

over the room? Granted it had been *their* room until a few weeks ago, but that didn't explain what just happened.

She reached for her magic again. Surely she could summon a mage light. Simplest of spells, it required almost nothing in the way of power. Finally, after she was shaking and sweating with effort, a wavery blue light formed, casting the bedroom in eerie shadows. Breana urged her light to burn hotter, brighter. Her teeth were chattering, and she felt as if she'd never be warm again despite icy sweat dripping down her sides.

She tugged the heavy, wool blanket around her shuddering form, but it didn't help so she dragged air hard into lungs that had nearly forgotten how to cooperate. And then did it again. And again, until she was able to clamp her jaws in a harsh, desperate line.

Her light flickered and brightened, and the ball of fear making it hard to breathe eased the slightest bit. Falling back asleep was laughable, so she dug her way out from under the covers and pulled a robe woven from soft, cream-colored wool over her linen nightdress. Sheepskin slippers came next.

At least the godawful chill that had permeated the air was dissipating, and the reek of evil along with it. Brimstone held a sulfur taint that burned the back of her throat and made her skin prickle with a million points of discomfort.

She blinked back tears as she made her way downstairs, her mage light bouncing over one shoulder. The dark had taken both her husband and her daughter, and robbed her of what had once been a warm and comfortable marriage. She hated Black Magick with a passion. Hated what it had almost done to her as she walked a tightrope between her husband's demands and her responsibility to the Coven.

"Yeah, and I did a shitty job all the way round," she muttered as she poured a cup of tepid coffee into a mug. It was bitter as all get out from sitting on the back of the woodstove since early the previous morning, but she gulped it down anyway, wanting the quick stimulation.

Too keyed up to sit, she wandered to a window and looked to the east. Dawn wasn't far off, but the horizon was still dark. Days were growing longer, but it was still winter, and it might not get light until seven. She'd sent a meticulous letter to Coven headquarters in New York. Within it, she detailed her sins in not turning her husband and daughter over to Coven justice—once she fully understood their allegiance had shifted to dark power.

That letter had certainly arrived by now.

What would they do to her?

A snort of derision curled her mouth into a bitter smile. She knew what she'd do to someone in her position. Banish them from the Coven for starters. After that, it would be anyone's guess, but the Coven wouldn't be out of line demanding her life as punishment for shielding her family from what they deserved.

Not much she could do. About any of it. No. She needed to keep going, day by day, and let the wheel spin as it would. She'd find out soon enough. Certainly by this coming summer when most—if not all—of the Coven had relocated to Utah Territory. At least she'd given Luke and Abigail a good start by marrying them. Memories of that day—and their joy—kept her going through the hardest spots.

She plodded back to the stove and poured the last of the coffee into her cup before she opened the woodstove door and sent a jot of magic to stir the embers. Once they crackled merrily, she added chunks of wood and refilled the kettle on the back of the stove with water from the pump next to the sink. The chores were automatic, and they settled her nerves enough to dissect what had driven her awake.

Coven enforcers, a group of hard-bodied, sharp-eyed men,

who kept witches on the straight and narrow, had seen to it that both Don and her daughter, Carolyn, met their end in mage fire, purging their souls of darkness. And they'd killed Alistair MacDuff, head of the Alchemical Council. She and Abigail had seen to the death of Alistair's henchman before he, too, was dumped in the purification of mage fire.

"Guess we didn't get them all," she muttered as she ground coffee beans with a mortar and pestle.

"If *them* refers to who I think it does," Joshua drawled from the kitchen doorway, "of course they're not all dead. That fresh coffee, I smell?"

Breana curved her mouth into a soft smile. "You know damn good and well it is. I drank the dregs from yesterday morning. Hang on till the water boils, and I'll brew a fresh pot."

"Don't rush. I got time." Joshua moved closer to the stove, extending his hands toward its warmth. Tight-fitting, buff-colored leathers, similar to what most Coven enforcers wore, hugged him like a second skin. Flame red hair hung loose to the middle of his back.

Breana turned to face him squarely and crossed her arms beneath her breasts. "Looks as if you got up in a hurry. Your hair's not braided."

"Hell, it's not even brushed," he countered. "Reckon whatever dragged you out of bed before the sun was likely the same disturbance that woke me."

"What about Chris?" She asked about the other enforcer living in the barn with Joshua. Both men had been part of a contingent that had shown up after her daughter died. While Sam and Luke had left, these two stayed on to help her run the ranch.

"Oh, he's up too, and ready if I say the word, but we didn't figure there was much call for both of us to charge on in here until we knew what was going on."

His words hung in the air between them, heavy with unspoken questions, and he impaled her with his shrewd hazel eyes as he straightened.

Breana uncrossed her arms and held her hands palms upward. "I have no idea what happened a little bit ago. I was deeply asleep, so far gone that at first I pulled magic to shield myself from Don. I'd forgotten he was dead." She closed her teeth over her lower lip. "Damn if it didn't feel like him though. That same rotten, Black Magick scent. The one that smells like dead things left in the sun too long."

"Did you notice anything else?" Joshua narrowed his eyes.

"Cold. Freezing cold. It took maybe half an hour for my teeth to quit chattering."

He set his mouth in a thin, hard line. "Not good. Means whatever it is can't be far away."

"Damn! You didn't recognize it, either." Fear shrilled her voice, and the fragile equanimity she'd established in her familiar kitchen frittered away.

"What Chris and I felt was nowhere near as strong as your encounter." He clamped his jaws together.

"So?" She made come along motions with both hands. "It means I'm the one they want, right?"

"Maybe. Although I can't imagine the Alchemical Council not wanting revenge against us all. We not only killed their leader. We purified his black, black heart and robbed the Dark Angel of Alistair's immortal soul. Come to think of it—" Joshua drew his red brows together "—we might have trouble from way higher up than the Alchemical leaders."

"Isn't that just peachy." Breana moved to the stove and poured hot water over the freshly ground coffee beans. "Nowhere we can hide from something that powerful, huh? I hadn't even considered the Dark Angel, but I should've."

"Hiding's never been my style. Yours, either, which is why I suspect it was hell to conceal what your husband turned into." A corner of his mouth twisted downward.

Breana ignored his comment. There wasn't any way to answer it. Not really. "How soon do you think the rest of the Coven might show up?"

"Not soon enough if you're hoping for help from that quarter. We have to solve this one on our own. Wagon trains move slow. I'm not thinking we'll see anyone until mid-summer at the earliest."

"Mmph. Not that they'd knock themselves out to help me anyway."

Joshua just kept his unreadable gaze locked on her, but held silence.

Breana busied herself sprinkling cold water over the coffee mixture to settle the grounds. After a few minutes, she poured a cup for Joshua and refilled her own. When she spoke, she picked her words carefully. "It's been kind of you and Chris to stay and watch over me, but I don't expect you to put your lives on hold until the rest of the Coven shows up. Besides—" she looked away from his direct gaze, "—like as not they'll either banish me or kill me when they do come. No reason to wait around for that."

"Hold up there." Joshua set his cup down and moved right in front of her, settling his hands on her shoulders. "Look at me, Breana," he commanded, and a compulsion spell eddied around her.

"Stop that." She writhed to break loose from his grip, but he held tight.

"How're you going to know what I say is true if you're staring at your slippers?" he demanded.

"Fine." She squared her shoulders and latched onto his unsettling gaze, trying not to think about how close he was—and how male—and how long it had been since anyone had touched her with anything even close to tenderness.

His eyes, more gold than green in the first rays of dawn creeping through the windows, softened, but he didn't let go of her. "Better. Me and Chris—Luke and Sam too—we didn't save you to walk away now. No matter what you say, we're staying until that Coven wagon train shows up. And we'll speak for you. I got letters from Sam and Luke before they left. So you'll have the word of four Coven enforcers saying you're a good woman, and the Coven should let you get on with your life—even if you're no longer part of our leadership."

Tears pricked, hot and bitter, just behind her lids. "You didn't have to do that, and you don't have to stay here, either."

"I know that. So does Chris. We got permission to remain with you for as long as we think you need us."

"That's only because the Coven didn't know about me then."

He scrunched his stark features into a frown. "You'd be surprised what they knew and didn't know. I shouldn't tell you this, but you and Don were the topic of many a conversation." She opened her mouth, but he shook his head. "Keep listening— for now. Do you honestly think no one noticed when you stopped showing up at the New York headquarters, except on rare occasions? Or when Don's energy changed?"

Anger flashed through her, bright and brittle. "If other witches knew, why didn't anyone reach out to me? Or to Carolyn?" The tears that had threatened fell thickly, too many to blink away, but Joshua still didn't let go of her.

"Keep talking. You got a lot of pain bottled up inside." His touch gentled, and he caressed her shoulder blades.

"My baby. She was my only baby. Maybe, if someone had

given a good goddamn—" Breana couldn't talk anymore. She was crying too hard.

Joshua drew her against him and stroked her hair. "Hush. Ssht. None of us knew about your daughter. Children never come to any Coven functions until they're of age, and she hadn't begun to bleed yet."

Breana slumped against his warm solidness as the fury bled out of her, washed away by her tears and weariness. Joshua held her, murmuring in Gaelic, until her emotional storm blew itself out.

"You haven't done much grieving for Carolyn," he said quietly and led her to a chair near the fire.

She sank into it and closed her hands around her coffee cup. It had felt good in Joshua's arms. Too good. He was a decent man, and magic ran strong in him. He deserved a woman who hadn't been tainted by evil and soured by loss. Better to not encourage so much as a sexual fling.

Better for him, not necessarily for me.

He shot an appraising look her way before settling across from her with his own mug. She was afraid he'd been inside her head. All the enforcers were competent mind readers.

Rather than saying anything about her inner turmoil over him, he murmured, "You need to find a way to keep living in a world without your daughter in it."

"It shouldn't be this hard."

"Why not? You tell me why losing a child should ever be easy."

"Because I bid my daughter farewell after Don seduced her with evil."

"Maybe so." He nodded sagely. "But you never gave up hope you could figure out a way to save her."

"You're sounding like a parent, but you don't have children."

"Don't have to. I had a mother, and I fully understand she'd have done murder to protect me and my brothers and sisters. Pa too."

"Of course. I wasn't thinking." Breana closed her teeth over her lower lip and bit hard. "The truth of it is I knew my daughter was lost forever when Don let that Salem witch have access to her body. If I'd played host to Sarah, I'd have had a hell of a time getting to the far side of something like that with my sanity intact—and Carolyn was only a child. Wickedness is seductive, alluring. The ones on that side, they don't have to spend the years we do learning to summon and control power. Black Magick flows through them like wildfire, impossible to resist."

"Abigail came close to succumbing when Sarah Osborne hitched a ride inside her," Joshua said, his voice grim.

"She told me. Scared the bejesus out of her too, and she's a seasoned witch. Strong as any we have in the Coven. Carolyn had no chance once Sarah possessed her. None at all. I still can't believe her own father offered her up like some sort of vestal virgin sacrifice."

"For all you know, that was part of his plans." Joshua's nostrils flared with disgust. "The dark like to take them young, and Sarah enjoyed her men. I still remember the unnatural heat from that bitch before we lured her out of Abigail and torched her with mage fire."

Breana laced her fingers together, pressing until the knuckles turned white. "Maybe that's part of why I haven't thought too long or too hard about any of this. I have no idea what my baby went through. Or if she suffered at all until the very end when she finally understood Sarah had no use for her."

"Sorry if I was too blunt, but no point pussyfooting around about evil. We need every ace in the deck, and for that we can't underestimate what the other side is capable of. You didn't hear

Alistair bargaining for his life with Sam. His exact words were: 'Want to switch sides, buddy? We have better pay, much better hours. All the women you can fuck. Young ones too. Untouched. The finest food—'"

"I get it. You can stop." Breana squared her shoulders.

"I can, but they never will. I want to make certain you don't forget that. We've been targeted, and before the day's out, we need to come up with a better defensive perimeter around this house than what we've got now."

Breana tossed back half her coffee. "I'll help every way I can with that."

"Anytime you want to talk about…well, about any of it. Don. Carolyn. Your fears about Coven justice. Find me. There's nothing so bad it doesn't go down a little easier when it's shared." He pushed to his feet. "I'm going to let Chris know we need to do some scouting. If The Dark Angel is about—or some of his henchmen—we're far from ready."

"I'll get something going for breakfast," she called after his departing back. "Come back in an hour."

"Thanks. See you then."

The kitchen felt empty without Joshua in it, but she didn't dwell on that. Instead, she trotted upstairs and dressed, trading her robe and nightgown for a simple homespun skirt, dark blouse, and a green sweater that had always been one of her favorites. Next she laced up a pair of stout boots and headed out to the henhouse to gather eggs. Her second stop was the goat pen where she filled a pail with milk and used magic to soothe the goats who wanted her to stay and visit.

Breakfast came together quickly. Cornmeal mush made with leftover cornbread from the previous night, milk and eggs with a few greens, and some sliced pork from a hog the men had slaughtered and salted a few weeks back.

Her head was full enough, she was grateful to have something else to focus on. One thing was certain. She needed to stop feeling sorry for herself. Breaking down and spilling her soul to Joshua was an indulgence. If evil had her in its gunsights, she'd damn well better keep her guard up, which meant sleeping shrouded in protection spells.

Or not sleeping at all.

Witches could get by with very little sleep, but only for short periods.

One of the worst parts of dealing with her husband once the dark got its claws into him, was he slithered away from direct confrontation. She didn't do well with enemies she couldn't face off against, and the stealth attack that had jolted her from sleep didn't set well.

"Better rein it in." She spoke to the empty kitchen. "The quickest way to get what you want is to ask for it. And I'm not ready for a full on fight. Not yet."

Joshua's observation had been deucedly accurate. She had to get to the far side of the hell she'd lived through. To do that, she needed to think about it. Talk about it. Open herself to the slashing emotional storm she'd held at bay. Until she could do those things, she'd be a shadow, a shell, and not strong enough to help the men mount a defense against whatever faced them.

At least she had a direction—finally. It might flay her raw, but she'd take the hard road until the demons that dogged her gave up and went home. Breana surveyed the pot bubbling on the cook stove. It was done enough, so she snapped up her wool cloak and went out to roust the men, determined to keep right on talking about both Don and Carolyn over breakfast. Talk was the first step. Once she could do that, accepting their choices— and their deaths—would be at least possible. Not easier, but within her grasp.